BLACK FRIDAY

Center Point
Large Print

Also by William W. Johnstone
with J. A. Johnstone and available from
Center Point Large Print:

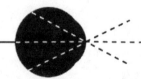

BLACK FRIDAY

William W. Johnstone
with J. A. Johnstone

CENTER POINT LARGE PRINT
THORNDIKE, MAINE

This Center Point Large Print edition is published in the year 2016 by arrangement with Kensington Publishing Corp.

Following the death of William W. Johnstone, the Johnstone family is working with a carefully selected writer to organize and complete Mr. Johnstone's outlines and many unfinished manuscripts to create additional novels in all of his series like The Last Gunfighter, Mountain Man, and Eagles, among others. This novel was inspired by Mr. Johnstone's superb storytelling.

The text of this Large Print edition is unabridged. In other aspects, this book may vary from the original edition. Printed in the United States of America on permanent paper. Set in 16-point Times New Roman type.

ISBN: 978-1-68324-165-2

Library of Congress Cataloging-in-Publication Data

Names: Johnstone, William W., author. | Johnstone, J. A., author.
Title: Black friday / William W. Johnstone with J. A. Johnstone.
Description: Center Point Large Print edition. | Thorndike, Maine : Center Point Large Print, 2016.
Identifiers: LCCN 2016034837 | ISBN 9781683241652 (hardcover : alk. paper)
Subjects: LCSH: Large type books. | GSAFD: Western stories.
Classification: LCC PS3560.O415 B544 2016 | DDC 813/.54—dc23
LC record available at https://lccn.loc.gov/2016034837

BLACK FRIDAY

Prologue

Tobey Lanning didn't know what was worse about Iraq: the heat, the sand, the bugs . . .

Or the people trying to kill him.

Considering that the air was full of flying lead and the thunder of automatic weapons fire, and shards of ancient brick were raining down on him from the crumbling wall behind which he crouched as bullets tore into it, he decided he might have to go with the last item on that list.

This sucked. Royally.

Tobey looked over at the man kneeling a few feet away from him and shouted over the roar of gunfire, "You gettin' anybody on that radio, Sagers?"

"Not yet, man. I'm transmittin', but I don't know if anybody's hearing me. I'm not getting a thing back."

Tobey bit back a curse and glanced at the truck that lay on its side in the road, next to the crater that the IED had left. The vehicle was just a burned-out shell now, sort of like the charred husks of the unlucky bastards who'd been caught inside.

A few minutes earlier, Tobey and Sagers had dropped off to relieve themselves. Seemed safe enough, since there was nobody around and nowhere for the enemy to hide except the ruins of some old building about fifty yards off the road. Hotchkiss, who was at the wheel, slowed down so the truck wouldn't get too far ahead.

Their business taken care of, Tobey and Sagers had been trotting after the truck when the improvised explosive device went off, toppling the vehicle, rupturing its gas tank, and creating a fireball that had engulfed it before any of the guys inside could get out.

That left Tobey and Sagers on their own.

Of course, there was an ambush to follow up the explosion. Tobey didn't know where the Iraqis came from. They were just there all of a sudden, shooting like madmen, mostly with AK-47s. Tobey and Sagers returned fire as they legged it toward the nearest of the abandoned buildings.

One stroke of luck was that Sagers was carrying the patrol's radio. That good fortune might have been canceled out by the slug that glanced off of the radio, inflicting damage it was impossible to assess under these conditions.

And it was also lucky, Tobey thought, that they had made it to the ruins without getting shot to pieces.

"Wasn't supposed to be like this!" Sagers yelled. He was a chubby East Texas boy, a redneck with an intellectual bent. "This sector was supposed to be peaceful and secure!"

"Ain't no such thing in this country, you

know that!" Tobey shouted over the gunfire.

He knew it was only a matter of time before some of the Iraqis circled around to catch them in a crossfire. Another half-fallen-down wall rose about twenty feet behind them. He needed to get over there so he could meet the inevitable attack that would come from that direction.

"I'm gonna crawl over to that other wall!"

"You better keep your head down!" Sagers warned him.

"No, I figured I'd stand up and dance a little jig along the way!"

"Better toss me that picture of your girlfriend before you do! I'll look her up when I get home and tell her I found it in the desert, like in that movie!"

Tobey made a colorful and somewhat obscene suggestion about what Sagers could do when he got home, then bellied down and started crawling, pushing his rifle ahead of him and being careful not to let the sand foul it. Behind him, Sagers's M16 barked occasionally as he tried to keep the enemy distracted.

No way in hell they were getting out of here. Not unless the radio actually was transmitting and help would soon be on the way, if it wasn't already. They had no way of knowing if that was true, so Tobey had to assume that it wasn't and that he'd be dying soon, probably sometime in the next few minutes.

That possibility scared him, but more than anything else it made him angry.

He still had things to do in his life, and he didn't want to lose it over some patch of sand.

A bullet whined past his head. He'd heard that eerie noise more times in the last few minutes than he liked to think about, but something was different about this one.

It was going the other direction.

Some of the enemy forces were behind the ruins now, as Tobey had expected. He stayed on his belly and tried to wriggle along like a snake in a hurry.

When he reached the wall, he thrust the barrel of his M16 over the ragged top and squeezed off a few rounds, more to keep the Iraqis honest than anything else. He didn't believe he would do much damage.

He thought about Ashley. Beautiful, golden-haired Ashley. They had dated for a year before he deployed. Things had gotten pretty serious between them.

Then Tobey had gotten his new orders. The relationship took a hit, but not one that they hadn't been able to repair before he went overseas. They sent thousands of e-mails, Skyped almost every day, and things were okay. She wasn't happy when he'd decided to stay on for a second tour, but he had smoothed that over . . . he hoped.

She had to understand: there were times when a guy just couldn't leave his buddies.

Now it appeared the choice had been taken out of his hands. Except for him and Sagers, the other patrol members were dead. Nothing he could do for them.

He had Sagers's back, though, and Sagers had his. That was the way it would end, just as soon as the insurgents decided it was time to rush the ruins.

The firing stopped suddenly. Tobey knew it might be a trick to get him to look, but he raised his head anyway. What he spotted made his eyes open wide in shock.

Fifty yards away, just behind a little rise, a guy knelt with what looked like a section of pipe balanced on his shoulder. Tobey recognized it as a bazooka, the same kind used in World War II. Lord knows where the Iraqis had gotten such an ancient weapon.

But the antique still worked, because smoke suddenly gushed from it and the heavy round screamed through the air toward the ruins. With an involuntary shout, Tobey surged to his feet, forgetting about all the bullets flying around as he dived away from the wall.

The shell slammed into the wall and exploded, blowing the part that hadn't fallen down already into a million pieces.

The concussion drove Tobey into the ground.

Debris pelted him. He was stunned, half-deafened. His muscles didn't want to work, and neither did his brain.

But he had held on to his rifle, and his mind was functioning just well enough to tell him that the Iraqis would be on top of him any second now. He forced himself to roll over and raise the M16. His grit-clogged eyes spotted dark figures swarming toward him. He barely had the strength to hold down the trigger and spray bullets toward them.

Slugs whined past his head and kicked up dirt around him. He dug his heels into the ground and scooted backward on his butt as he continued firing. When he put pressure on his legs, his right thigh screamed in pain. Glancing down, he saw the blood on his trousers. There wasn't a lot of it, and it didn't seem to be spreading fast, so he was hit but maybe not seriously.

Didn't matter. The enemy was still coming.

Tobey's back bumped into something. He glanced over his shoulder, saw that Sagers had retreated the same as him. The Texas boy said, "Gotcha, buddy," as they sat back to back and fired at the attackers charging them from both directions. Tobey felt Sagers's body jerk as bullets pounded into it, but Sagers's rifle kept chattering until it fell silently empty.

Tobey's hearing had returned quickly after the explosion from the bazooka round, so he was able to hear the sudden rumble. Blood was running into his eyes. He seemed to be peering through a red curtain as machine gun fire swept through the Iraqis, shredding them and knocking the grisly corpses off their feet.

More explosions made the desert shiver. Tobey knew he was badly disoriented, but the only explanation that made any sense to him was that help had arrived. The call for help over Sagers's radio had gotten through after all.

The insurgents who hadn't been chopped down in the first volley turned and ran. All but one of them, who stood maybe fifteen feet in front of Tobey, staring death in the face.

He was just a kid, probably not out of his teens yet, no beard or mustache, so skinny the AK he held seemed almost as big as he was. His dark eyes locked in on Tobey's flinty blue ones. He was frozen in place by fear.

All Tobey had to do was press the trigger, and he'd stitch a line of slugs right across the kid's torso. He wanted to. For Hotchkiss and the other guys in the truck, for Sagers, who was slumped forward, no longer shooting or moving, for everybody this little shit and his friends had hurt.

But he didn't, and after a heartbeat or two that seemed much longer, the kid broke and ran. Tobey lost sight of him quickly as troops in desert camo thronged around him, some of them giving chase, others securing the area around the ruins.

A lieutenant dropped to a knee in front of Tobey and asked, "How bad are you hit, soldier?"

"Don't know, sir. What about . . . Sagers?"

"Your buddy behind you?" The officer shook his head. "Sorry, son."

"Hell." A wave of weakness washed through Tobey. Maybe he'd lost more blood than he thought. He started to topple to the side as darkness closed in on him, like curtains drawn to shut out the bright daylight.

"Hang on, soldier," he heard the lieutenant say as he passed out. "You're going home . . ."

Chapter 1

Thanksgiving, Springfield, Illinois, eight months later

"I'm just saying that the system is broken and it's time we tried something else, that's all."

"Damn right the system's broken! If it wasn't, the country wouldn't keep electing presidents who hate America!"

"You can want America to be better without hating it."

"Not if what you mean by *better* requires changing everything that made this country great in the first place. My God, Robbie, do you really

14

think less than half of the population can go on carrying everybody else *forever?*"

"If all the rich people who can afford it will just pay their fair share—"

"Fair share? You mean, everything they have? Because even if they did that, it wouldn't keep this country from going farther in the hole for even one day! Not one. Damned. Day."

Ashley looked over at Tobey, shrugged slightly, and mouthed the words *I'm sorry.*

He gave a tiny shake of his head to let her know it was all right. He was used to hearing her father and brother argue. It went on at every gathering of the Parker family, and Tobey had assured her he considered it a feature, not a bug.

Norm Parker was an electrician, an old-school guy who would have been right at home as a member of the Greatest Generation. His youngest son Robbie was a computer whiz who made three or four times the money his dad did, a fact of which Norm was quite proud. Politically, however, they were poles apart.

Emily Parker, Norm's wife and Robbie's mother, said, "Speaking of one day . . . Can't you two stop fighting for one day? It's Thanksgiving, for goodness' sake!"

"Holidays never stopped them before, did they, Mom?" Ashley asked. "We always have to sit at the dinner table and listen to those two butt heads."

Tobey said, "Hey, you shouldn't call your father and brother names like that."

Ashley burst out laughing.

Her ten-year-old niece Danielle said, "I don't see what's so funny."

"Hush, dear," Danielle's mother Betsy said. "Eat your cranberry sauce."

"Don't like cranberry sauce," the little girl said, pouting.

"I'll take it!" her twin brother Danny said.

Betsy slapped his reaching hand back and told him, "Eat your own food."

Family life, Tobey thought dryly. Wasn't it wonderful?

Actually, he answered his own question; it was. Annoying at times, but it still beat the alternative.

He looked around the long table, Norm at one end, Emily at the other, him and Ashley and Robbie on one side, Ashley's older brother Jeff, his wife, and the twins on the other side. Growing up, Thanksgiving dinners had consisted of Tobey and the old man eating whatever they could find at the grocery store off of old-fashioned folding TV trays that had been in the family for generations, while they sat in front of the TV watching football. The old man, Tobey's grandfather, chain-smoked cigarettes and drank beer, and by evening he'd be drunk and half-asleep. But there was always food, always a roof over their heads, and Tobey hadn't been one to complain.

His home life sure didn't give him any reasons not to enlist, though, once he'd stuck it out for a couple of years of junior college. He didn't want to go on with his education. Maybe in a few years, after he got out, he'd told himself.

Well, he was out now, and it was time to start thinking about those things. And a lot of other things as well, the most important being the beautiful, blond young woman sitting beside him.

Norm said, "Seriously, Tobey, can you believe the way the media and the politicians have brainwashed this kid?" He waved a fork at Robbie.

"I'm not brainwashed, Dad," Robbie said. "I just know how to think for myself."

"Think for yourself? You believe every lie those lefties spout! Haven't you ever learned anything about history? Don't you know that communism is responsible for more evil and more deaths than anything else in the history of the world?"

Robbie rolled his eyes and said, "You can't just yell about Communist boogeymen and refuse to see how income inequality and the tyranny of the one percent have ruined this country. True socialism has never been tried—"

"Sure it has, and it always turns into a dictatorship. Ever hear of the Soviet Union? Ever hear of Cuba?" Norm grimaced and shook his head. "Oh, that's right, they don't teach

17

anything in the universities anymore except how those places were workers' paradises. They leave out all the stuff about gulags and mass executions. Wouldn't want to upset any of the students or hurt their delicate little feelings! I guess they should start posting trigger warnings in all the delivery rooms, so babies can start learning to be victims as soon as they're born!"

Robbie waved his hands and said, "Now you've just gone off into madness. Why don't you save your rants for another time, Dad? We're trying to eat Thanksgiving dinner here."

"Yeah, well, I'm not sure there's much to give thanks for in this country anymore."

The genuinely bitter edge in Norm's voice shut down conversation around the table for a few minutes. The only sounds were the clink of silverware against china. Finally Danny said, "Can I go watch the football game?"

"The Bears aren't playing," Norm said. "What does it matter?"

"Nobody's going to watch football yet," Emily decreed. "Nobody leaves the table until we've all had pumpkin pie."

"That sounds like a pretty good rule to me," Tobey said. "I remember one Thanksgiving over in Iraq, we always had turkey and dressing and pumpkin pie, and there was a rocket attack but we stayed right where we were until we'd finished Thanksgiving dinner."

"An immoral, unjust war based on lies," Robbie muttered.

Tobey let it go. He could have argued the point, but it would have been a waste of time and energy and he knew it. You couldn't explain some things to a guy like Robbie.

He'd never had pure evil staring him in the face, wanting nothing more than to kill him, the way Tobey had.

Betsy changed the subject by saying, "I hear that they're expecting record crowds at the mall tomorrow."

They all knew which mall she was talking about: the American Way Mall, the biggest and best in the entire country, sprawling over acres of what had once been farmland just outside Springfield. People came from all over the country to shop there.

"You couldn't pay me enough to go to the mall on Black Friday," Emily said. "I don't care how good the deals are."

"Rampant consumerism," Robbie said under his breath.

Norm shook his head and said, "Eh, I don't like crowds."

"I have to work," Jeff said. From the look on his face, Tobey thought he was adding silently, *Thank goodness.*

"I was thinking we might go," Tobey said.

"Really?" Ashley asked with a slight frown.

"You didn't say anything to me about it. I know how you hate crowds and shopping."

"I don't *hate* shopping. I'm just more the sort of guy who likes to go into a place, get what he's after, and then leave."

"Oh? Are you after something in particular? Is that why you want to go to the mall?"

"Maybe," Tobey said.

He wasn't going to tell her what he had in mind. Not yet.

But he remembered how she had been there for him when he got back, the way she had helped him through months of rehab on his leg, giving him the strength to keep working at it when he was so disgusted he wanted to quit. He was back to normal now, and he knew he had her to thank for it.

She had been there for him as well when he woke up yelling and shaking at night, reliving the ambush that had cost Sagers's life and nearly cost his. He saw all those terrible sights, heard that murderous cacophony, in his dreams, and when they jolted him back to reality, Ashley was there to hold him until his pulse slowed down. If he was ever going to be right again, she was the path to normalcy.

So, yeah, damn right he wanted something at the mall. He was going to the jewelry store there so he could get her the best engagement ring he could afford. Come Christmas Eve, he would pop the question and ask her to marry him.

Because more than anything else, he wanted to spend the rest of his life with Ashley Parker, and nothing would stand between him and that goal.

Chapter 2

"You can't be a security guard," Calvin Marshall's mother said. "You're too young."

The no-nonsense tone of her voice allowed absolutely no room for argument.

"Actually, you only have to be eighteen," Calvin told her. "And I just turned nineteen last week."

He tried not to sound smug about it, because he knew that would annoy her faster than anything else. And once his mother was annoyed about something, she tended to dig in her heels and refuse to be budged.

She gave him a superior look and said, "I think I know how old you are, young man. I gave birth to you, after all. Eighteen hours of labor—"

"Yeah, I think the boy's heard that eighteen-hours-of-labor story a time or two," Calvin's father Eddie said. "Look at him." Eddie pointed at Calvin. "College boy."

"I'm in college for now," Calvin said. "Until the end of this semester."

"We'll come up with the money to keep you in

school," his father promised. "Don't you worry about that."

"Yeah, but it would be a lot easier if I could carry some of the load myself. That's why I applied for that security guard job at the mall. I can work overtime these next three days and make quite a bit, and then go on working part-time after that and still keep up with my classes."

"But they'll give you a *gun*," Christina said. "I don't like the idea of my boy carrying a gun."

Calvin shook his head. "No, they won't. Some of the guards are armed, but not all of them. I won't be. Hey, I'll just be there to be a body in uniform, to discourage shoplifters and such. They don't really expect me to, I don't know, fight crime."

"Are you sure about that?"

Calvin nodded solemnly and said, "I'm sure. The only dangerous thing about it will be the risk of getting trampled by hordes of bargain-hungry shoppers when they open the doors in the morning."

Christina looked worried and opened her mouth to respond when Eddie said, "The boy's joking."

"Oh. I knew that." She frowned at Calvin. "But those crowds really are pretty bad. I've gone shopping a few times on the Friday after Thanksgiving, and I thought I was going to be crushed! You'll need to be careful." She sighed.

"That is, if you're really going through with this."

"I am," he said. "It's all set up. I'm supposed to be there at six o'clock in the morning. The mall opens at eight."

Calvin went back to eating. Instead of turkey and stuffing and all the trimmings, his mother always made chicken and dumplings for Thanksgiving. The meal was always delicious, so this was a holiday tradition he was just fine with. Maybe she had started doing it because it was cheaper, back in the early days of their marriage when they didn't have much money and it had taken most of the wages Eddie made as a mechanic to pay the mortgage on this house in a decent part of town. Eddie had worked a lot of overtime back then, too.

Calvin knew his pop wasn't just an average mechanic. He was really, really good at what he did, and so the jobs and the wages had gotten better over the years. Not so good, however, that the family could be considered well-to-do. But they always got by.

For a time, when he was in junior high, his father had hoped he would be good enough at sports to get a scholarship to a decent college. Calvin had played football, basketball, and baseball, and he'd run track, to boot. He was always good enough to make the team, but never good enough to get much playing time or stand out when he did manage to get on the field or the court. Nor were his grades outstanding enough to garner an academic scholarship, although he had passed all his classes without any trouble and graduated in the top half of his class.

Still, his parents were determined that he should go to college and make something of himself, so when the time came, they had borrowed money, and along with grants and student loans, it was enough for right now.

But they were skating on the thin edge of financial disaster, and it wouldn't take much to push them over. One large, unexpected expense would do it. That was why he was determined to make some money and help out.

That was why he had gotten the security guard job at the American Way Mall.

He knew his mother was worrying needlessly. Other than the enormous crowds, nothing much was going to happen at the mall this weekend.

Chapter 3

Jake Connelly picked up the tray from the kitchen counter and double-checked to be sure he had everything on it he was supposed to. Turkey, mashed potatoes, gravy on one plate. Adele didn't like stuffing or cranberry sauce. Green bean casserole on a saucer. A slice of pecan pie on another saucer. A cup of decaf. A glass of water and a little paper cup beside it that held all her meds.

Yep, Jake thought. Happy Thanksgiving.

He carried the tray out of the kitchen, through the dining room and the living room, then down the hall to the master bedroom.

Some days, Adele spent in the recliner in the living room, the recliner so big it was more like a bed than a chair, she had said when he bought it for himself a few years earlier. So big it almost swallowed her, now that she'd wasted away to nothing, propped up by pillows and swaddled by blankets. Now that she was so thin, she was always cold. He kept the heater up high enough that he went around with his sleeves rolled up most of the time, but she still needed the blankets.

The chair was comfortable, though, and that was his main concern these days, keeping her comfortable. This morning, however, she'd said she was too tired to make the trip down the hall to the living room.

"We can use the wheelchair," he had told her. "You don't have to use the walker. I thought you might like to watch the parade." He paused. "You always loved the Thanksgiving Day parade."

Adele had sighed and nodded, then said, "I know, dear. But I just don't feel up to it this year. Maybe next year."

"Sure," Jake had said, the crack in his heart widening just that much more. Both of them knew good and well that she wouldn't be here for next year's parade. There was a good chance that her cancer-ravaged body wouldn't last even until Christmas.

Neither of them spoke of that. Acknowledging the inevitable did no good. They just took things a day, an hour, a minute at a time. What else was left?

Her eyes were closed when he came into the bedroom. He paused just inside the door and wished it was a little brighter in here. The thick curtains shut out most of the weak November sunlight. Jake stood there for a moment, silent and unmoving, the fear that was always with him rising inside his chest, until he was able to detect the faint rising and falling of her chest under the covers.

The relief that went through him then was strong enough to make him weak in the knees. This wasn't the first time he had felt such a reaction, and he knew that it wouldn't be the last.

"I'm not asleep," she murmured as he crossed the room with the tray. "I'm just resting." She opened her eyes, and her voice was a little stronger as she said, "Oh, Jake, you fixed Thanksgiving dinner. How sweet of you."

"I told you I would. They have lots of stuff in the stores now that make it easier for guys like me who are no great shakes at cooking. It's not as good as what you would have fixed, but . . ."

"But you did." She sighed as she looked up at him. "You shouldn't have to waste your time taking care of me, Jake."

"Hey, you took care of me all those years."

She scoffed and said, "You were a big, tough cop. You didn't need any taking care of."

"That shows how little you know. I would've been a mess without you, kid."

"I'm afraid it's been a long, long time since either of us could be called a kid."

"What're you talkin' about? I look at you and that forty years goes away, just like that."

"It's nice of you to say so, but there are so many other things you could be doing . . ."

"Better than spending time with my best girl?" Jake shook his head. "I don't think so. Now, stay there. I'll go get my food and be right back."

"All right. Thank you, Jake."

He pointed a thick, blunt finger at her and said, "Don't go anywhere."

She smiled and said, "I'll be right here."

He had fixed another tray for himself and left it in the kitchen. Whenever it was possible, they ate their meals together. For so many years their schedules had been pretty hectic, what with him on the job and her working at City Hall, and they had missed out on a lot of meals together.

When they'd retired and moved from Chicago down here to Springfield, he figured it would be different, and for a few years—*good* years—it had been. All those old jokes about guys retiring and getting underfoot and annoying their wives, hadn't applied to them. They enjoyed each other's company, and life had been a breeze.

Until Adele got a cough she couldn't shake and a doctor had looked across a big desk at them and said words like *Stage 4* and *metastasizing* and *a year, perhaps eighteen months.* Adele, who'd never smoked a day in her life and never been around it much, either. Just the luck of a very, very bad draw.

That was in late September of the previous year, so things were proceeding according to the grim diagnosis. They had been through chemo and radiation, trying to slow the bastard down, and there had been a couple of clinical trials, but nothing had done much good. *Keep her comfortable,* the doctors said. *Try to enjoy the time you have left.*

She had a special, short-legged table she could use for eating in bed. He helped her sit up, got her situated, put everything from the first tray onto the table. She picked up the paper cup with the pills in it. Her hand shook, but she could still control it well enough to dump the meds in the palm of her other hand. She picked up the glass of water and said, "Down the hatch."

"Down the hatch," he repeated seriously.

Adele swallowed the pills, then set the glass down and looked at the food.

"It all looks so good. You're just too wonderful to me, Jakey." The pet name she had called him since the early days of their marriage made him feel warm inside.

"That's me," he said, trying to keep it light. "Wonderful Jakey. A lot of scumbags I arrested up in Chicago would disagree with you, though."

"Oh, what do they know? They're just scumbags."

That got a genuine laugh from him. Adele smiled at him.

And the years fell away, and she was young and beautiful again, and the life they would share was all in front of them . . .

"Jake, I want you to do something for me."

The image in his mind's eye faded. He sat down in the chair beside the bed, perched the second tray on his lap, and said, "Sure. Anything."

"Tomorrow I want you to go to the mall and get some different curtains for this room. One of the stores there has a sale on some that will really brighten up this space. I looked it up on the phone."

She had a smartphone she kept on the bedside table, so she could still get online when she felt like it. Some of her old friends from work sent e-mails to her, and when she had the strength she tapped out replies to them.

"The mall?" Jake said. She wasn't thinking this through. Tomorrow was the day after Thanksgiving. The biggest shopping day of the year, with the biggest crowds. Everywhere was going to be busy, of course, but the mall would be the worst. He said, "Maybe I could go to Hypermart—"

"No, there are some particular ones I want. I know you've done your best, dear, but it's too gloomy in here. Honestly, I could use some cheering up."

Jake opened his mouth but stopped himself before he asked if it would be all right to wait until after the holiday weekend. Of course it wouldn't be all right. She might be gone by next week, he told himself with the same sort of brutal honesty he had displayed in his years on the job.

Just go and get her the damn curtains, and stop whining about it.

"If it's cheering up you want, it's cheering up you're gonna get," he said. "I'll be at the mall bright and early in the morning. A few crowds don't scare me."

"That's my big, tough cop," she said.

Chapter 4

The van eased to a stop at the curb in front of the apartment house in the lower-middle-class neighborhood. The dark November night had settled down hours earlier. The Laundromat next door, along with the other businesses along the block, would have been closed by this hour even if it hadn't been Thanksgiving.

Habib Jabara considered Thanksgiving a sin against Allah, like all the other American holidays, most of which had their roots in pagan superstition.

In the months he had been here, he had studied a great deal about America, its people, their customs, their holidays. He wanted to know as much about his enemies—Allah's enemies—as possible, so it would be that much easier to destroy them.

Of course, in doing so one had to be careful not to allow those Western ways to pollute one's soul. Habib was convinced he had been successful in that. The Chicago Bears sweatshirt he wore was merely a disguise. He had never seen an American football game, although he was familiar with their obsession with the sport.

But when he wore the sweatshirt, people saw only a clean-cut young man who was a fan of "Da Bears," so their eyes passed right over him and they never paused to think that his fondest wish might be to see all of them die screaming in agony.

A few of them, of course, might take heed of his dark skin, hair, and eyes, and wonder about his ethnicity, but there were plenty of his people here in this country already, with more coming all the time, urged on by Americans who congratulated themselves on their "tolerance," never stopping to think that they might be inviting in their own destruction.

And there was no getting around it—Habib looked like a kid who ought to be bagging groceries at the local supermarket.

Mahmoud Assouri, behind the wheel of the van, grunted and said, "This is where he lives."

Assouri was ten years older than Habib, stockier, swarthier, and generally more threatening-looking. That actually came in handy because people tended to watch him more closely and ignore his younger companion. If they were going to be suspicious of anybody, it was Assouri.

"He doesn't have a roommate, you said?" Habib asked. "No girlfriend who might be staying over?"

Assouri shrugged and said, "No roommate. I can't say for sure whether he might have gotten lucky down at the pub."

The older man was an interesting blend. He had been in the United States for eight years and most of the time sounded like an American, but he had also spent several years in England before that and occasionally a British word or expression cropped up in his speech, like "pub."

"Well, if there's a girl up there with him, that's her bad luck," Habib said. He opened the passenger door and stepped out of the van. "Come on."

Chapter 5

Aaron Ellis's eyes never stopped moving. That was a habit he had acquired all the way back in juvie, not that many years time-wise but an eternity in the way it seemed to him. He hadn't spent half his life behind bars, but he hadn't missed it by much.

You couldn't afford to not pay attention in prison. As much as possible, you had to watch in all directions, all the time, because you never knew where or when trouble would come at you. Even in juvenile corrections, there were plenty of guys who wanted to mess you up—or worse.

It hadn't taken long for Aaron to learn to be alert. The guys who tried something failed to take him by surprise, so they lost any advantage they might have had.

Aaron was just a medium-size guy, not some muscle-bound hulk, but he fought like a berserker when he had to. Living with the old man had taught him that. Every stint inside he'd done, he had come out relatively undamaged.

At least physically.

Mentally, he wasn't so sure. A lot of the time these days, he worried that he was going crazy.

He jumped at the slightest sound. He kept seeing things from the corner of his eye, but when he turned his head to look, there was nothing there. He heard laughter, and sometimes crying, from empty rooms.

He slowed down as he drove through the suburban neighborhood. On the lawns in front of several of the houses on this block, kids were playing football. One of them overthrew a pass, and the ball bounced into the street, causing Aaron to brake as another kid dashed after it. The little punk scooped up the ball, waved at Aaron, and ran back to the game.

He cursed bitterly as he drove on. Why were all these people around? It was Thanksgiving. Weren't people supposed to go over the river and through the woods to freakin' Grandma's house on Thanksgiving?

Traditionally, holidays were a good time for guys like him to find empty houses to burglarize. This year it looked like everybody had stayed home.

Or maybe these were freakin' Grandma's houses in this neighborhood, so the rest of the family had come here. That would be just his luck, Aaron thought.

He hadn't wanted to go back to burglarizing houses. When he'd gotten out of juvie he had sworn he would never do anything to get sent back there or anywhere else like that, but it hadn't taken him long to see that nothing had changed while he was inside.

The old man was still a jerk who liked to get drunk and knock his wife and kids around. Aaron's friends still stayed high on weed or crack or booze. His school was still a crumbling hellhole that wasn't much better than a prison itself. The temptations—drugs, stealing, fighting —were still too much. All the vows he'd sworn to go straight were soon forgotten.

Since then, going in and out of the system for various offenses, he'd realized that there was no point in making such promises to himself or anybody else. There was a good reason prison gates were known as revolving doors.

Last time inside, though, an utter weariness had gripped him, so that he felt like he was three or four times older than he really was. He'd seen some of them, the old cons who had spent most of their lives behind bars and didn't really know what it was like to breathe free air anymore, and he'd decided it was time to grow up and break that pattern.

He wasn't a kid anymore. He was twenty-two years old, after all. Almost twenty-three.

But then his little sister Jennie, who was a senior in high school, got an early acceptance to college. Nobody in the family had ever gone to college, but she was smart. Really smart.

Aaron didn't see how that was possible, since she had come from the same parents he did and he knew he was dumb as dirt, but it was true. She could do it, could succeed and make something of herself, if she got the chance. She thought she had a pretty good shot at some partial scholarships.

But that wasn't going to be enough. Not hardly.

She deserved the break, and Aaron was going to do whatever he could to see that she got it, even if it meant going back on his word to himself.

Besides, he was already sort of in debt to the guy who had fronted him the weed he and Henry had been smoking a few days earlier, and that dude had a bad reputation when it came to guys who didn't pay what they owed, so Aaron figured if he could bust into a few places, find some good stuff to hock . . .

Well, two birds, one stone, right?

All he had to do was get over these damn nerves. *And* find a place that looked like nobody was home.

Wait a minute, he thought as he eyed a house on the left side of the street. No kids on the lawn, no cars in the driveway, all the curtains closed. When you broke into enough houses, you developed an instinct about which ones were safe and which ones weren't. This one *felt* safe to Aaron.

Best of all, it backed up to a concrete-lined drainage ditch, and on the other side of the ditch was the alley behind a strip shopping center where all the businesses were closed today.

That was one reason Aaron had chosen this

street. He could park in the alley, out of easy sight from the surrounding streets, cross the drainage ditch, and get into the backyards of the houses. Most of them had wooden fences around them, so that would give him even more concealment.

He counted the houses until the end of the block so he'd know which one was his target, then turned left at the intersection and left again into the alley behind the shopping center. A moment later he was sliding down the ditch's sloping concrete side.

It hadn't rained in a while, so the ditch was dry except for a few puddles here and there. Quite a few leaves had drifted into it. They crackled under his feet as he crossed the bottom.

Getting up the other side was easy enough. The wooden fence had a back gate in it. He took a screwdriver with a thick, heavy shaft from his pocket and worked it into the gap between the fence and the gate. When he got it in the right position, he leaned on the tool, putting enough strength and weight into it to pull the screws holding the lock's hasp out of the wood. They barely made any noise as they came loose, certainly not enough to be heard over the football games playing on TVs in most of the houses along here.

Before swinging the gate open, Aaron put his eye to the gap and looked around the backyard as best he could. No dog was in sight. Not even a doghouse. That was good. He pushed the gate back, stepped into the yard.

The back door had a chain on it, but he kicked it open anyway. He stepped inside, feeling that little shiver go through him, the knowledge he was somewhere he didn't belong. It was a good feeling and a bad one at the same time.

He looked around. It was on the dim side in the house, but there was enough light for him to see that he was in a kitchen. Probably nothing in here worth stealing. If he had time, he'd take a quick look around on his way out.

He was about to head for the living room when he heard a squeaking noise from his left. He glanced in that direction and instinctively crouched and stiffened as he caught a glimpse of movement in the gloom of a hallway. Slowly, a grotesque shape rolled closer to him.

It wasn't so grotesque as it came closer and Aaron made out the details. It was just a guy in a wheelchair. Kind of sickening, though, because he was old, with just a couple of tufts of white hair sticking up from his bald scalp, and twisted up like he couldn't sit straight.

The old man had had a stroke, Aaron realized. The left side of his face hung down like melting wax. A string of drool hung from that corner of his mouth. The wheelchair was motorized, and the control was mounted on its left arm. The old man had a hand like a chicken claw hooked around it, pushing on it so the chair moved slowly forward.

As soon as Aaron realized somebody else was in the house, his pulse had kicked into high gear. Now, as he saw that it wasn't anything to be worried about, he relaxed a little. He held up both hands, palms out, and said, "Hey, old-timer, just take it easy. I won't hurt you—"

"Damn right . . . you won't," the old man wheezed from that crooked mouth. His right hand and arm looked like they hadn't been affected by the stroke as he raised them and pointed a heavy, silver-plated revolver with a long barrel at Aaron. "Get outta . . . my house . . . you little punk."

Aaron's eyes widened. He stood there frozen for a split-second, considering his options. He could rush the old man and try to take the gun away from him. The revolver might not even be loaded, and it might not work if it was. And could the old guy really see well enough to shoot him?

It wasn't worth risking his life to find out, Aaron decided.

He turned and bolted for the door between the kitchen and the dining room.

The gun went off behind him, so loud it was like a giant had clapped his hands against Aaron's ears. He yelled in a combination of shock, pain, and fear but kept moving. He hadn't felt a bullet hit him, so he knew the old man had missed.

The gun blasted again as Aaron reached the door between the kitchen and dining room. Splinters flew from the jamb.

Aaron knew if he had charged the wheelchair, the old man would have blown a big hole right through him.

He sprinted through the kitchen, out the back door, and across the yard. He expected to hear the gun go off again at any moment, but it didn't. That wheelchair had been moving so slowly the old man probably hadn't reached a spot where he could draw a bead on him again. But he might, so Aaron didn't slow down.

He went through the broken gate, slid down the side of the drainage ditch, charged across and up the other side, and ran to his car. He fumbled the keys into the ignition, started the old rattletrap, and gunned along the alley.

When he came out at the far end of the shopping center, he slowed down a little, pulled out onto the street, and headed away from the neighborhood.

His hands were clamped hard around the steering wheel because he knew that if he let go of it, they would start to shake. This wasn't the first time in his life he'd been shot at, but it had been a while. Maybe he really had lost his nerve. The way he'd been seeing and hearing things that weren't there lately, he wouldn't doubt it for a second.

"Screw it," he said out loud. "No more jobs today." He still wanted to get some money for Jennie's college, and he still needed to pay off that guy he owed, but he would worry about that tomorrow.

Tomorrow . . . Black Friday, he had heard people call it. The day after Thanksgiving, when all the stores had sales and people crowded into them.

Maybe that was just what he needed: a crowd. With a bunch of people around him, whatever phantoms were pursuing him couldn't get to him, could they? Normally, he didn't like crowds, but right now he sensed that was exactly what he needed to get his mind off everything.

"Screw it," he said again. "I'll just go to the mall tomorrow."

Chapter 6

Sister Angela DiNardo wiped some drool off Pete McCracken's chin and said, "My, you certainly had yourself some excitement tonight, Peter."

"Too much excitement," the uniformed cop with the '70s-style mustache said. His belly bulged against the blue shirt he wore. "You can't go around shootin' off guns in a neighborhood like this. You got everybody for a couple of

41

blocks all stirred up, like a war was fixin' to break out."

"It was . . . a home invasion," Pete said, fighting for breath as usual. Since the stroke, his left lung didn't work correctly, so the right one had to take up the slack—and it was ninety years old like the rest of him. "I got a right to . . . defend my property."

"Sure you do, old-timer, but not with a cannon like that." The cop nodded toward the Ruger Redhawk .44 Magnum revolver that he'd placed on the table in an evidence bag.

"It worked . . . didn't it? Damn little weasel . . . took off runnin' . . . like the devil was after him." Pete glanced at Sister Angela. "Sorry, Sister."

"That's all right, Peter," she told him. "I know you're upset about what happened."

"I'm just upset I missed the little sh—I mean . . . the sonuva . . . the . . . the . . ."

His voice trailed off into a frustrated growl, as he couldn't come up with any way to describe the kid who had broken into his house without using profanity. Sister Angela wasn't a stickler about such things, but he knew she was disappointed in him when he cussed. He didn't like letting her down.

For one thing, he depended on her. She came around nearly every day to check on him. She took him to the grocery store and helped him handle any other errands that needed done, and when he didn't feel up to that, she took care of those chores herself and delivered the groceries to him.

That semblance of independence was important to him. He wanted to be able to stay here in his own house for as long as possible. He knew that if they ever stuck him in one of those damn *homes,* he wouldn't last a month.

Home. That was a stupid name for them, when they were anything but.

For another thing, he had a rule about not making good-looking young women mad at him. Sister Angela had that dark-haired, dark-eyed, olive-skinned Italian beauty, like that Sophia Loren and Gina Lollabrigida in those movies he'd watched fifty years ago.

Or Claudia Cardinale. Pete sighed. Claudia Cardinale, now there was a woman!

Sure, Sister Angela was a nun, but they didn't wear those habits that covered everything up anymore, and she was a hot number. He supposed it might be a little sacrilegious for him to think of her like that, but at his age he couldn't do anything but look, and anyway, he wasn't sure he'd ever believed what the priests said about lusting in your heart being as bad as doing the real thing.

If that really was true, then hell was surely full up by now, and there wouldn't be any room for him!

"You say the guy kicked the back door open?" the cop asked as he looked at the damaged door.

"Yeah. I heard the crash . . . and came in here . . . to see what was up."

"You had the gun with you?"

"I keep it . . . with me . . . nearly all . . . the time. Never know . . . when you'll need it."

"No offense, Mister . . . uh . . ." The cop consulted the notebook where he'd written down Pete's name. "No offense, Mr. McCracken, but a fella your age, you don't need a gun. Period."

"If I hadn't had it . . . that kid would'a killed me."

"I don't think—"

"I got a good look . . . at his face. I could'a . . . identified him in court. I would have . . . too . . . if I'd ever had the chance. Yeah, he would'a . . . killed me . . . to shut me up . . . if I hadn't had the gun."

"You're in illegal possession of a firearm," the cop said stubbornly. "You got no Firearm Owners Identification Card. I got to confiscate this weapon."

"Are you going to arrest him?" Sister Angela asked anxiously. "You can see for yourself, Mr. McCracken is really in no shape to be arrested."

"What?" The cop shook his head. "No, I'm not gonna arrest him. I'll just file a report. It'll be up to the DA to decide what to do about the case."

"Put me in jail," Pete said, mustering as much defiance as he could. "See if I . . . care."

Sister Angela rested a hand on his shoulder and said solemnly, "Nobody's going to put you in jail, Peter. I'm not going to let that happen."

"Well . . ." The cop scratched at his jaw and frowned in thought. "I've got your statement, Mr. McCracken. I'll file a report, and we'll go from there."

"You gonna look for . . . that punk who tried to . . . rob me?"

"He could be fifty miles away by now. But I've got the description you gave me, and we'll circulate it—"

"Not gonna do . . . squat . . . in other words." The pause he had to take to drag in a breath had given him a chance to come up with a suitable substitute for what he'd almost said.

"I'll file a report," the cop said yet again, like something a priest repeated several times during Mass. He sounded exasperated now. "You'll need to get this back door fixed, and the gate in your fence, too."

"How is he supposed to do that on Thanksgiving Day night?" Sister Angela demanded. "Nobody's working today."

"Not my problem, Sister. Helping people, that's more in your line of work."

He picked up the bagged and tagged revolver, gave them both a curt nod, and, walking out of the kitchen, headed back toward the front of the house.

"I'll let myself out," he added over his shoulder.

When the front door had closed behind the cop, Sister Angela said, "Ooh, I am so mad right now."

"Not . . . at me . . . I hope," Pete said.

Quickly, she shook her head.

"No, of course not. I don't care what that officer said, you didn't do anything wrong."

"I don't have a permit . . . for that gun."

"Well, technically that may not be legal, but as far as I'm concerned, you earned the right to do whatever you please as long as you don't hurt anyone else. You helped save this country. In fact, you helped save the entire world."

Pete liked hearing that. Not many people seemed to remember those things anymore. World War II was ancient history. He said proudly, "I did . . . didn't I?"

Of course he hadn't done it alone. He'd had a few million other GIs giving him a hand, spread out all the way from the South Pacific to Berlin.

But he'd been there, too, from the bloody, screaming hell of Normandy to the frozen hell of Bastogne—"Nuts!"—to those god-awful concentration camps they'd liberated that truly were hell on earth. He'd seen an ocean of blood spilled and had added to it himself in more than one battle. He'd been just a raw, eighteen-year-old recruit on June 6, 1944, when he went ashore on Omaha Beach, and a seasoned veteran of nineteen when the war in Europe ended less than a year later.

By then, his eyes were a lot older than that when you looked into them. A thousand years older.

But when it was over, he'd come home and got on with his life, like most of the guys who had been overseas with him. He had worked, married, raised a family, seen his kids move away, buried his wife, married again, buried that wife as well, and kept on keepin' on until the stroke meant that he couldn't anymore.

These days, sure, he was just playing out the hand he'd been dealt and waiting for the game to be over. He knew that, but even so, he was damned if he was going to let some punk bust into his place and steal his stuff and maybe try to kill him.

Life might not be what it once was, but anybody who tried to take it from him was gonna get a fight.

His thoughts had wandered off. They did that a lot these days. Sister Angela was talking again. He forced his attention back onto her and heard her say, ". . . guest room, all right, Peter?"

"What? I'm sorry."

She smiled, never losing her patience with him.

"I said I'd stay in the guest room tonight, so you won't be here alone."

"I'm used to . . . bein' alone."

"Yes, but we won't be able to get that door repaired until tomorrow, and you don't need to be here by yourself."

Yeah, like a twenty-six-year-old nun who weighed maybe 110 pounds was gonna be much help in a fight, he thought.

He shook his head stubbornly and said, "No, you . . . go on home. I'll be . . . fine."

"You're sure?"

"I'm . . . positive." He tried to make his tone firm enough that she'd know there was no use arguing with him.

"Well . . . all right. I might be able to fix the doorknob enough to keep the door shut for tonight," she went on, "and we can prop a chair under it for added security. Then tomorrow morning I'll call someone to repair it and the gate."

"It'll be . . . expensive."

"Don't worry about that. I can take care of it if I need to."

"I thought nuns were . . . poor."

"Well, it's true that I'm not rich in anything except faith and friendship, but we're not as poverty-stricken as people always think we are."

"I guess . . . I appreciate it, then, Sister . . . everything you're doin' for me."

"I'm happy to do it. Will you be all right while I try to fix up the door?"

"Yeah. I guess I'll . . . watch some TV . . . or something."

"All right." As he started out of the kitchen, she added, "You know, I was planning on doing some shopping tomorrow. Would you feel up to going with me? I know you enjoy a little outing now and then."

"Yeah, I suppose . . . I could do that."

"It's settled, then . . . depending on when someone can come to work on the door, of course." Impulsively, she came over to him, bent down, and kissed him on top of the head. "Don't worry about a thing, Peter. I'll take good care of you."

"Thanks," he rasped. This was the first time a pretty girl had kissed him in, Lord, he couldn't remember when. Nun or no nun, he wasn't going to complain.

She was wrong about one thing, though, he thought. He got hold of the knob on the chair's left arm and pushed it forward, then to the left so that the slowly rolling chair went into the hall instead of the living room. He went back to his bedroom and stopped the chair beside the dresser.

With his good arm and hand, he opened the top drawer and reached into it, sliding his hand under the pile of underwear until his fingers closed around cool metal. The side of his mouth that still worked curved upward in a grin.

That damn cop might have taken the Ruger with him, but Pete still had the Browning Hi-Power.

Sister Angela's heart might be in the right place, but if there was ever any real trouble to be dealt with, a few well-placed 9mm rounds would be a hell of a lot more effective.

"Heh," Pete said happily as he looked at the semi-automatic pistol. They would just see who was gonna take care of who.

Chapter 7

Charles Lockhart looked at the turkey dinner he had just nuked in the microwave of his apartment kitchen. What a sad, pathetic thing dinner for one was. For a second he considered picking it up from the counter and dumping it in the trash . . . but he was hungry. And public schoolteachers didn't make enough money to afford such extravagant gestures as throwing away perfectly good food.

Charles's father had always accused him of having his head in the clouds, but he had a practical side, too. He carried the previously frozen dinner from the counter to the table and set it down, then got himself a bottle of non-alcoholic beer from the refrigerator.

Happy Thanksgiving, he told himself as he sat down to eat. He recognized the bitterness in the thought, but there wasn't anything he could do about it right now.

Besides, there was a part of him accustomed to the bitterness, almost like it was an old friend.

The hour was fairly late for Thanksgiving dinner because he'd slept in, then watched what was left of the parade, followed by the dog show that was on every year. Charles liked dogs, and if he'd had a house, he would go to one of the shelters and adopt a rescue dog. Maybe two. It would have been all right for him to have one pet here in the apartment, but that didn't really seem fair to him. He was saving up for a down payment on a house with a nice backyard, so one of these days . . .

Yeah, just like one of these days he'd be married and have a family and be a respected educator. People would actually listen to him.

The day before, when the bell rang for early dismissal, he had tried to tell the juniors and sophomores in his English II class good-bye and wish them a happy Thanksgiving break, but nearly all of them dashed out the door before he could say a word. They might not be little kids anymore, but sometimes they still acted like they were, and one of those occasions was when school was dismissed early for a break.

In this case, that break was only four days. They'd been bitching all week because they had to go to school on Wednesday. None of the other districts in the area did. In fact, some of them were out all week and called it Fall Break.

The calendar in the district where Charles taught was a little fluky, though. He'd tried to explain to them that they would get out a day or more earlier than those other districts at the end of the school year, but that was months off and didn't mean anything to the kids. Not much did other than the here and now.

Probably it never occurred to any of them that he wanted out of there just as much as they did. The kids all thought that teachers *liked* school, and Charles knew that some did.

He wasn't one of them. He didn't *dislike* it. There were lots worse jobs in the world, and he was well aware of that. And there were those rare times when one of the kids actually understood what he was trying to get across, and that was gratifying.

For the most part, though, he was doing the same thing they were: putting in the time.

As he started to eat, he picked up the book lying on the table, a paperback edition of *The Great Gatsby*. It was one of his favorite novels. The curriculum allowed him only a few authors of his picking each year, and, he usually opted for Hemingway or Fitzgerald, as they were accessible. Sometimes Faulkner or Henry James, if he was feeling in a particularly perverse mood and wanted to torture the kids.

Today he just read the ending of *Gatsby* while he ate. He knew it pretty well by heart but always enjoyed letting his eyes travel over the words anyway. There was something so poignant about being a boat beating against the current. He suspected that was a good description of him as well.

When he was finished, he set the book aside, went into the living room, and turned the TV on again.

The first thing that came on was a commercial for a local gun store. They were having a big Black Friday sale, like every other business in town. Charles had never fired a gun in his life and hadn't even held one in his hand, nor did he have any interest in them.

He flipped through the channels. Football game. Football game. Football game. Commercial for a huge, daylong sale at the American Way Mall, with new specials every hour.

That was a little interesting, he decided. At some point, he would need to buy Christmas presents for his family, so he might as well get started on that. Sure, it would be crowded, but he didn't mind parking at the edge of the mall lot. The walk would do him good.

He spent enough time alone here in his apartment. Being around a lot of people might be just the thing he needed to perk him up and bring him out of this gloomy mood.

A little excitement would be a welcome thing, he told himself.

• • •

The SAM arced up from the brown, gray, and tan landscape below, trailing smoke as it tore through the hot air toward the chopper.

Jamie Vasquez's co-pilot yelled, "Incoming!" but Jamie was already leaning on the controls, sending the helicopter veering sharply down and to the left. Startled cries came from the troops she was ferrying.

Jamie wasn't surprised, though. Intel said that the Taliban wasn't active in this area right now, but she was in her third tour in Afghanistan and had learned a long time ago that intel could be trusted only so far.

She kept the chopper swooping hard to the left, hoping the surface-to-air missile wasn't a heat-seeker. Most of them weren't. In large part, the Taliban forces were still using weapons left over from the ill-fated Russian invasion more than thirty years earlier. Many of them weren't very advanced.

This missile didn't appear to be changing course in response to her actions. In the pair of heartbeats Jamie had to spare as the SAM streaked toward the chopper, she recognized that and heaved a mental sigh of relief. Her reflexes had been fast enough to get them out of harm's way.

Then the missile barely clipped the chopper's tail and detonated.

The explosion jolted the helicopter as if a giant hand had tried to swat it out of the air. Men yelled curses as the aircraft began to spin crazily.

Jamie fought the controls as they tried to tear themselves out of her hands, using all the skill and strength she had developed during thousands of hours in the air. In the other seat, the co-pilot shouted readings from the instruments.

The sandy, rocky ground was coming up fast.

The chopper was still level, though, which was good. If Jamie could stop the spin and get just a little forward momentum, she could set them down without a catastrophic crash. She hoped. There would at least be a chance . . .

Of course, even if they got on the ground, Taliban fighters would probably be waiting for them.

She lowered her chin to key the mike strapped to her throat and called in the Mayday, giving headquarters their position. A few fighter planes might be able to keep the enemy off of them long enough for another chopper to get here for an evac.

If they didn't . . .

Well, those soldiers back there had signed up to fight. Looked like they might get their chance a little sooner than they'd expected.

The spinning slowed. Servomotors whined as they responded to Jamie's skillful touch. She coaxed a little more stability out of the controls.

The chopper lurched forward, clearing a pile of jagged rocks by no more than twenty feet. A gentle, sandy slope loomed ahead of the aircraft. Jamie thought she might be able to set it down without too much damage . . .

Then it tilted with no warning and rammed starboard side first into the ground.

She came up gasping for air, as if she were fighting against a literal tide that threatened to drown her.

"Whoa, honey, take it easy," her husband Tom told her. "You just dozed off." He frowned. "Were you dreaming that you were back there again?"

She sat up in bed. The light on Tom's side was still on. He'd been reading a paperback Western that he must have set aside when she startled awake. It was sitting facedown on the covers, open to a page about halfway through the book.

Jamie glanced at the clock. 10:50, it read. She had gone to sleep almost immediately when her head hit the pillow at 10:30, exhausted after a long day of kids and Thanksgiving festivities.

That meant she had been asleep for twenty minutes. How in the hell could she have had such a detailed dream—or nightmare, to give it its rightful name—in only twenty minutes? In real life the incident hadn't taken as long as that. Among the ones who had been killed was Master Sergeant Benjamin Farley. He had saved Jamie's life at least twice, then lost his defending the makeshift stronghold from the enemy. In addition to Jamie, only four soldiers had lived through that fight.

Various medals had been passed out, some of them posthumously. Jamie had gone home and taken the medical discharge they offered her. She had been on her third tour when she was wounded, so nobody pressed her to stay in.

Besides, she had a husband and four kids between the ages of eight and seventeen, and she had been away from them long enough already. Somebody else could handle the fighting from here on out.

That didn't mean it was easy to leave the past behind, though. A couple of times a month, on average, she had these painfully vivid dreams where she relived that day in the desert. Those rocks were on the other side of the world from her suburban Springfield home, but to her they might as well have been just down the street.

She pushed the covers back on her side of the bed and said, "I'm taking something."

"Are you sure that's a good idea?" Tom asked.

She swung her legs off the bed and was struck by the asymmetry of them. The right one ended just below the knee. She had assumed she would be used to that by now, but sometimes she wondered if she ever would be.

The doctors had done a top-notch job all the

way around, from the amputation to the rehab to the prosthesis to the therapy that taught her how to get around on it. People who only saw her in jeans might not even realize she was missing part of her leg.

She would always know it, though.

She didn't bother putting on the prosthesis just to go to the bathroom and open the medicine cabinet. The crutch she kept by the bed was good enough for that. She shook a pill from the prescription bottle into the palm of her other hand and closed the cabinet, then swallowed the pill dry and looked at herself in the mirror.

Her sandy blond hair was still cut short to fit in a flight helmet, even though she wouldn't be taking the controls ever again. There weren't any more lines around her eyes and the corners of her mouth than you'd find on the faces of most women in their late thirties.

Once she had overheard one of her oldest son Andrew's friends telling Andrew how hot she was, which had embarrassed Andy, of course and almost started a fight.

Where the image broke down was her eyes. They had seen too much.

Luckily, she had come home to a loving husband, good kids, and a peaceful life. She had figured she would put everything else behind her.

She was trying, but so far the results had been mixed.

Tom was pretending to read again when she got back to bed, but she saw the way his eyes cut toward her now and then in a sideward glance.

"I know I've probably been taking a few too many pills," she said as she climbed into bed. "I'll cut back on them. I really need to get some decent sleep tonight, though. I've got Christmas shopping tomorrow."

"You don't *have* to go shopping the day after Thanksgiving, you know," he said. "It'll be all right if you wait until next week when the crowds aren't so bad."

"No, you and the kids had to celebrate Christmas without me for too many years already."

"Hey, we always Skyped."

"It's not the same thing and you know it," Jamie said. "I promised myself that the first Christmas I was back, I'd go out the day after Thanksgiving and buy presents for all of you. You know how it is when you set a goal for yourself."

"Sure," he said. Tom Vasquez knew about goals. He was the vice president of a corporation that made machine parts for the U.S. Air Force through various Department of Defense contracts, so he had to be goal oriented and diligent. Jamie was the same way. She'd always thought that was one reason they got along as well as they did.

He went on, "But if you get up in the morning and don't feel like it, you don't have to go. Hey, you can always buy stuff online. You can get almost anything that way now."

"No," Jamie said, shaking her head stubbornly. She felt the pill beginning to take effect already, so she slid down in the bed and pulled the covers over her again. Drowsily, she said, "I'm going to the mall tomorrow, just like I promised myself. I did three tours in Afghanistan . . . after all . . . How bad . . . can a shopping mall . . . be?"

Chapter 8

Habib and Assouri went into the apartment house lobby. No one was around. One of the lights in the small lobby was burned out, so it was only dimly illuminated. Habib could see well enough to make out the names on the labels under the buttons. He pushed the button marked REED.

The voice that came scratchily from the intercom speaker sounded annoyed as it asked, "Who's there?"

"Habib and Mahmoud," the younger man answered.

"Oh. Come on up, then."

The buzzer sounded, signaling that the inner door was unlocked. Mahmoud pulled it open and held it for Habib.

Donald Reed lived on the third floor. The two men were in good shape, so the climb didn't bother them. When they reached the hallway, they walked quietly down it to the door of 307, Reed's apartment. He was waiting for them with the door open a couple of inches. He swung it back as they approached and smiled.

Habib saw the small, semi-automatic pistol in the American's hand. With a smile on his own face, he asked, "Expecting trouble, Donald?"

"You mean this?" Reed gestured with the gun. "Nah, just being careful. I wanted to make sure you guys were alone."

"Who else would be with us?"

"I dunno." Reed stepped back so they could come in, then closed the door behind them. "I guess I'm just paranoid. I was afraid Homeland Security or the FBI or somebody like that might have grabbed you and forced you to lead them to me."

As if anyone would ever care about such a tiny cog in the machine as Donald Reed, Habib thought. It wasn't like Reed was the mastermind behind the plan.

No, that was Habib.

"No one has discovered the plan. No one has reason to suspect a thing," he said. "Everything is going exactly like we want it to go. That is, if you've done your part."

"Hey, of course I have." Reed sounded a little offended at the thought he might not have carried out his assignment. He set the pistol on a table and went on, "Everything is locked up in that supply closet just like it's supposed to be. As far as anybody knows, it's just cases of industrial-strength cleaning supplies."

Mahmoud said, "The janitors will not bother it?"

"No reason for them to. I stacked the boxes in the very back, like you told me. Under normal circumstances, it would take a couple of weeks before anybody would touch them." Reed grinned. "And of course it'll all be over with long before that, praise Allah."

Habib managed not to wince at the sincere but awkward sound of the phrase. He hated to hear that name in the mouth of an American, even a deluded fool like this one who considered himself an ally of the holy jihad.

He knew that Donald Reed had drifted in and out of a dozen different religions and movements in his life before deciding that Islam was the answer for which he had been searching all along. Habib was certain Reed had thought that about all the other impulses he had followed.

Someone who honestly converted to Islam could be accepted, even an American. Reed probably had visions of fighting the Great Satan alongside his new Muslim brothers. To Habib, though, he would never be fully trustworthy. The blood of too many infidels ran in his veins.

Better to make use of him, then be certain that

he wouldn't lose his resolve at the last moment and ruin everything.

That was why Habib and Mahmoud were here tonight.

"You're sure your people will have a way out for us?" Reed asked now.

There, Habib thought. He's already wavering. Worrying about his own life, instead of being happy to give it up as a martyr to their glorious cause.

"Everything is arranged," Habib lied. "Once we have carried out the mission, helicopters will land on the roof of the mall to carry us away from there. We'll take hostages with us, so they won't dare shoot us down. Then there will be planes waiting at the airport."

"I can't wait to actually see Mecca," Reed said.

There would be no helicopters, no planes, no Mecca for Donald Reed. Not for any of them. Reed thought this plan had originated with the leaders of the movement in the Middle East, but in truth it had come from an entirely different place.

It came from the brain of Habib Jabara. He had planted the seeds, cultivated them, nursed them along, adding a piece here, a piece there, recruiting this man and that, building an invisible organization right under the noses of the Americans, right here in the heartland of their country.

Let others protest, hold press conferences, file lawsuits. Let them infiltrate the government, worm their way into the corridors of power, exploit the foolish obsession many Americans had with "diversity" and "tolerance." In the long run, Habib knew, that was a better, more effective way to crush America once and for all, but it was also slow. Too slow for the hatred that burned inside him.

Let others worry about politics.

He was here to spill infidel blood.

And what better time to start than now?

While they were talking, Mahmoud had been easing around behind Reed. At a slight nod from Habib, he struck.

He grabbed Reed from behind, locking an arm like an iron bar across his throat to choke off any outcry. Reed seemed to be completely shocked and didn't even fight back except to paw feebly at the arm clamped around his neck.

Habib pulled up the front of the Bears sweatshirt enough to reach under it and grasp the handle of the knife sheathed on the inside of his blue jeans' waistband. He drew the knife, stepped closer to the suddenly horrified Reed, and drove the razor-sharp blade into the American's chest, angling it up so that it missed the ribs and went into the heart.

Reed's eyes opened as wide as they could, almost impossibly wide. He jerked a couple of times as Habib leaned his weight into the knife to make sure the point penetrated the heart. Reed lifted his hands but didn't strike out with them. All he could do was shake them uncontrollably.

Then his body went limp. His eyes still stared at Habib as the young man eased the blade out, but they no longer saw anything. Habib stepped back as Mahmoud carefully lowered the body to the floor. There was a little blood on the front of Reed's shirt, but not much.

The American had died without a sound, too. That was good. They would lock up the apartment when they left here, and the body probably wouldn't be discovered for several days. Not that it would matter, as long as it wasn't discovered before eleven o'clock tomorrow morning.

Habib took a handkerchief from his pocket and wiped the blood from the knife before putting it away. Mahmoud leaned over and checked Reed for a pulse, although it really wasn't necessary. He gave Habib a curt nod.

Feeling quite pleased with the way things were going so far, Habib went into the apartment's small bedroom, looked in the closet, and came back carrying a uniform, black trousers, and gray shirt, on a hanger. The shirt had AMERICAN WAY stitched over the right breast pocket.

He held up the security guard's uniform, smiled at Mahmoud, and said, "I think it will fit me quite well, don't you?"

Chapter 9

Black Friday

Calvin Marshall tried not to yawn as he stood in the chilly, predawn darkness with the other security guards waiting to enter the American Way Mall on the Friday after Thanksgiving. He knew that if he started yawning, he might not be able to stop.

He hadn't slept very well the night before. Whether that restlessness was from being nervous about starting this new job today or because he had eaten too much of his mom's good cooking, he didn't know. Either way, he was tired and the day hadn't even gotten started good yet.

He stuck his hands deeper in the pockets of the brown bomber jacket he wore over the uniform he'd been issued. A faint line of gray showed in the eastern sky, down close to the horizon.

It was supposed to be a sunny day, warm for November, perfect for shopping, but at the moment the temperature hadn't started to warm up yet. It was close to freezing. Breath-fog hung in clouds in front of the guards' faces.

They would go into the mall through one of the service entrances. People were already lined up at the regular entrances, eager to get inside and get their hands on some bargains, even though those doors wouldn't open for more than two hours. The parking lots around the mall were close to a fourth full already.

The man standing beside Calvin must have noticed him looking at the parked cars. The guy said, "By ten o'clock there won't be any empty spot, except maybe out on the farthest edge of the lot. By noon those will be full and there'll be a traffic jam of people circling and looking for a place to park."

"That bad, huh?" Calvin said.

"Oh, yeah. It won't ease up until late afternoon, when people start to get worn out and go home. I've seen it every year for the past five years. That's how long I've been working here." The man stuck out a gloved hand. "Dave Dixon."

"I'm Calvin Marshall," Calvin replied as he shook Dixon's hand. The older man was taller, rawboned, with a lantern jaw and bushy eyebrows.

"First time, Calvin?" Dixon asked.

"Yeah. First time working here, and first time as a security guard, period."

"You ought to do okay. You play football?"

"Why? Because I'm black?"

"No, man, because you look like an athlete," Dixon said. "You just got that jock vibe about you, you know?"

"Oh. Sorry. Yeah, I played ball in high school. Barely made second string, though."

"That's all right. You've got experience chasin' people down and tacklin' 'em."

Calvin frowned and said, "You think I'll have to do that here?"

"Well, part of our job is to watch for shoplifters, pickpockets, people like that, and there are always some of them who'll try to run when you confront them."

Calvin looked at the holstered pistol on Dixon's hip and said, "You're one of the armed guards. I'll bet they don't run from you."

"You'd be wrong there, my friend. The gun might scare the amateurs into cooperating, but a lot of these lowlifes are professionals. They know we're not gonna haul out a gun and start shooting in a crowded mall. Hell, that'd be a huge lawsuit —a *bunch* of huge lawsuits—just waitin' to happen. So if they take off, we have to chase 'em just like you guys who aren't carrying. The only time this gun comes out is if some civilian is armed and threatening people."

"Has that ever happened?" Calvin asked. He knew his mother was worried about things like that.

"Not since I've been here," Dixon said. "We've had some fistfights, but no shootings or stab-bings."

"That's good."

"Yeah, for the most part people come here to shop, not to cause trouble. Other than the petty thieves, of course." Dixon paused. "Where they got you workin'?"

"Food court," Calvin said.

Dixon made a face and said, "Ohhh. I'm sorry."

"What's wrong with the food court?"

"That's where most of your fights break out. People get all hyped on frozen yogurt and soft drinks."

Calvin frowned at the older man for a moment and said, "You're joking."

"I wish I was, old buddy. You'll see."

Before Calvin could say anything else, the service door opened and a beefy, white-haired man stepped out. He wore a mall jacket as part of his uniform. Calvin recognized him as Raymond Napoli, the supervisor in charge of the security guards. Calvin had had to interview with Napoli before he got the job.

"Let's go," Napoli said, waving the guards into the mall with the clipboard he held in his left hand. "We've got a lot to go over before the regular doors open in a couple of hours."

The uniformed men and women filed in. The service door opened into a corridor with offices on both sides of it. A time clock was mounted on the wall at the far end of the hall. One by one, the guards punched in for their shift.

Napoli appeared to be counting them as they moved past him, Calvin noticed. A frown creased the supervisor's forehead, as if something was wrong.

When they had all punched in and were gathered just inside the doors that led out into the mall proper, Napoli looked at the rows of cards in their slots, then turned to the guards and said, "Where the hell's Reed? Anybody seen him?"

Some of the guards shook their heads while others muttered in the negative. Dixon, who was taller than most of the group, craned his neck and looked around. He said, "I don't see him, Skipper."

An annoyed growl came from Napoli. He reached in his jacket pocket, brought out a phone, consulted his clipboard, and thumbed in a number. He stood there listening for a few moments, then broke the connection.

"No answer. Is he friends with any of you? Anybody talked to him since Wednesday?"

Again he got only headshakes.

"I knew it," Napoli said. "I knew he was too much of a flake for me to depend on him. I never should've scheduled him for a shift today." He made a disgusted sound and shook his head. "We'll just get by with being short one man, I guess. Shouldn't make much difference. For us, anyway. Reed's gonna be out of a job for this holiday season, though."

That seemed a little harsh to Calvin. Maybe this

guy Reed, whoever he was, was sick or something. Or his car broke down. There could be all sorts of reasons why he didn't show up.

But it might have been different, Calvin supposed, if Reed had called Napoli to let him know there was a problem. Calvin didn't intend to miss any of his shifts while he was working at the mall, but if he had to, he would be sure to let his boss know as soon as possible. That was just common sense.

"All right, everybody should've gotten your assignment," Napoli went on. "Spread out and go to your posts, and I'll be coming around to talk to all of you before the doors open, especially you new people."

Calvin felt like Napoli was looking right at him when he said that, although maybe that wasn't the case. Maybe he was just a little nervous, he told himself.

"Where are you working?" Calvin asked Dave Dixon as the group of guards began to disperse.

"Downstairs by the north entrance," Dixon replied. "By the calendar and smoked sausage kiosks." He grinned. "So I get to look at swimsuit calendars and mooch samples off the girls at the sausage place. It's a tough job, kid, but somebody's gotta do it. Come down and see me on your break if you want. I'll get you a piece of kielbasa if you're lucky."

"Yeah, I'll do that," Calvin said, lifting a hand

in a wave of farewell as he started toward the food court.

Calvin had spent a lot of time in this mall with his friends, and walking through it now while it was closed and mostly empty, before a lot of the lights were turned on, caused a distinctly eerie feeling. It reminded him of some of those zombie movies he had seen, where some catastrophe had wiped out most of the human race and left the survivors at the mercy of a horde of ravenous monsters.

Yeah, that was kind of like the crowds of shoppers on the day after Thanksgiving, he thought with a wry smile. The Black Friday Apocalypse.

He reached the food court and stopped to look along it to the customer entrance at the far end. The sets of big glass doors were still locked.

A humming noise caught his attention. He looked toward the far side of the area and saw one of the mall's maintenance crew running a buffer. She was a young woman with her dark hair pulled back in a ponytail, petite enough that the buffer seemed almost as big as she was. She seemed to be handling it with no trouble, though.

With nothing to do at the moment, Calvin strolled across the food court toward her. She glanced up, saw him coming, and switched off the buffer.

"Almost done here, okay?" she said. She had some sort of Eastern European accent that made her sound exotic to Calvin. She was pretty, too.

"It's okay by me," he said with a shrug. "The mall won't be open for a while yet. I just thought I'd come over and say hello."

"Hello," she said. "I must get back to work."

"Okay. I'm Calvin, by the way."

"Irina."

"Good to meet you."

"Likewise." She switched the buffer on again and started working it back and forth across the floor.

Well, that didn't go just great, Calvin told himself as he walked slowly back toward the opening between the food court and the rest of the mall. Not that he had gone over there to flirt with her or anything. He really was just being friendly and passing the time.

He forgot about Irina as he spotted Raymond Napoli striding toward him. The boss nodded to him and checked off something on the clipboard, probably his name, Calvin thought.

"You squared away here, Marshall?"

"Yes, sir. I know what to do."

"Keep your eyes open, that's the main thing. If you look like you know what you're doing, people will assume that you do."

"Yes, sir." Calvin hesitated, then went on, "I heard that there's more trouble here at the food court than anywhere else. Fights and such."

"This is where the kids hang out, so yeah, there

are squabbles you'll have to break up. Most of your shoplifters, purse snatchers, and the like, though, hang out around the main entrances, where they can run right out to a waiting car. So you shouldn't have to deal with much of that."

"Okay, thanks," Calvin said, nodding.

Napoli handed him a walkie-talkie and said, "Push that button and you get me. Push this other one and you broadcast to all the other units in the mall. That's your panic button. Bad trouble breaks out, you yell for help right away."

"Yes, sir. But I thought you said you're not expecting much trouble."

"I'm not. But you put that many people in one place . . . well, you just never know, kid." Napoli chuckled. "They don't call it Black Friday for nothin', you know."

Chapter 10

Vanessa Hamilton knew her sons would sleep late on Friday morning. As much turkey as they had eaten the day before, they were liable to be groggy all weekend, especially since there was plenty of leftover turkey as well.

Tomorrow morning and Sunday morning, she would get up early and make pancakes and bacon and eggs, and they would have a big family breakfast both days.

Today Jon, seventeen, and Mark, sixteen, would have to fend for themselves. That would be good practice for them.

Mitch would just grab some coffee and toast and be fine with that. He'd be in a hurry to get to the store, anyway. He always opened at eight o'clock, so today would be no different for him.

Vanessa woke Kaitlyn at seven. The girl moaned and groaned but got out of bed. Shopping had a powerful pull on a fourteen-year-old girl.

"We're leaving in forty-five minutes," Vanessa told Kaitlyn's back as she disappeared into the bathroom.

"We'll be there before they even open the doors," Kaitlyn replied, her voice muffled by the closed door.

"And we'll have a place to park, too."

Vanessa hoped that was true. She wasn't sure how quickly the parking lot would fill up. Well, if they had to park a long way out, that would be all right. The day was supposed to be nice, and the walk wouldn't hurt them.

Mitch was already up and had the coffee on when she got downstairs, bless his heart. He was leaning on the counter with both hands, watching the strong black brew drip from the coffeemaker. Vanessa came up beside him, put a hand on his shoulder, and kissed him quickly on the cheek.

"I hope it's a good day," she said.

"At the store, you mean?"

"Everywhere." She smiled.

He grunted and said, "It'll be all right. We've made a little less every Black Friday for years now, so I'm expecting the total to go down again this year. If it doesn't, it'll be a pleasant surprise. We've got stuff on sale, of course—you've got to, this time of year—but hardware's not like a lot of other businesses. We do a year-round trade. We don't have to do half of our gross between Halloween and Christmas like those other places."

The store's real competition came from the big nationwide hardware/lumberyard chains. Mitch couldn't afford to match their prices. They sometimes sold items for less than Mitch had to pay for them wholesale. It was like everything else. The mom-and-pop stores were on their way out. Couldn't fight the future. But there was nothing wrong with hanging on to the way things used to be for as long as possible, and Vanessa was proud of her husband for doing so.

That small business pride wouldn't stop her and Kaitlyn from heading for the mall today. Some of those prices were just too good to pass up.

"I was thinking that after Kaitlyn and I are finished at the mall, we'd come by and see how things are going, maybe give you a hand if you need it."

Mitch smiled and said, "Now that really *would* be a pleasant surprise."

"It's a date, then. We ought to be done by the middle of the day. Tell you what, why don't we stop by Dutch's and get some hamburgers? We'll bring you one."

His smile widened into a grin as he said, "I knew there was a good reason I married you."

"Only one?"

"Well . . . quite a few, actually."

"You'll have to go through the list with me sometime. But not now. We both have things to do."

Mitch nodded and started to pour coffee in his travel mug.

"Indeed we do," he said.

Kaitlyn came into the kitchen wearing jeans and a University of Illinois sweatshirt. Mitch frowned and said, "People are going to think you're a college coed."

"Nothing wrong with that," Kaitlyn said.

"There is when you're only in the eighth grade," Mitch countered.

Vanessa said, "I think you look fine, honey. Don't worry, Mitch, nobody's going to mistake her for a college girl."

"Hey!" Kaitlyn objected.

"I just meant, you're going to be shopping with your mother."

"Yeah, about that. I was thinking that maybe we could split up once we got to the mall . . ."

"Forget it," Vanessa said. "I'm not letting you out of my sight."

Chapter 11

Aaron hadn't slept much. Being shot at like that had a way of getting a fella all wired, so that he couldn't relax. The sun wasn't even up yet when he crawled out of bed.

His eyes felt like their sockets were lined with sandpaper. Every time he blinked, he wanted to scream. He rubbed at them, but that just made them feel worse.

Something moved in a dim corner of his room. He saw it from the corner of his eye and turned sharply in that direction as he caught his breath.

For a terrible second he seemed to see that crazy old man sitting there in a wheelchair, cackling and pointing the big revolver at him. Damn, the barrel of that gun had looked like a freakin' cannon!

Of course, nothing was there in the corner that wasn't supposed to be. Aaron knew every inch of this room. He ought to. He had grown up here. It was completely humiliating that he'd had to move back in with his parents instead of being out on his own, but as broke as he was, he didn't have much choice.

He groaned as he swung his legs out of bed and stood up. Dressed in his underwear, he stumbled around the room until he found the pair of jeans he had taken off the night before and pulled them on. He struggled into a T-shirt and went down-stairs barefooted.

Where was he going again? Oh, yeah, the mall. He'd decided to go to the mall. He couldn't afford to do any shopping, but he could hang around. Maybe some of his old friends would show up. They'd all spent a lot of time at the mall when they were kids, and some things hadn't changed. A lot of people his age seemed to be trying to hang on to their high school days, even though they'd been out of school for years.

Aaron hadn't finished his education. He'd been behind bars when the rest of his class graduated and hadn't even gone for a General Education Development test. For a while, after he'd gotten out of jail, his mother had been after him to get his diploma, but he guessed she'd given up, because she hadn't said anything about a GED for a while now.

His mother was sitting by herself at the old Formica-topped table in the kitchen, with a cup of coffee in front of her. Aaron knew his dad had gone to work already. The old man would be nursing a hangover from all the beers he'd put away the night before, but at least he'd been drunk enough that he spent the evening in a half-stupor from which he hadn't roused. Be grateful for small favors, as Aaron's mom always said.

The old man drove a bus. How he hadn't had a

wreck and gotten himself fired or thrown in prison, Aaron didn't know.

Aaron liked the idea of his father being in prison, though. Try being such a big jerk there and he'd find out real quick what a pathetic joke he really was.

"There's coffee," his mother said as Aaron sat down at the table. "You want some?"

"I'll get a cup in a minute," he told her. He had a sour taste in his mouth, and his stomach was sort of jumping around. He wasn't ready to put anything inside it yet.

"I can fix you something to eat."

He shook his head and said, "No, I'm not hungry."

"What are you going to do today?"

Man, she was just full of questions. He felt like telling her that his plans were none of her damn business, but he suppressed the impulse. He was living in her house, after all, and other than letting the old man get away with all the crap he'd gotten away with over the years, she'd tried to do a decent job of raising him and his sister, he supposed.

"I dunno," he finally said. "I thought maybe I'd go out to the mall."

"Really? There'll be a big crowd there today. I thought you didn't like crowds."

Normally, he didn't. He didn't explain that he wanted a bunch of people around so he'd be less likely to see and hear things that weren't there. He hadn't ever told her about that. He hadn't told *anybody*.

Life was crappy enough without people thinking he was going crazy.

"I need to pick up a few things," he lied.

His mother leaned forward and said, "You know what you need to do? You need to take Jennie with you."

Aaron sat back and frowned in surprise as he said, "What? Take Jennie?"

"I'm sure she'd enjoy it. And it's been a long time since the two of you did anything together. When the two of you were little, you used to play together all the time, even though there was more than four years difference in your ages. I never saw a brother and sister who got along as well as you did."

That was because Jennie was the only real ally he had in this house, and he was hers, he thought. What was that old saying? The enemy of my enemy is my friend; that was it. The old man was definitely the enemy of everybody else in the family.

But as he and Jennie got older, they weren't as close. That had been inevitable, he supposed. They each had their own interests. His had been drugs, sex, hanging out with his friends, and getting whatever he wanted without having to work for it, which had led inevitably to crime.

Jennie, on the other hand, loved school and wanted to excel at everything she attempted. Aaron couldn't imagine caring that much about anything.

They still got along—if that meant they didn't fight—but the idea of spending the day at the mall with his sister didn't really appeal to him.

On the other hand, having her come along meant that he wouldn't be alone on the drive to and from there. As jumbled up as his mind was these days, he didn't really want to be alone any more than he had to.

Once they were at the mall, they could split up and go their separate ways, rendezvousing later at the food court or something. Maybe they could even have lunch and talk some about her plans for college.

Those thoughts went through his head in a flash. He shrugged and said, "Sure, if she wants to, that's all right with me, I guess."

"I don't think she's up yet. Do you mind waiting for her to get ready?"

Aaron shook his head and said, "Nah, I don't have anywhere I have to be at any certain time."

Wasn't that the truth?

Pete McCracken got himself up and dressed, into the wheelchair, and made his own breakfast. He still had enough use of his left arm to pilot the chair with it, although sometimes he had to use his right hand to move his left one into place where it could grasp the control knob. His right arm worked just fine, about the only part of him that still did on a consistent basis.

Sister Angela had helped him move everything in the kitchen down low enough that he could reach it. He actually enjoyed getting his own meals. It told him that if Sister Angela ever stopped coming for any reason, he could survive without her.

Whenever he thought about that possibility, however, he felt a cold, empty spot inside him. Whether he wanted to admit it or not, the nun was his only friend. He didn't want to lose her.

Luckily, in the time he had left he might not have to. Unlike most young women, she wasn't going to get married and go off somewhere with her husband, her already being married to God and all.

He supposed her bosses in the Catholic Church could move her to another parish or something. Not being Catholic himself, he wasn't sure how all that worked, just like he wasn't sure why she had ever "adopted" him the way she had.

Maybe she was just a good person. It was possible, he told himself . . . although not too common, in his experience.

When he had finished breakfast, he went back to the bedroom and got the Browning Hi-Power from the drawer. There was a little pouch on the inside of the wheelchair's right arm where he slid the gun and an extra loaded magazine.

Loading magazines was a pain in the butt in his condition—that was why he liked the Ruger revolver so much, a wheel gun was easy—but he managed, just like he managed everything else that was a physical challenge since the stroke.

He'd be damned if he was going to roll over and die because of some blood clot in his brain.

The doorbell rang while he was rolling out of the bedroom. He said, "Hold your . . . damn horses," even though it was unlikely whoever was on the other side of the door could hear his croaking voice.

Couldn't be Sister Angela. He had given her a key when she started taking care of him, and she would have let herself in. Pete couldn't think of who else might be visiting him on the morning of the day after Thanksgiving.

Maybe that fat cop had come back to return his Ruger Redhawk to him. Pete didn't think that was very likely, but it would be welcome if that turned out to be the case.

It didn't. He unlocked the door, swung it open, and glared as he saw the man standing there. He said, "Who the hell . . . are you?" then noticed too late the white collar around the man's neck.

"We've met, Mr. McCracken," the priest said with a patient smile. "I'm Father Steve."

He had been with Sister Angela once when

she'd stopped by, Pete recalled. They had been on their way to run some errand. The guy was young, little more than a kid—although at Pete's age, almost everybody seemed like a kid. He had tousled blond hair and looked like he ought| to be surfing in Southern California instead of being a parish priest in Springfield, Illinois.

Pete didn't like Father Steve, he also recalled. Maybe he was jealous. Not in any sort of romantic way, since he didn't feel like that about Sister Angela and likely Father Steve didn't either, considering his calling, but the priest got to spend a lot of time with her, the lucky son of a gun.

"Yeah, I . . . remember you," Pete said. "What do you want? Where's . . . Sister Angela?"

"I'm afraid she's under the weather."

"She's . . . sick?"

"It's nothing serious, she assured me."

"Oh. Well, I guess . . . bein' a nun . . . don't excuse her from havin' lady troubles."

Father Steve flushed and said, "I don't think it's anything like that—"

Pete waved his right hand to stop him.

"It's all right. Thanks for . . . comin' to tell me . . . I guess. She could'a just . . . called me . . . and not bothered you, Father."

"It's no bother. And I didn't just come by to tell you. Sister Angela said that the two of you had an outing planned for today." Father Steve stepped aside a little and waved toward the handicap-equipped van parked at the curb, the van that Sister Angela carried Pete around in on their excursions. "She asked if I'd mind taking you to the mall, and I told her I'd be glad to."

"What?" Pete started to shake his head. "Oh, no, that's . . . not necessary."

"I really don't mind, sir," Father Steve said. He didn't sound completely sincere. Pete would have bet that Sister Angela had had to talk him into this.

He started to roll the wheelchair back from the open door and said, "No, forget it—"

"She told me you'd say that."

Pete paused where he was.

"She did, did she? What else . . . did she say?"

"That you like to pretend to be a cantankerous old curmudgeon, but that you're really not. She said that you're actually a kind, generous man who doesn't like to allow anyone to get too emotionally close to you."

Pete narrowed his good right eye and said, "Yeah, that sounds just like . . . the kind o' bleedin' heart claptrap . . . she'd come up with, all right."

Father Steve took a deep breath and went on, "She told me to ask you to go ahead and carry on today just as the two of you had planned. She said it's been a while since you've gone any-where and that it'll do you good to get out of the house."

"That sounds like her, too," Pete admitted grudgingly. "If I don't . . . do like she says . . . she'll go and get her feelin's hurt . . . won't she?"

"She'd never say so, but I suspect that she would."

Pete sat there for a long moment, then muttered, "Oh, the hell with it. I guess we're goin' . . . to the mall . . . Father."

Chapter 12

Tobey woke up with his arms full of firm, warm female flesh. That sure was an improvement over the way he emerged from slumber most mornings in Iraq. Too many of those had been rude awakenings involving gunfire and explosions.

As he stirred into wakefulness, Ashley did, too. They were spooned together, but she rolled over so she was facing him. She nuzzled her face against his shoulder as his arms tightened around her again.

"This is wonderful," she said in a sleepy murmur. "I could stay like this all day."

"So could I," Tobey agreed, "but we've got things to do. We're going to the mall, remember?"

"I remember. It still seems a little odd for you to suggest doing that."

"Maybe I'm just glad to be home. I want to

revel in all the things I didn't know if I'd ever get to do again."

She kissed his shoulder and then bit it lightly.

"I know something we could both . . . revel in," she suggested in a husky voice.

Tobey wasn't going to argue with that, although a part of his brain was still occupied in thinking about how he was going to slip away from her once they were in the mall and go to the jewelry store to pick out her engagement ring.

Certainly, it would have been easier if he had gone by himself sometime, but he kind of liked the intrigue and excitement of doing it this way, as if this were some sort of secret mission he had to carry out.

Then, considering how she was kissing him with growing urgency, he stopped thinking about other things for a while.

They didn't get in any hurry leaving Tobey's apartment. It wasn't like they could beat the crowds to the mall. By nine o'clock, the place would already be packed and so would the parking lot. But it was a nice day, looked like, so Tobey didn't mind if they had to walk quite a way to one of the mall entrances.

Ashley was as beautiful as ever in jeans, a silk blouse, and a lightweight jacket. Tobey wore jeans, a snap-front shirt, and a denim jacket.

Ashley sometimes tried to accuse him of

dressing like a cowboy, but the clothes were comfortable, he'd explained. That was the only reason he wore them.

And if they made him look a little like a cowboy . . . well, so much the better, as far as he was concerned.

The denim jacket had a good inside pocket, too, where he carried a Smith & Wesson M&P 9mm Shield, along with an extra loaded eight-round magazine. The little semi-auto was light-weight and accurate. It didn't have the stopping power of a .45, but with hollow-point rounds it would be pretty effective.

He was glad Illinois had started issuing concealed carry licenses. After being armed nearly all the time in Iraq—and having his life depend on his skill with those weapons on a number of occasions—he would have felt positively naked if he'd had to go around without a gun.

He didn't expect to ever actually *need* one again, at least he hoped not, but if bad trouble ever cropped up, he'd be prepared for it.

To that end, he made it out to the range at least a couple of times a month and did plenty of dry fire exercise between sessions. He had a good eye and didn't want to lose it.

This morning, Ashley saw him slipping the Shield into his pocket and said, "Are you expecting to have to shoot your way through a horde of crazed shoppers?"

"Hey, you never know when a zombie apocalypse might break out. There's a good reason why they shoot so many of those movies in shopping malls. People are more likely to be insane to start with when they're trapped in them."

"It was your idea to go today, you know," she pointed out dryly.

"I know, and I still want to. Come on."

One of the first things he'd done when he got back was to buy a pickup with the money he'd saved. He had worked construction before he enlisted and figured he'd go back to that, and having a vehicle he could use for hauling things might come in handy. He'd been right about that, too. He worked steadily and was pretty much a master carpenter.

Tobey liked the feeling of having the pickup's substantial chassis around him, too. Not that he expected to encounter any ambushes in suburban Springfield.

He opened the pickup's door for Ashley. She was a tall girl, so she didn't have any trouble climbing in, although Tobey was right there to give her a hand if she had.

"I'm still curious what it is you want to buy," she said as they started toward the sprawling mall on the edge of town.

"Nothing in particular," he lied. "I just thought it might be fun to look around."

"Uh-huh," she said, clearly not believing him.

"You're hoping I'll see something and talk about how much I like it, so you'll know what to buy me for Christmas."

"If that's what I was doing, I probably wouldn't admit it, now would I?"

"Probably not. But it doesn't really matter. Being sneaky is not your strong suit, Tobey Lanning."

"I'll remember that," he replied. He almost said, *I'll remember that when we're married,* but he caught himself in time.

They had discussed marriage, but not all that seriously yet, at least as far as Ashley knew. If Tobey hadn't been serious, he never would have brought the subject up in the first place.

"You're not thinking about buying me a gun, are you?" she asked a few moments later. She wasn't an anti-gunner. In fact, she had gone with him to the range a few times and shot some with his weapons, proving to be decently accurate at five to ten yards. She had seemed to enjoy herself, too. But she'd never expressed any interest in having a gun of her own.

"I wasn't planning to, no," Tobey answered, honestly this time.

"Good. I don't mind being around you when you're carrying, but I don't see any reason for me to have one. I couldn't ever shoot another person."

"I wouldn't be so sure about that."

"I am. No matter what the circumstances, I

91

couldn't pull the trigger on another human being."

Tobey didn't see any point in arguing with her, so he didn't say anything else about the subject.

He didn't believe she was right, though. If she ever found herself in a situation where the instinct for self-preservation ought to kick in, she would fight to defend herself or some other innocent person. He hoped that was true, anyway.

A few minutes later, they came in sight of the mall and the parking lots that surrounded it. Tobey's eyes widened a little as he said, "Wow."

"I warned you."

"Yeah, I know." He laughed. "There's no turning back now, though. Remember that poem by Tennyson we had to study back in high school?"

"It's the mall, Tobey. It's not the valley of death we're charging into, like the Light Brigade."

"We'll see," he said.

Chapter 13

A few minutes before eight o'clock, a woman in short heels, a skirt, and a blouse had come around the corner into the food court and walked toward Calvin, her heels clicking on the tiles. Normally he'd never be able to hear such a sound because of the hubbub in the mall, he thought, but without customers in here the place was a lot quieter. The clicking even echoed a little.

While waiting for the mall to open, Calvin had drifted through the food court to the entrance doors. There were eight of them, four sets of two, all glass with metal dividers between them. One set was handicap-equipped with a motor to open the doors, the large round switch to activate them being mounted on the wall close by.

Because the doors were glass, Calvin could see the crowd of shoppers walking in from the parking lot and gathering on the other side as they waited for the mall to open. Right now they were just kind of milling around, not lining up or anything. When the doors were unlocked, they would have to form rough lines, though, in order to come in.

Unless they all tried to stampede through at once, in which case there would be trouble and somebody might be hurt. It would be part of Calvin's job to prevent that, and he suddenly felt a little surge of worry. He didn't much like the idea of being responsible for people's safety.

But if that was going to bother him, he shouldn't have gone to work as a security guard, he supposed, no matter how much he needed the money.

In the meantime, though, watching the crowd was fascinating in a way. Calvin saw people of all shapes, sizes, sexes, and colors. Everybody came to the mall, especially on Black Friday. Couples trying to keep unruly children from running all over the place. Groups of moms pushing strollers. Rich people. People who, judging by their clothes, didn't have much money. Young people. Old people. Teenage girls. Calvin noticed plenty of *them,* but not many boys. Most guys his age were still asleep, he figured, unless they had to work like he did. It would take more than shopping to get them out of bed this early, unless there was some brand-new, eagerly awaited video game involved.

Now eight o'clock loomed, and the doors would soon be open. The woman approaching Calvin smiled at him. She was in her thirties, which seemed fairly old to him, but nice looking, with brown hair that fell to her shoulders. He figured she worked for the management company that ran the mall. She had a key in one hand.

"Hello," she said. "You're one of the temporary guards, aren't you?"

"Yes, ma'am. Calvin Marshall."

"I'm Emily Thorn. Nice to meet you, Calvin. I work for Rand Properties."

"Yes, ma'am. I figured as much. Are you here to unlock the doors?" He glanced at the crowd. The shoppers must have sensed that something was going on. They had surged closer to the doors, like a rising tide. "I think those folks would appreciate it if you did. They're ready."

"We can hope so," Emily Thorn said. She lifted her head a little and cocked it to the side in a listening attitude as Christmas music suddenly filled the air. Calvin looked up and realized the music was coming from speakers on the ceiling.

"Somebody in the office just pushed a button, didn't they?" he asked.

"That's right. But it's not exactly a *Winter Wonderland* out there, is it?"

Calvin looked at the hundreds of eager customers standing in the sunshine and said, "I guess that all depends on your state of mind." He held out his hand and went on, "Why don't you let me unlock the doors? I think everybody's going to be orderly, but you might get trampled by accident."

"No, this is my job," Emily said. She went to the far right-hand set of doors first, quickly and smoothly unlocking them, then moved efficiently along the line, unlocking the other pairs.

By the time Emily reached the motorized doors at the left end, Calvin estimated that at least a hundred people had come into the mall. A little pushing and shoving had taken place, but not much, and all he had to do was stand next to the wall and smile and nod at the shoppers as they streamed past him.

"Morning, folks," he said to some of them. "Good morning." During his training, he'd been instructed to greet the customers if he wanted to, but not to be overly friendly. It was important to retain an authoritative presence, too.

Emily came over to him and said, "See, that went fairly smoothly, didn't it?"

"Yes, ma'am, it sure did. I'm guessing this wasn't your first time to do this."

"No, I've been working here at the mall for six years, so this is my sixth Black Friday." She cocked her head slightly to one side. "I'm sorry. Does calling it that offend you? Because I can call it something else—"

His chuckle stopped her. He said, "No, ma'am. It doesn't bother me a bit. My dad raised me not to get upset at things that nobody means any offense by. He says there are enough macro-aggressions in the world that folks ought to worry about them and not imaginary micro-aggressions."

"Well, I can't really comment on that—corporate HR policies, you know—but I don't see any harm in saying that your father sounds like a smart man."

"Yes, ma'am, he is."

She smiled again, mindful of human resources policies, and said, "Really, you don't have to call me ma'am. I'm far from being your boss, Calvin. It's okay just to call me Emily."

"All right . . . Emily." That sounded a little funny to Calvin, but he didn't want to argue with her.

"I'll see you around," she told him, then started back through the now packed food court. Some of the franchises weren't open yet, but some were, and people were already lined up to buy soft drinks, ice cream, frozen yogurt, cookies, pretzels, hot dogs, and even Chinese food. The breakfast of the modern-day bargain hunter, Calvin thought.

He crossed his arms over his chest, leaned against the wall, and watched the steady procession of humanity.

Dressed in the uniform of the murdered Donald Reed, Habib Jabara walked into the American Way Mall with a confident stride and a smile on his face.

The mall had been open for a while, but there was still a constant stream of people going in and out. Habib had considered getting there while the doors were still locked, so he could mingle with the crowd waiting to get in, but he'd decided that it might look odd for a security guard to be *outside* like that. By waiting, he had an even better chance of not being noticed. The shoppers who saw him would think he was arriving for a later shift than the guards who were on duty when the place opened.

The trick was going to be avoiding other guards and mall employees who might see him and know that he wasn't Donald Reed. Luckily,

Habib knew from conversations with Reed that the man hadn't had many friends among his fellow workers. Reed's level of intensity in his attitudes had been enough to put most people off.

Once he was in the mall, he tried to be as unobtrusive as possible. He walked along briskly among the shoppers, not hurrying but trying to make it look like he was on his way somewhere, bound on some errand. He kept a good distance between himself and the real security guards he passed, so they wouldn't be as likely to be able to read his name tag.

Habib knew that the mall hired quite a few extra guards for the holiday season, and it was unlikely those temporary workers would be acquainted with all of their fellow employees. The full-timers would think he was one of the new part-timers. The part-timers probably didn't know much of anyone, maybe two or three of their coworkers at most.

Habib had thought it all out, spending hours and hours, even days, considering every possibility. That was how he approached things, logically and thoroughly.

The leaders of the network that had brought him to this country didn't consider him anyone important, anyone to be listened to. As far as they were concerned, he was just another soldier in their holy cause, a warm body to be sacrificed if need be while they continued their slow, deliberate takeover of the United States.

Habib was going to prove them wrong about him, and he was going to demonstrate that bold, decisive action was the way to proceed, as well. Allah demanded the blood of the infidels, and Habib was going to deliver it.

Once he had decided on that, he had set out to gather allies, forming his own organization of men and women who shared his belief that they ought to strike swiftly and brutally against the enemy. Nothing cowed the Americans as much as the sight of their dead families.

Habib had studied history. He knew that there had been a time when an attack such as the one he planned would have united the Americans in righteous anger, would have roused them to a fury so fierce that their giant rage would have crushed any in opposition to them.

Many of the older men in the network secretly feared the infidels and worried that if they moved too fast, the Americans might still rise up and swat them down like bugs.

Those days were long gone, Habib knew, eaten away by the acid of craven, greedy politicians and members of the news media so pompous and self-righteous that they were utterly blind to their own foolishness.

Habib knew that the country's heart was hollow now. The United States no longer posed any real threat to the caliphate. So why wait?

Why not start the killing now?

No one looking at him would see the thoughts going on in his head. He smiled and nodded at the Americans as he passed them, and they smiled and nodded back, the idiots.

He opened a door marked AUTHORIZED PERSONNEL ONLY and went along a maintenance corridor to another door that led into a storeroom full of janitorial supplies. This was where Donald Reed—the real Donald Reed—had been hiding the weapons, a few at a time, for weeks now.

Habib just had to make sure they were there, where they were supposed to be, and then he would return to the main area of the mall and signal Mahmoud, who was also dressed in one of Donald Reed's uniforms, and who was now waiting to start spreading the word to the others.

Habib had a hundred men inside the mall, give or take. Something might have happened to delay a few of them, or even prevent them from showing up. But for practical purposes, he was going to call it one hundred men ready to kill.

Not only to kill. One hundred men ready to die for their cause.

One hundred men, in the right place and time, could change the world.

One man could change the world.

Habib was convinced he was that man.

He went into the unlocked storeroom and moved several crates, exposing the stack of them with the special markings he recognized. Reed had been telling the truth, Habib thought with a smile.

He reached out, rested a hand on one of the crates with automatic weapons hidden inside it, and he seemed to be able to feel the raw power emanating from within, the power to take the lives of scores of infidels and demonstrate to the Americans once and for all that their day was over. Now was the time for the Sword of the Prophet to strike.

"Whatcha doin' there, pal?" a voice asked from behind him.

Chapter 14

Tobey cruised the parking lot for several minutes, looking for an empty space.

"I think I saw some spots out along the edge," Ashley said, not sounding like she was complaining, just pointing out facts. "You might as well park out there and we'll walk."

"Are you sure?"

"I'm perfectly capable of walking that far. Unless you enjoy driving around and around in a crowded parking lot and dodging pedestrians."

Tobey grunted and said, "Not hardly." At the

end of the row, he turned toward the outer edge of the lot, instead of back toward the mall.

Ashley was right. There were empty spaces on the outer fringes of the parking lot, although even there they weren't in abundance. Tobey backed the pickup into one of them. He had gotten into the habit of being able to get out of wherever he was in a hurry if need be, although he didn't anticipate that being necessary today.

So much of being prepared for trouble was being ready to do things you didn't expect to be necessary. A reasonable person hoped they *wouldn't* be necessary. But one of these days, they *might* be, and the person who was best prepared was generally the one who survived.

Tobey and Ashley joined the shoppers heading into the mall. He had devoted considerable thought to how he was going to handle this. He didn't want to suggest that they split up as soon as they got inside. She would be suspicious of that, for sure. In fact, it would be better if the suggestion came from her, and he had an idea of how to go about achieving that end.

"It was your idea to come here today," she said as they walked into the mall. "What do you want to look at first?"

"How about that place that sells nothing but calendars? They always have some good ones."

"All right. That's pretty close, I think. And they're probably giving out samples at the cheese and sausage place down there at that end of the mall, too."

"I wouldn't say no to that," Tobey replied with a smile.

They spent a good twenty minutes looking at calendars catering to all interests and talking about the various subjects. Ashley made a comment about the time Tobey spent studying the swimsuit calendars, to which he told her, "None of those girls look as good in a bikini as you do, Ash."

"You're just flattering me."

He shook his head and said, "Nope, it's the absolute truth, and I'll swear to it on a stack of Bibles if you want me to."

"I don't think that's necessary," she said. "And I appreciate the sentiment, whether it's true or not."

"Oh, it is. You don't have to doubt that for a minute."

They moved on to the cheese and sausage kiosk nearby, where teenage girls dressed in German milkmaid outfits were indeed passing out samples to shoppers. Tobey tried a couple of different kinds of cheese, as well as a slice of sausage.

"It's good," he told the girl in the elaborate costume who gave him the food. Her piercings and the purple streaks in her blond hair didn't exactly go with the innocent milkmaid outfit, he thought, and then he told himself not to be judgmental.

"Thanks," she said. "The cheese is on sale today."

Ashley said, "You'd just as soon not be here, wouldn't you, honey?"

"It's not that obvious, is it?" the girl asked worriedly. "I don't want to get fired."

"No, it's not obvious," Ashley assured her. "I just know what it feels like because I've been in the same place."

"Really? I need the money—"

"Oh, I know. Believe me. Tobey, let's buy a few things."

He shrugged and said, "Sure, whatever you want." They picked out several items and paid for them.

Then as they walked on toward the middle of the mall, Tobey told Ashley, "I didn't know you'd worked at a place like that. I'm trying to imagine you dressed up like a German milkmaid. It's kinda sexy."

"I never wore one of those silly costumes," she said now that they were out of earshot of the girl they'd been talking to. "You can tell she was embarrassed, though. She's probably hoping none of her friends sees her."

"Nothing embarrassing about honest work."

"That's where you're wrong. There are all kinds of honest jobs that are plenty embarrassing. Especially if you're a teenage girl."

"That's something I never had to worry about." They had reached a sporting goods store. Tobey slowed down and looked at the place with interest.

Ashley noticed what he was doing, just as he figured she would. She said, "Why don't you go on inside and look around to your heart's content? We can meet up later."

"But we came to spend the day together," Tobey protested, hoping the objection sounded genuine.

"There'll still be plenty of the day left. I was thinking I'd go look at earrings and purses. You don't really want to do that, do you?"

"Well . . ."

"It's settled, then. We'll meet in the food court in, say, an hour?"

"Sounds good to me," Tobey said with a nod.

That was true. Things were working out just the way he had planned. The jewelry store was close by, and once Ashley was out of sight, he could go over there and pick out her engagement ring.

She was going to be surprised in just a few weeks when he asked her to marry him.

Habib didn't panic when the man spoke to him unexpectedly. For a split second his pulse spiked and he was afraid that the plan had been discovered, but then his iron will took control and forced a sense of calm to flow through him.

He even managed to put a smile on his face.

This took place in a matter of heartbeats, so there was hardly a discernible delay between the question and Habib's response to it. He turned his head, smiling, and saw an American standing in the doorway of the storage room.

The man was tall, rawboned, lantern-jawed, with bushy eyebrows, and he wore the uniform of a mall security guard, including a pistol strapped into a holster at his waist. Habib had never seen him before, but that didn't stop him from sounding like the two of them were old friends as he said, "Oh, hi."

"Hi, yourself," the American said. He seemed more puzzled than actually suspicious, but he wasn't going to let go of that curiosity. "I asked what you're doin' in here, pal."

How Habib hated the infidels' habit of addressing each other as "pal" or "buddy"!

On the other hand, that instinctive urge of theirs to believe that, deep down, everyone liked them was one reason it was going to be so easy in the long run to conquer them. You have to be able to recognize your enemies before you can defeat them.

"One of the janitors asked me to come in here and look for something for him," Habib lied easily.

"That's not your job," the American said in a somewhat disapproving tone.

"I know, but it didn't seem like much trouble. I mean, why not help out a fellow mall employee, you know?"

The American grunted and said, "You're one of the new guys, right?"

"That's right. Why do you ask?"

"Because if you'd been here very long, you'd know not to trust them custodians. Biggest bunch of connivin' con men you've ever seen."

"I'm sure they say the same thing about us guards," Habib replied with a chuckle.

"Yeah, maybe." Instead of going away, the American did the one thing Habib didn't want him to do. He took another step into the storage room and asked, "What is it you're looking for, anyway?"

Habib wasn't prepared for that question. He said the first thing he could come up with off the top of his head.

"Um . . . urinal cakes."

"Urinal cakes?" the American repeated. "They're not even kept in here! Somebody should've warned you about those custodians."

"I . . . I'm sorry," Habib said, getting angrier all the time as control of this situation slipped further from his fingers. Why wouldn't this infuriating infidel just go away?

The man laughed suddenly and said, "Ah, don't worry about it, kid, I'm just screwin' with you. There's no such thing as the urinal cake scam."

"Oh. It was just a joke then." That didn't make Habib feel relieved. In fact, it made the flame of his rage burn that much brighter.

"Yeah. I'm Dave Dixon, by the way." So far Habib had been standing with his back to the American, so the man couldn't read the name tag pinned to his shirt. But now the American stepped even closer and leaned forward so he could see the front of Habib's uniform. "And you're . . ."

The man stopped short and frowned.

"Wait a minute. I know Donald Reed, and you're not—"

While the American was voicing his unfortunate discovery, Habib slid out the combat knife from inside the waistband of the uniform trousers.

Before this day was over, he was going to kill hundreds of Americans anyway. He might as well start now, he thought again.

A flick of his wrist opened the blade. He brought it up, the move almost too fast for the eye to follow, and plunged it into the man's chest, angling the knife up to reach the heart, the same way he had killed Donald Reed some twelve hours earlier.

At the same time, his other hand shot out and closed around the American's throat to choke off any outcry.

Habib rammed his weight into the man and forced him back against the wall. The man's skull thudded hard against the wall, but it was unlikely he felt much of the impact because he was already dying. His eyes bulged and his mouth hung open.

Habib's knife hand pressed against his chest. Every bit of the blade was buried inside the American's body.

Habib twisted it and took savage pleasure in the action. Given better circumstances, he would have preferred to slit the American's throat and let him bleed to death, or even more satisfying, drive the knife into his belly and rip it from side to side, creating a huge, gaping wound through which the man's entrails would spill.

It would have been nice, seeing the American staring in horror at his own guts before he died.

But right now, killing this man quickly and silently was best, Habib knew.

Later, there would be plenty of time for him to luxuriate in watching Americans die.

Chapter 15

Tobey hadn't planned to get distracted, but it was difficult not to once he was in the sprawling sporting goods store that was one of the mall's anchors. There was just so much to look at.

The store carried every sort of camping equipment anybody could ever need, a vast array of fishing gear, bows and arrows, exercise apparatus, balls, bats, nets, shoes, boots, waders, camo clothing, trail mix, granola, water purifiers, and around the outside walls were dozens of glass-fronted cases filled with edged weapons and guns.

Bowie knives, skinning knives, axes, hatchets, and personal defense blades. Revolvers, semi-autos, shotguns, hunting rifles, AR-15s, replicas of famous guns from the Colt .45 Peacemaker to the Winchester '73 and the Sharps Big Fifty. Calibers from .22 on up. Shelves and shelves of boxed ammunition.

For a guy like Tobey, it was a little slice of heaven.

In the meantime, he knew he needed to get over to the jewelry store and buy Ashley's engagement ring, but he found himself looking at a display of beautifully made 1911s and had trouble tearing himself away.

The guy working behind this section of counter came over to him and said, "The classic, iconic handgun of the twentieth century, just like the Peacemaker was the classic of the nineteenth."

"You'll get no argument about either of those things from me, amigo," Tobey said.

"You want a closer look at any of them?"

Tobey looked at the prices on the guns, sighed, and shook his head. He had enough money for that ring, but not if he spent it on some fancy 1911.

"No, I guess not," he said regretfully.

"Come on," the salesman urged. "What are you

gonna spend it on that's nicer than one of these babies?"

Tobey thought about Ashley. Guns were nice, but he was in love with her and always would be.

"I've got something in mind," he said. "Sorry."

"Well, come on back any time. We'll be here."

Tobey nodded and turned to head for the jewelry store, where he planned to spend the money he'd saved on the true love of his life.

Habib had stopped Dave Dixon's heart so quickly that when he withdrew the blade from the wound, only a small amount of blood welled out to stain the American's uniform shirt.

Carefully, Habib lowered the body to the floor, sliding it down the wall until Dixon was in a sitting position. Habib wiped the blood from the knife with the inside of the man's jacket, then put the weapon away.

He had to move quickly now. One of the mall's maintenance workers could come in and ruin everything, as the guard almost had.

Habib started moving the stacks of crates around. He needed to create an open space big enough that Dixon's corpse would fit into it. Once he had done that, he could move the crates back in front of the dead man to hide the grim sight.

Urgency nibbled at the edges of Habib's brain

as he worked. Everything had gone perfectly until now, and this glitch in his plan annoyed him.

Of course, he had known from the beginning that he couldn't control everything, couldn't account for every possibility. At some point, like it or not, he would have to trust to luck.

Luck was sometimes good, sometimes bad, but always capricious and unpredictable. Habib had to count on his swift wits and determination to overcome any setbacks.

Just like he was doing now. In a matter of minutes he had fashioned a hiding place for the corpse. He pulled the dead man away from the wall and got behind him, so there was no chance he would get blood on his own uniform as he grasped Dixon under the arms and lifted him. Grunting with the effort, he picked up the limp weight and hauled it backward into the little space behind the crates.

He stretched Dixon out along the wall and rolled the body on its left side to face the cinder blocks. Then, holding Dixon in place, he used his foot to shove one of the heavy crates against the body to keep it from rolling back. Another crate and then another formed a barrier. Habib began to stack them again.

A few minutes later, he was finished, and no one had disturbed him. If anyone glanced into the storage room now, all they would see were the crates of janitorial supplies.

No one would suspect that a dead man was hidden behind them.

Or a small arsenal of automatic weapons.

Beads of sweat covered Habib's face. It was cool back here in the areas of the mall off limits to the public, but you couldn't prove that by him. He heaved a sigh of relief as he sleeved some of the drops off his face. The speedy recovery he had made from this potential disaster told him that Allah was still on his side, still guiding his actions with the divine hand of vengeance.

Leaving the body hidden there worried him, but he couldn't stay and watch the place. He had other things that had to be done if the plan was to go forward. He eased the door open, checked the service corridor, and finding it empty, stepped out and pulled the door closed behind him.

A moment later, he was out in the mall again. He walked toward the bank of escalators in the center of the mall, and when he reached them, he looked up and saw Mahmoud Assouri standing on the second level, resting his hands on the black plastic top of the clear glass railing.

Habib's eyes met Mahmoud's. Slowly, Habib nodded his head just a little. The gesture was so small, so commonplace, so innocent, that no one would notice it.

Mahmoud smiled slightly, but that was his only reaction. He turned away from the railing and disappeared from Habib's angle of sight.

Habib didn't have to see his second-in-command to know that Mahmoud was carrying out the next step in the plan.

And none of the Americans had any idea what was about to happen.

An instinct for trouble was maybe the most important quality a good cop could have.

Jake Connelly had learned that over the years, and his own instinct was honed to a keen edge. He could pick out a troublemaker a mile away.

Because of that, he was suspicious as the gray-haired woman approached him in the home furnishings store and asked, "Could I help you, sir?"

"Yeah," Jake said. "I came to get a set of these."

He held up his phone to show her the picture of the curtains Adele had sent him to buy. He didn't want a lot of other stuff. No shams or flounces or whatever the hell they were called. Just plain, old-fashioned curtains.

"Oh, those are very nice," the woman said as she looked at the webpage Jake's phone displayed. "And they're on sale today, so you can get a good deal on them."

"Yeah, that's what my wife said."

"She sent you to get them?" the woman asked knowingly.

"That's right."

"Well, I'll be sure and take good care of you, then."

Jake figured that meant she planned on selling him a bunch of things he didn't need. She was going to be disappointed, though. He was no pushover for a sales pitch.

"They're right over here," she said, turning and pointing. "You'd better not waste any time getting them. Those curtains are a popular item, especially today."

"Thanks," Jake said, trying to sound sincere instead of surly. He hated to ask for any favors, but he went on, "Maybe you could show me . . ."

The woman smiled and said, "Of course."

The aisles were crowded, just like every other place in the mall. Jake wasn't sure why she had singled him out to approach, unless it was because he looked a little lost and she took him for an easy mark.

Or maybe she actually was trying to be helpful, he told himself. It wasn't easy to break through the shell of cynicism that years on the job had given him, but he knew, logically, that there were still some nice people in the world.

Just because he hadn't dealt with them very often didn't mean they weren't out there.

It could have been worse, he mused. The parking lot was crowded, but he'd been lucky and had come up on a fairly close spot just as a shopper was backing his car out. Jake had waited and then swooped in, beating a car coming from the other direction to the punch.

Inside the mall, pedestrian traffic was heavy, but people were moving along with a minimum of standing around. They were bent on their errands as much as he was, he supposed.

"Here are those curtains," the saleslady said. "What color do you need?"

Jake's brows drew down in a frown. Adele hadn't said anything about the color.

He held up the phone again and said, "This one, I guess. The one in the picture."

"Well, this style comes in five different colors. If you look at the webpage, you can see the drop-down menu where it asks you to pick a color if you're ordering online."

"You mean you can order these online?"

"Of course. You can get any merchandise in our stores from our website, and other options, besides."

Then why in the hell hadn't Adele just ordered what she wanted and had it delivered to the house, he asked himself. Why send him out into this . . . this hellhole of good cheer?

Maybe she just wanted a break from him, he realized. He supposed he *did* tend to hover a little. Or maybe she honestly thought it would do him some good to get out of the house for a while. She probably wished *she* could get out of the house and go somewhere besides doctors' offices and treatment centers and hospitals.

Feeling foolish and a little embarrassed all of a sudden, he said to the saleslady, "The room where these are going is a pale blue, I guess you'd call it. I don't know the fancy name for that particular shade."

"Then I believe these will do just fine," she said as she picked up a set of curtains in a clear plastic package. She handed them to Jake and asked, "What do you think?"

He held them up, squinted at them, and tried to imagine what they would look like hanging over the windows in the bedroom. That wasn't easy, because he had about as much visual sense as a rock when it came to things like that.

But after a moment he nodded and said, "Yeah, I think they'll look okay," even though he still wasn't a hundred percent certain.

"Excellent. What else can we get for you?"

Here came the sales pitch. He shut that down right away by saying, "That's it. This is all I need."

"The checkouts are at the front of the store, then," she told him with a smile. "Thank you, and have a wonderful holiday season." She glanced around and added in a slightly conspiratorial tone, "Is it all right if I wish you a Merry Christmas?"

"It's all right by me, lady," Jake said. "Merry Christmas to you, too."

For a second he was tempted to buy something else, just because she hadn't been cowed completely by the forces of political correctness. But he didn't know what it would be—he didn't exactly need new throw pillows or anything—so he just smiled and nodded and headed for the checkout.

Long lines stretched from all of them. Jake passed the time while he waited by playing solitaire on his phone. He might be a crusty old curmudgeon most of the time, but some aspects of modern technology were okay, he supposed.

When he finally made it out of the store, he paused in the mall and drew a deep breath as he tried to think of anything else Adele might like. A little surprise of some sort might brighten her day.

He hadn't come up with anything yet when he noticed the security guard.

The guy was standing over by the main escalators in the center of the mall, looking up at the second level. The intensity on the guard's face made Jake think something might be wrong, so he lifted his gaze as well. If there was some sort of trouble, he might be able to help out, although those rent-a-cops often resented the real thing, even retired ones.

Jake didn't see any trouble, though, just another guy leaning on the railing up there and looking down at the guard. Or maybe they weren't looking *at* each other, but only in each other's general direction.

Jake didn't think so, though, and then when the guard nodded a little—such a faint movement of his head that most of the busy shoppers hurrying around him never would have noticed it—Jake was sure there was a connection between the men.

Those two were up to something, he told himself.

And to a guy like him, such a thought was like waving the proverbial red flag in front of the proverbial bull. Jake wanted to know what was going on here.

There was one way to find out. When the guy on the second level walked off and then the guard turned and sauntered away, Jake followed him, staying back in the crowd so he wouldn't be spotted, but close enough that he wouldn't lose his quarry.

The thought that he needed to get home to Adele prodded the back of his brain, but Jake put it aside for the moment.

This wouldn't take long, and hell, it probably wouldn't amount to anything, anyway.

Chapter 16

Tobey wasn't the sort of man who second-guessed himself. He knew there was a possibility Ashley wouldn't like the ring he picked out. If that happened, they would just bring it back and return it, and she could select her own ring.

She ought to give him credit for trying, though, he thought as he stood in the jewelry store, looking down through glass at glittering diamonds and bands of shining silver and gold.

A sleekly attractive, well-dressed young woman stood on the other side of the counter, smiling at him. Her expertly manicured hands rested on the glass on her side. She wasn't wearing an engagement ring or a wedding band, and Tobey had seen the way she eyed him appreciatively.

Didn't matter, he told himself. He was taken. And once he had told her he was looking for an engagement ring, she hadn't bothered trying to flirt with him. Instead she had settled for being friendly and professional.

"If you told me how much you want to spend, I can show you the rings in that price range," she suggested. "Just a ballpark figure is fine."

Tobey hesitated, then said, "I've got three thousand dollars."

Actually, he could go as high as four thousand,

but he didn't see any reason to tell her that.

"You can get a very nice ring for three thousand," she said. "Let's look at these right along here . . ."

Tobey glanced toward the throngs passing by in the mall. The store was open all the way across the front, like most of the businesses here, with heavy gates that would be drawn across to close it off after hours. He figured that they probably had a safe somewhere in back, too, where they locked up the most valuable items.

The important thing was that Ashley could walk by, glance in here, and see him. He mentally muttered curses at himself for lingering so long in the sporting goods store, looking at guns. He should have gotten this done as quickly as possible, before she finished what she was doing and came searching for him. She might do that even though they had agreed to meet at the food court.

Then he told himself to relax. She'd said she was going to look at purses and accessories, and he knew from experience how long *that* could take. He just didn't need to waste any more time than he already had.

He couldn't afford to rush this decision, though. Ash might be wearing this ring for the rest of her life—he certainly hoped she would be—so he had to find just the right one . . .

"Do you see any you like?" the woman asked.

"I dunno, they're all really pretty," Tobey replied without looking up. His eyes went from one ring to the next in this section as he tried to imagine how each of them would look on Ashley's finger.

His scrutinizing gaze paused on a ring with a simple but classically beautiful stone in a setting that was fancy but not gaudy, with three smaller stones in a line on each side of it. The main stone wasn't huge, but it was a nice size, he thought. The band was a deep gold color.

"I can afford this?" he asked.

"You can," the woman said. "Although the tax might make it go a *little* over your budget."

"That's all right," Tobey said.

"You think your girlfriend—I mean, your soon-to-be fiancée—will like it?"

"I believe she will," Tobey said. "She's beautiful, and so is this ring."

"I've never even met her, and I know you're right about her. Do you want a closer look?"

"Yeah. Yeah, I do."

She unlocked the case and took the ring out, then lifted it from its velvet nest in the box and extended it toward him. Tobey took it gingerly. The thing felt tiny and delicate in his big, blunt fingers, even though he knew that diamonds were among the hardest substances on earth.

"Think about slipping that onto your girl's finger."

"That's just what I'm doin'," Tobey said. Everything about it felt right. "I'll take it."

"That's wonderful. I'm sure you're both going to be very happy." She gave him a dazzling smile, but not as dazzling as the ring. "Now, what about the size?"

"Oh, crap," Tobey said before he could stop himself.

The young woman laughed, a genuine sound that made him like her.

"You don't know her ring size, do you?" she asked.

"Well . . . no."

"What about my finger? How does it compare to hers?" She took the ring from him and slipped it on the third finger of her left hand.

For a second he wanted to say, *Hey, don't do that! That's Ashley's ring!*

But it wasn't yet, and anyway, he figured other women had tried it on in the past, so this was nothing to get upset about. The woman was just trying to help him.

Her fingers were a little skinnier than Ashley's, he thought, and the ring was a little loose on her. He said, "I think it might fit her okay."

"You want this to be a surprise, don't you? So you can't very well bring her in and have her try it on."

"That's right. I plan to ask her to marry me on Christmas Eve."

"Aww. That's sweet. Well, if it doesn't quite fit, you can have it resized later. From what you're saying, though, it should be pretty close."

"I hope so." He hated to bring up the next subject, but he had to. "Uh . . . what if she hates it?" Quickly, he added, "I don't think she will, but just in case . . ."

"I know, this is a substantial investment. As long as the ring is in the same condition it is now, you can return it for full credit within thirty days and she can pick out something else."

"That's fair enough, I guess. Cutting it a little close on the thirty-day business, but Christmas Eve falls inside that window."

The woman smiled again, shook her head, and said, "I don't think you have a thing to worry about. She's going to love it."

"You really think so?"

"She loves you, doesn't she?"

"Yeah," Tobey said. "I believe she does."

A few minutes later, he left the jewelry store three grand poorer but with the little black box in his pocket, a light step, and a grin on his face.

Mission, as they say, accomplished.

Despite the sunshine, the temperature was cool enough today that most of the shoppers were wearing jackets. Habib had studied the weather forecast and was counting on that, but he had a backup plan as well.

Now, on the spur of the moment, he decided to combine the two.

The mall had displays of shopping bags set up in various places. They were simple, cheap bags with the mall's name and logo printed on both sides. Their handles were looped into a coin-operated machine. Shoppers fed in a certain amount of quarters and could then pull one of the bags loose.

Habib wandered through the mall until he found one of the shopping bag displays in an isolated area. He had a pad of paper, a marker, and some tape in his pocket, items he had brought along in case the weather was too warm and people were in shirtsleeves. He brought them out and quickly printed a makeshift sign that read OUT OF ORDER.

After taping the sign to the display, he picked up the whole thing. Tending to a problem like this was probably something the janitorial staff would more likely do, but that didn't matter. The shoppers who saw a guard carrying a bag machine like that wouldn't think anything of it.

Habib started back toward the storage room where the guns and Dave Dixon's body were hidden.

He got there just in time. One of the men who had joined in this holy effort with him was approaching the entrance to the service corridor. Habib caught his eye, and the man slowed down, loitering in front of a toy store for a moment while Habib carried the bag display into the corridor and along it to the storage room.

The area was deserted, he saw. Relief went through him. Dixon's body and the arsenal hadn't been discovered.

He opened the door and confirmed that everything was in place. The Americans hadn't found out what was going on and set a trap for him.

They would have been surprised if they had. Enough explosives were strapped to his body under his shirt to make a nice big blast. He had known right from the start that this was a necessary precaution. If anything went wrong, he was not going to be taken alive, and he would take as many of the infidels with him as he could.

He set the shopping bags down, moved a crate, and opened one of the special ones. He took out a small but deadly, fully automatic Steyr TMP, one of a shipment that had been bought on the black market in Europe, shipped on a freighter to South America, smuggled northward and finally across the border from Mexico into Texas, and then transported up here to Illinois.

The door eased open. Habib turned and handed the gun to the man he had seen out in the mall a few moments earlier. The man took it, smiled as he hefted it, and said, "Allahu akbar."

"Allahu akbar," Habib replied.

The man reached behind him and stuck the Steyr into the waistband of his trousers, under the jacket he wore. The weapon was small enough that it wasn't very noticeable. The man already had a dozen fully loaded thirty-round magazines hidden around his body. When the time came to strike, he and his fellow warriors would have plenty of firepower.

No sooner had he gone, after wishing Habib good luck and saying that they would meet again in paradise, than another man was there to pick up his weapon. Habib broke open the shopping bag display and slipped the machine pistol into the bag.

"If you carry it by both handles, the bag will be closed enough that no one will look in and see the weapon," Habib told the man, who nodded in understanding.

That was how it began, and for the next hour Habib continued distributing the weapons that Saudi oil money had paid for. Another example of how the stupid Americans had sown the seeds of their own destruction, he thought, by doing business with men who wanted them all dead.

Habib felt excitement growing inside him. Everything was going so well. He began to get the sense that a great victory was inevitable here today, that Allah had touched him and bestowed a special destiny on him with which nothing could interfere.

His name would be known from now on.

When the clerics spoke of the martyrs who had done the most to further the holy cause of Islam, the name of Habib Jabara would be first among them.

Nothing could stop him now.

Jake was more torn than he had been in a long time. He should have headed for home an hour ago, he told himself as he sat on one of the benches the mall had put out so shoppers could rest for a few minutes before going off to spend more money.

Jake had been on the bench for more than a few minutes, though. It was located diagonally across from the entrance to a service corridor with an AUTHORIZED PERSONNEL ONLY sign on it. He was pretending to look at stuff on his phone, but in reality he was watching the steady stream of Middle Eastern–looking guys going in and out of that corridor.

That security guard he had noticed earlier had made his radar go off, and nothing that had happened since then had done anything to silence those alarm bells. Jake had followed the guy and seen him put an OUT OF ORDER sign on that thing that dispensed shopping bags. That didn't really seem like something a guard would have done, but Jake supposed it was possible.

He had been twenty yards back in the crowd as

the guy carried the bags back to the service corridor near where Jake had first seen him. Jake had spotted the bench and gone over to sit down on it.

And then the parade had started.

Jake's last fifteen years on the job, he'd heard more than he ever wanted to about racial profiling and how bad it was and how the police and other authorities could never be allowed to carry out such evil, disgusting, racist behavior.

Which was all bullcrap, of course. There was nothing racist about being able to look at the plain and simple facts right in front of your eyes and recognize them for what they were.

One of those facts was that nearly all Islamic terrorism was carried out by young, Middle Eastern males. It was crazy to think that anything else might be true. Worse than that, it was a waste of time and resources.

There were plenty of Muslims in the country now, more than ever before, in fact. Jake supposed that most of them were law-abiding folks who just wanted to be left alone to go about their lives, like anybody else. Maybe it wasn't fair to look at somebody like that and wonder if he was a terrorist.

But when a bunch of them suddenly started acting in odd ways . . . Hell, forget about fair. It wasn't *prudent* not to wonder about them. Jake was willing to bet that none of the guys he had seen going in and out of that service corridor in the past hour were *Authorized Personnel.*

So what were they doing? What was their connection to the security guard Jake had first noticed? To be honest, that guy could be Middle Eastern, too, although Jake had taken him for Hispanic or Indian at first.

Jake didn't have any answers, but the hunch was growing strong in him that somebody needed to start looking for some.

That wasn't his job. He was just an old, retired cop with a sick wife at home. He put his phone away, rested his hands on his knees, and heaved his body to his feet. He knew where the mall offices were. The head of security would be there, too.

A few minutes later, Jake found who he was looking for. The burly, white-haired man was standing behind a counter in one of the offices, wearing the same sort of uniform Jake had seen on all the guards. He had some papers in front of him, but he glanced up from them and asked, "Help you, sir?"

"Jake Connelly," Jake introduced himself as he stuck his hand out. "I used to be on the job in Chicago."

Jake saw the flash of wariness in the man's eyes. *Some ex-cop who's got his nose out of joint about something,* he was probably thinking.

But the man kept his voice level and noncommittal as he shook Jake's hand and said, "I'm Ray Napoli, head of security for the mall. Is there a problem, Mr. Connelly? Did you witness some shoplifting or an incident like that? We're always happy to take reports from our shoppers—"

"That's not it," Jake interrupted. "I think maybe you've got yourself a situation here . . . and it's not a good one."

Chapter 17

Calvin started to get tired as the morning wore on. He had played football, run track, and done plenty of athletic stuff, but he'd never had to just *stand* for long periods of time. He was surprised by how tiring doing that turned out to be.

Not only that, but it was boring as well. He wouldn't have thought that watching thousands of people—all varieties of people—walk past him could get monotonous, especially when many of them were attractive young women, but that was exactly what had happened.

He found himself wondering where that girl Irina was and what she was doing. She probably wasn't even here at the mall anymore, he thought. She might work the night shift and could have come in right after midnight to get the place ready for the onslaught of shoppers on Black Friday. Chances were, she was home asleep by now.

He kept an eye out for her anyway. He wasn't sure why, other than the fact that she'd seemed nice and he wouldn't have minded talking to her again. That was reason enough, he supposed.

But he didn't see her, and that was a little disappointing. He could have missed her in the crowd, he reasoned. He had thought the mall might get less busy after that first opening rush, but that hadn't turned out to be the case. If anything, the place was even more crowded now.

Calvin smiled and nodded to everyone who made eye contact with him. That wasn't many people. The shoppers who had come to the mall today were too intent on getting what they were looking for to care too much about what was going on around them.

To them, Calvin thought, he was just another mall fixture, like a bench or a potted plant.

He knew where he could find at least one friendly face, though. He had a break coming up soon, and when he had the chance, he intended to walk down to the end of the mall where Dave Dixon was posted. Even though he and Dave had talked for only a few minutes early that morning, Calvin had sensed that the other guard would be glad to see him.

They had been taught in their training to remain at their posts until someone came to relieve them, so that was what Calvin did. The time for his break came and went, but it was only five minutes past the time when another guard walked up to him and said, "You're Marshall, right?"

"That's right."

"Okay, you can take twenty minutes."

This guard was an older man and had a holstered gun on his hip. Calvin wondered if his job was to go around the mall and relieve the other guards so they could get their breaks. That actually wouldn't be a bad assignment, he thought. It would be better than standing in one place for hours.

Of course, this guy appeared to be a full-timer, and a veteran of the security force, at that, so that was probably why he got this particular job . . . if, indeed, that was what he did.

Calvin thanked the man who had relieved him and headed for the end of the mall where he hoped to find Dave Dixon. As he walked along, he met a man and woman who were armed and wearing the uniform of the Springfield Police Department. They nodded to him as he passed.

That was something else that had been covered during training. The PD assigned three units to the mall for this long holiday weekend. One patrol unit cruised the parking lots constantly, while the officers from the other two units circulated through the mall all day. They were there to handle any actual arrests that had to be made, whether for shoplifting, disturbing the peace, public intoxication, or other crimes.

Calvin found it hard to believe that anybody would actually get drunk to come to the mall on the day after Thanksgiving . . . but maybe that was the only way some people felt like they could face it.

He spotted the calendar kiosk and the cheese and sausage store up ahead and knew Dave ought to be around here somewhere. Calvin looked all around, however, and didn't spot the tall, raw-boned guard.

Someone else was on duty, though: a short, pale, redheaded man who didn't look happy.

Calvin walked up to him, nodded pleasantly, and said, "Hello."

Without returning the greeting, the man snapped, "Are you here to tell me what the hell happened to Dixon?"

Calvin frowned in surprise and shook his head.

"No, I'm looking for him myself. Isn't he supposed to be here?"

"Damn right he is. I gave him his break a little while ago, and he never came back."

So the guard who had relieved Calvin wasn't the only one doing that job, but Calvin hadn't thought that he was.

"You a friend of his?" the man asked.

"Well . . . we just met this morning . . ."

"Doesn't matter. Dixon's one of those guys who's your friend right away, as soon as he meets you." The man glared. "I hate guys like that."

"I wish I knew where he might be—"

"You're on your break, right?"

"Yeah."

"Take a look around for him, okay? Hate to ask you to do it, but we gotta find the guy. If he's flaked out and left, Napoli can call in somebody to replace him."

"I don't really know him, but that doesn't seem like something he'd do," Calvin said.

The redhead shrugged his beefy shoulders and said, "Yeah, you're right about that. All that bein' chipper is annoyin' as hell, but Dixon's good at his job, I'll give him that. If he'd gotten sick or something, he would've let the boss know."

"I'll look for him," Calvin said. He wasn't exactly *worried*—he didn't know Dave Dixon well enough for that—but he was concerned. And curious. He asked, "Which way did he go when you relieved him?"

"That direction," the man said, pointing to a section of the mall that contained a toy store, a shoe outlet, a couple of hip, trendy clothing stores, a place that sold leather handbags, and a makeup and beauty supply store.

"I'll go have a look around," Calvin said. He put his hands in the pockets of his jacket and started in that direction.

This wasn't the way he had intended to spend his break, he thought . . . but it was still better than just standing around.

Tobey looked at his phone to check the time. It hadn't been as long since he and Ashley split up as he had thought. Maybe it had just seemed like he had wasted too much time in the sporting goods store because he was nervous.

You wouldn't think anybody who had gone through what he had, anybody who carried around battle scars and still limped a little when the weather got too damp, would get nervous under circumstances like these, but hey, asking somebody to marry him was scary stuff!

He had some time left before he was supposed to meet her at the food court. Maybe he would stop at the sporting goods store and look at those 1911s again. Now that he had spent nearly all his money, he thought as he patted the bulge that the ring box made in his jacket pocket, he could look at the pistols without being tempted to buy one and just appreciate them for the works of art they were.

He headed in that direction.

Napoli's expression had changed from one of distracted tolerance to frowning interest as he listened to Jake explain about the men going in and out of the service corridor where they didn't really belong.

"Are you sure they were Middle Eastern guys?" Napoli asked when Jake was finished.

"Looked like it to me."

"Not Hispanics?"

"I don't think so," Jake said. "But hey, either way they were where they're not supposed to be, acting suspiciously."

"Yeah, but if they're Middle Eastern—" Napoli stopped short.

"Look, you don't have to worry about me reporting you to HR or anything like that," Jake told him. "I'm a cop, or at least I was. I know that profiling is a useful tool, and that all those bleedin' hearts who say we shouldn't use it are full of crap. I know what you're thinking, too. Terrorists."

Napoli rested his big hands on the counter, drew in a deep breath, and said, "Aren't you thinking the same thing?"

"Damn right I am."

Napoli walked around the end of the counter, saying, "Tell me again where you saw these guys."

"I don't know what the official designations are, but it was the door to the service corridor on the northern side of the mall's west wing, about three-fourths of the way down to that fancy department store."

The creases in Napoli's forehead deepened.

"You know, I've got a guy down at that end of the mall who went on his break and didn't come back."

"That's kinda odd. You think there might be something hinky about him?"

"Dixon?" Napoli grunted and shook his head. "Hell, no. He's one of my best men. Worked here since the mall opened. I trust him completely. But something might've happened to him. It would've had to, for him not to do his job."

"We'd better go down there and check it out," Jake suggested.

"That's exactly what *I'm* going to do. You need to go on with your shopping, Mr. Connelly. You brought this matter to my attention and I appreciate it, but looking into it is my job."

"You'll be outnumbered."

Napoli hesitated and asked, "How many did you say there were?"

"Once I realized what was going on and started counting . . . eighty-eight. There could have been as many as a dozen guys before that."

"So maybe a hundred." Napoli grimaced.

"Yeah. Maybe what you'd better do is call the cops or, I don't know, Homeland Security."

Napoli shook his head and said, "Not until I've had a look for myself. I'm not gonna throw the mall into a panic. Not today. If it all turned out to be nothing, management would kill me."

"Suit yourself. I still think I should come with you, though."

"You got anti-terrorist experience?"

"No." Jake shrugged. "But bad guys are bad guys, right?"

Napoli grunted again and jerked his head toward the office door.

"Come on," he said. "But if things go south, no suing the mall."

"Things go south and I probably won't be around to sue anybody," Jake said.

Mahmoud was the last man to come to the storage room. Habib greeted him with a tense nod and handed him one of the machine pistols.

"Everyone is in position?" Habib asked.

"I have walked from one end of the mall to the other, on both levels," Mahmoud replied solemnly. "Our men await the signal."

Habib picked up one of the Steyrs for himself and checked it, sliding a fully loaded magazine into the well in its grip. There was one more question he felt like he had to ask, but he was uneasy about it and so he delayed.

But there was no more time, and so he took a deep breath and said, "You're sure about your part?"

Not a flicker of emotion showed on Mahmoud's stolid face.

"What true follower of the Prophet could be unsure at a time like this?" he asked. "It will be my honor and privilege to strike this blow against the infidels on their own soil."

"You are a good man, Mahmoud," Habib said. He gave in to impulse and quickly hugged the older man. As he did so, he felt the explosives strapped under Mahmoud's tightly closed jacket.

The bomb he carried was larger than the one on Habib. The explosion when it detonated would be enough to wreck the main escalators at the convergence of the mall's four wings, plus it would kill everyone on them at the time. Mahmoud would set it off when he was halfway up to the second level.

There was another set of escalators in each wing, but Habib had men on all of them to gun down the Americans riding on them and take control. The stairs at the end of each wing were covered as well. With thousands of shoppers in the mall, the only way to deal with them was to isolate them, cut them into small groups so that they couldn't help each other or mount a coordinated effort against their attackers.

Each of Habib's men knew his job. Each would take over the area assigned to him and get all the Americans down on the floor. This control would be enforced with bloody ruthlessness. Men were posted at the entrances and exits as well, to keep anyone from fleeing the mall, and more important, to keep everyone else out.

Then, once any scattered opposition was quickly crushed—Habib didn't expect the soft, cowardly Americans to put up much of a fight—

and the mall was completely under his command, he would begin to issue his demands. There were political prisoners to be freed, frozen assets to be released, statements to be made.

But in the end, the biggest statement would be this: Before the day was over, thousands of Americans would die, their lives snuffed out in the middle of their secular, materialistic wasteland, and Habib and his followers would be in paradise, heroes in the glorious cause of Islam.

No one—*no one*—was getting out of the American Way Mall alive.

Habib slapped Mahmoud on the back a couple of times and then stepped away from him. The older man gave him a curt nod and turned to leave the storage room.

Habib would follow him momentarily. He wanted to take this last moment for himself, alone, to reflect on what was about to happen. It was the greatest thing he had ever done, he thought. The greatest thing he ever would do.

He took a deep breath, picked up one of the shopping bags, and placed the automatic pistol in it. Then, carrying the bag, he left the room and stepped out into the corridor.

Mahmoud would wait until he saw that Habib was in position, then start up the escalator to detonate the bomb halfway to the upper level. The blast would signal all the other men to open fire. Knowing that everything was waiting on him now, Habib didn't dawdle but rather strode briskly along the corridor.

He was halfway to the door leading out into the mall itself when it swung open and two men appeared there. The one slightly in the lead was tall, broad shouldered, and had a shock of white hair. He wore a security guard's uniform, like the one Habib had on.

The other man was shorter and wider, with a face like a bulldog. He was dressed in civilian clothes, but he didn't carry himself like a civilian. Like his companion, he had an air of authority and command about him.

Habib felt a second of panic at the sight of the men. They moved with determined strides, and he knew they were here because of him. Somehow, they had guessed that something was wrong, and they were determined to find out what it was. Habib considered trying to bluff, to brazen out the impending confrontation.

But the security man would know that he wasn't Donald Reed, Habib realized. There was no way he could make the man believe otherwise.

Well, he had planned to kill Americans today anyway, he thought as he reached into the shopping bag and closed his hand around the pistol's grip. As he started to lift the gun, bringing the bag up with it, the white-haired security man yelled, "Hey, you! What are you—"

The man was already reaching for the gun on his hip as he spoke. Habib didn't let him draw the weapon. He squeezed the trigger, sending a burst of fire through the bottom of the bag.

Chapter 18

Even all the handicapped parking places were full, something that almost never happened . . . except on Black Friday, Pete McCracken supposed.

As Father Steve circled through the lot, Pete said, "Look, Father, why don't you just . . . forget about it? You can take me home . . . and we'll tell Sister Angela . . . you brought me to the mall like she wanted. Hell, it'll be . . . the truth. We're here, aren't we?"

"No, Mr. McCracken, I'm sure we'll find a place soon," the priest said. "I have faith." He grinned over his shoulder. "That's my job, after all."

"Yeah, yeah," Pete muttered.

"Look, I was right." Father Steve pointed through the windshield. "There's an empty spot now."

He pulled into the parking place, then got out to operate the van's wheelchair lift. Pete could tell he had done it before. It took only a few minutes for the priest to get him out of the van and onto the ground. Father Steve put the lift away, then locked the van with the button on the key fob.

"I'll push," he said as he moved behind the wheelchair.

"I can . . . do it myself." Pete felt the wheelchair start to move before he could hook his withered hand around the knob. "Ah . . . hell. What's . . . the point?"

He sat there and let the priest push him into the mall. Father Steve used the automatic doors so he wouldn't have to hold them open while he maneuvered the wheelchair through them.

Once they were inside, Pete said, "Holy—" then stopped himself before he fully expressed the thought that went through his mind at the sight of all those people.

"Quite a crowd, eh?" Father Steve asked cheerfully.

"Yeah, you could . . . say that. I think the last time . . . I saw this many people . . . in one place . . . was on a troop ship . . . headed for Europe."

"That's right. You were in the war, weren't you? The Great War?"

"No, that's what . . . they called World War One . . . before they knew there was . . . gonna be another one. Don't they teach you kids . . . history anymore?"

"I guess I was getting confused, what with you being part of the Greatest Generation."

"Not gonna . . . argue that part . . . with you. We were just . . . a bunch of average joes . . . but we saved the world. Your . . . pansy ass generation . . . couldn't do that."

Gently, Father Steve said, "I hope my generation will see to it that the world never needs saving like that again. I don't think it will ever come to that."

"Don't kid yourself . . . Father. It always . . . comes to that . . . as long as there are guys . . . who think they can . . . run roughshod over everybody else."

"Disagreements can be solved without going to war."

"Not talkin' about . . . disagreements. I'm talkin' about . . . evil. You believe in . . . evil, don't you . . . Father?"

"Yes, of course. But I believe it comes from outside of ourselves and that human beings can always be freed from its influence."

"Maybe. But some of 'em . . . the only way you can free 'em . . . is by shootin' 'em in the face."

Father Steve made a scoffing sound. Pete knew without looking around that the young priest was shaking his head. He was wasting his breath arguing with Father Steve . . . and in his condition he didn't have much breath to waste.

Father Steve had been pushing the wheelchair through this wing of the mall. He changed the subject by asking, "What would you like to look at, Mr. McCracken?"

Pete didn't really want to *be* here, let alone look at anything, but he knew that if he indulged the kid and pretended to be interested in something, he would get back home sooner. So he raised his good arm, pointed at a sporting goods store, and said, "Over . . . there. Might bring back . . . some good memories . . . of when I could still . . . hunt and fish."

Father Steve angled the wheelchair in that direction and said, "That's fine."

As the priest pushed him toward the store, Pete looked idly around, and suddenly he stiffened as much as his atrophied muscles would let him. He had just spotted a familiar face in the crowd.

It was that damned punk who had tried to break into his house the day before!

"You didn't have to bring me with you if you didn't want to, you know," Jennie said as she and Aaron walked toward the mall.

"Nah, I don't mind," he told her, which wasn't entirely true but close enough. Even though they hadn't talked much on the way over here, it had been sort of nice, the two of them being together in the car. He'd had the radio on, and it turned out they both liked some of the same music, which had surprised him a little.

"You *look* like you mind, the way you're frowning," she said now.

"I didn't know we were gonna have to go on a freakin' hike once we got here, that's all."

"It's not that far. Only a couple of hundred yards. If you'd let me drive your car, I could've dropped you off at the door . . . Grandpa."

She was smiling at him. Aaron laughed and said, "Let you drive my car? No way!" Although in truth, there was actually no way she could hurt that old rattletrap, he added silently.

He went on, "You're plannin' on ditchin' me as soon as we get in there, right?"

"I figured you'd be the one to ditch me."

"I don't care. We can hang if you want. I just thought you might want to see if any of your friends were here."

"I don't have that many friends," Jennie said, and what was bad was the matter-of-fact way she said it. Aaron felt a pang of sympathy for her.

He'd had plenty of friends in high school, what little time he'd been there. There were always guys who wanted to hang around with him since his time behind bars had given him a reputation as a badass. Also, he knew where to find the best weed.

Jennie was a nerd, though, and despite the fact that nerds were a lot cooler than they used to be—Aaron didn't understand how that was possible, but he'd witnessed it for himself—they still tended to be outsiders.

"I do know this one girl, though," Jennie went on. "Her name's Holly. She's working at one of the seasonal stores in the mall. You know, the one that sells cheese balls and beef sticks. Maybe I'll stop there and say hi to her. She could probably use some cheering up. They make her wear this silly costume."

"She might not want her friends coming by to see her. She might be embarrassed."

"Well, we'll just go by and say hello. I don't think she'll mind."

They had reached the doors. Aaron opened one of them and shrugged.

"Whatever you want to do," he said.

He was just here to avoid the phantoms, and so far it had worked.

"What do you think?" Kaitlyn asked as she held a short, black dress in front of her.

"I think that's way too old and revealing for you to wear," Vanessa answered without hesitation. "Anyway, where would you wear it? It's not appropriate for anywhere you go."

"Oh, I don't know," Kaitlyn said as she turned to study her reflection in a full-length mirror. "I think it might make a few eyes pop out at school."

"You mean the junior high you go to?" Vanessa

took the dress and hung it back on the nearby rack where it had come from. "None of this stuff is appropriate. We're in the wrong section."

"Yeah. The *cool* section," Kaitlyn muttered as her mother turned away. Vanessa heard the comment but chose to ignore it.

Even the good kids had to be a little rebellious, she thought. In the long run, it wouldn't do any harm.

He needed a hobby, Charles Lockhart told himself as he walked through the mall, trying not to bump into people. He'd never been very comfortable with human contact. He liked books and he liked the Internet, but people . . . not so much. Which made dealing with his students and fellow teachers difficult at times.

So maybe he needed to do something that would get him out of his comfort zone . . . although to be honest, that was a really stupid name for it, he thought, because he'd never actually been that comfortable, no matter what zone he was in. The socially awkward zone, that was a better name. He always seemed to be in that one.

But what sort of hobby could he get involved in? He thought about model railroading. That appealed to the old-fashioned side of his nature. But he could do that in his own apartment. A hobby, even if it wasn't one that brought him in contact with other enthusiasts, ought to be something that would get him *out*.

He was looking around when he saw the sporting goods store. At first his gaze started to pass right over it. Camping didn't appeal to him—as far as he was concerned, *Roughing It* was the title of a Mark Twain book, and that was all—and he knew he could never be a hunter.

But fishing . . . maybe. The idea of sitting on the bank of some slow-moving stream with a hook and a line in the water, waiting for a bite, wasn't too bad. It sounded peaceful. Like something out of a Norman Rockwell painting.

And he wouldn't actually kill the fish, of course. If he happened to catch one, he'd take the hook loose and throw it back into the river. That way he wouldn't have all the mess and bother of cleaning and cooking it, two things he didn't really know how to do, anyway. Having a hook in its mouth would still be painful for the fish, Charles supposed, but it would get over that.

He didn't have to decide today. He could go over there to that store and look at the fishing poles and the tackle and think about it some more.

Every hobby had to start somewhere, he supposed.

Tom Vasquez was a hard man to shop for, Jamie thought. Her husband made good money, and if there was something he wanted, he was in the habit of getting it for himself most of the time. Her kids didn't really want for anything, either.

Except maybe a mother.

She frowned and forced that thought out of her head. She had done the best she could for her kids, and that included doing her duty as a soldier.

Anyway, those days were over now. She was home, with an honorary discharge and some medals that were tucked away in a drawer, and she wouldn't be going overseas to fight the enemy anymore.

Right now her job was to figure out what her husband might like for Christmas. She wandered through the men's wear section of one of the department stores, looking at robes and pajamas. A man could always use a nice, comfortable robe, right? Especially when it got cold in the winter. Despite the nice weather outside, Jamie knew those days were coming soon.

Pete felt his heart pounding. He struggled to draw in a deep breath, something he couldn't do very well these days. His good hand dropped to the little pocket inside the wheelchair's right side where the Browning Hi-Power was hidden. His first impulse was to draw the gun, throw down on the punk, and yell for him to stay right where he was. Then Father Steve could call the cops.

Only the priest wouldn't *need* to call the cops, Pete realized. The threat of some old geezer waving a gun around would be enough to bring them rushing to the scene. People would panic and rush around and trample each other. These days, most people went crazy just at the sight of a gun.

Something else made Pete stay his hand.

The punk was with a girl.

She was a few years younger, a teenager, from the looks of her. Pretty, in a girl-next-door sort of way, with chestnut hair that fell around her shoulders. Kinda skinny. She wore glasses, too, and reminded Pete of one of his granddaughters. Or was it one of his great-granddaughters? He had a little trouble keeping up with that.

This girl sure didn't look like she ought to be hanging around with a punk who'd bust into people's houses on Thanksgiving.

Then Pete thought he detected a faint resemblance between them. Hard to say, since his eyes weren't what they once were, but that would explain things. They were brother and sister. Hell, even punks could have sisters, he supposed.

It wouldn't do to shoot her brother right in front of her.

Then the two of them split up, with the girl veering off toward the place that sold cheese and sausage while the punk ambled toward the sporting goods store that was already Pete's destination. Pete's eagerness to confront the little son of a bitch was enough to make him lean forward a little.

"Are you all right, Mr. McCracken?" Father Steve asked.

"Just keep pushin', Father," Pete said.

As Tobey walked toward the sporting goods store, he scanned the crowd around him, searching for Ashley. If they ran into each other, they wouldn't have to rendezvous at the food court. That would be okay with Tobey, since he had done what he came to do and the ring was resting securely in his pocket.

Whatever else Ash wanted to do here at the mall, however she wanted to spend the rest of the day, that was fine with him.

Without thinking about it, he did more than keep an eye open for Ashley. He studied the other people around him. He had gotten in the habit of doing that in Iraq, where the enemy looked just like everybody else on the streets, and the only way to spot them in time was to watch what they were doing. Noticing any suspicious behavior could easily mean the difference between life and death.

Tobey reminded himself that he was back home now and didn't have to do that anymore. There were a few guys around who looked like they could have come from Fallujah or Tekrit or Baghdad, of course, and honestly, he paid more attention to them than anybody else.

They weren't doing anything unusual, though. The guy walking along about a dozen feet in front of Tobey actually looked more dangerous, with his close-shaven head and the hoodie he wore and the way he kept turning his head from side to side so he could look around, like he was nervous and watching for something. The girl with him said something to him and then angled off.

Tobey watched her go, and then his eyes moved past her to the old man in a wheelchair who was being pushed in this direction by a priest. They struck Tobey as an unlikely pair. The old man had a really intense expression on his face, and he reminded Tobey of a vulture, the way he hunched forward a little in the chair.

There was a tall, skinny guy approaching the store, too, and he really looked out of place in his corduroy jacket with leather patches on the elbows. Tobey hadn't seen a jacket like that in ages and didn't know they even made them anymore.

A young black man wearing a security guard's uniform came out of the store and paused in front of it. He pushed his jacket back and put his hands on his hips as he looked around with a baffled frown on his face. Whatever he was searching for, he hadn't found it in the sporting goods store, and now he didn't know what to do next. That was what his attitude told Tobey, anyway.

They were all there in front of the store, within twenty feet of each other, when Tobey heard a sound he'd never expected to hear again.

Cutting through the hubbub of the busiest shopping day of the year, blotting out the good cheer of the Christmas music playing over the mall's PA system, a burst of automatic weapons fire stopped Tobey in his tracks.

Chapter 19

When the kid in the guard uniform started to raise the shopping bag, the alarm bells already going off in Jake Connelly's head set up a real clamor. The way Ray Napoli stiffened and reached for his sidearm told Jake that the mall's head of security was experiencing the same sensation.

Neither of them reacted fast enough, however, and with blank corridor walls on both sides of them, they had nowhere to go.

The noise was loud—a swift, deadly chatter as muzzle flame shredded the bottom of the shopping bag.

Napoli had taken a quick step to his right as he tried to draw his weapon. That was the only thing that saved Jake's life. The kid swung the gun he was firing from left to right, stitching a line of bullets from one side of the corridor to the other. The slugs thudded into Napoli's chest and drove him back against Jake. Napoli's body shielded the former cop from the unexpected onslaught of lead.

Jake clawed under his jacket for the .357 holstered at his waist. He had been under fire before and knew not to panic. The impact of Napoli falling against him threw him off balance, though, and the gun stubbornly refused to come clear.

Jake's feet slipped. He realized the floor was slick from the blood pouring out of the wounds in Napoli's chest and midsection. With his free hand, he grabbed instinctively at the other man's jacket. That just succeeded in getting him dragged down, too, when Napoli fell.

Only a handful of heartbeats had passed since the kid opened fire, but already the mall was full of screaming because of the sound of a gun going off. Jake heard it as if from a great distance. His ears rang like somebody was pounding on a giant drum right next to them.

Napoli was lying on top of him now, pinning Jake's gun arm so he couldn't use the .357 even if he could have gotten the weapon out of its holster.

The shooting stopped. The kid stalked forward along the corridor toward the chaos erupting out in the mall.

Jake stopped trying to get his gun out. Instead, acting purely on instinct, he stayed as still as possible, holding his breath so that not even his chest moved. If he had any chance, it lay in making the killer think that he was dead, too. With so much blood, it would be difficult to tell for certain.

The shooter fired another short burst into Napoli's body as he strode past. Jake felt the corpse shudder as the bullets struck it, but the slugs didn't go all the way through.

Jake knew without having to check that Napoli was dead. Nobody could absorb that much lead and live more than a second or two.

He expected the kid to slow down and make sure of both of them, but as he passed them he broke into a run. The adrenaline had to be pumping so hard in him that he might not be thinking straight. Jake stayed where he was until the kid had gone by, then he shoved hard against Napoli's weight.

The security chief was a big guy. Jake had to grunt and strain to roll him to the side. Jake rolled, too, through the pool of blood that had already gathered, and finally succeeded in getting the short-barreled revolver out of the holster. He lifted the gun, hoping to get a shot off . . .

His head came up just in time for him to see the shooter vanish around a corner at the end of the corridor.

•••

Mahmoud wasn't supposed to start up the escalator until he saw that Habib was in position, but the shots changed everything, Habib knew. They had discussed the possibility of something going wrong and what to do if it did. Mahmoud was supposed to act on his own initiative if he could tell that everything wasn't going according to the plan.

So when Habib emerged into the mall after gunning down the two Americans and looked toward the bank of escalators at the center of the building, he wasn't surprised to see Mahmoud fighting his way up the middle of the three escalators that rose to the upper level.

Mahmoud grabbed the clothes of the people above him and slung them back and to the side, sending them tumbling over onto the flanking escalators. Screaming, yelling, and shrieks of agony as the escalators caught hold of flesh and chewed it like giant mechanized jaws filled the air. Mahmoud ignored all of it as he lunged higher on the moving steps.

When he neared the halfway point, he stopped and turned so he could look back toward the spot where Habib stood. Just for an instant, their eyes met across that distance, and then Mahmoud's hand moved sharply to his chest.

He disappeared in a blinding burst of flame. The explosion shook the floor under Habib's feet. He staggered.

When he caught himself, he saw that Mahmoud was gone. So were the escalators, except for small, twisted remnants at the top and bottom. Dozens of Americans had been blown to bits in the blast, as well. The righteous smoke of holy destruction rolled through the mall.

Habib's heart leaped joyfully at the sight. With an incoherent yell, he pivoted around and pressed the Steyr's trigger, exulting as the weapon leaped and pounded in his hands.

The sudden chaos, accompanied by screams and shots, was like being back in Iraq. Tobey twisted toward the chatter of an automatic weapon and at the same time reached into his jacket to close his hand around the solid grip of the 9mm Shield.

The action was purely a reflexive one. His muscles knew what to do.

His brain was shouting *Ashley! Where's Ashley?*

He hoped she was at the far end of the mall, far away from whatever madman was doing this.

Then the huge blast rocked the very earth itself and almost knocked Tobey off his feet. He staggered and threw out his good arm to catch his balance. He knew an explosion that big, in a place this crowded, must have claimed dozens of lives, but there was nothing he could do for them now.

Instead he grabbed the arm of the closest man, who happened to be the tall, skinny guy who looked like a professor. Tobey practically threw him toward the sporting goods store and yelled, "Get in there! Find some cover!"

The guy stumbled right into the kid wearing the hoodie. They nearly fell down but held each other up.

"Go! Go!" Tobey shouted at them. He waved his arm to emphasize the words.

Suddenly he remembered the old man in the wheelchair and looked around to see what had become of him.

The priest was already heading for what he must have hoped was safety, pushing the wheelchair at a run in front of him. The old man looked like he was trying to yell but couldn't find the breath.

More shots hammered in a full-auto staccato.

The worst part, though, was that they were coming from different directions.

Tobey could figure out what that meant. This was a coordinated attack involving multiple shooters. That, along with the explosion, said one thing to him.

Terrorists.

Again he thought about Ashley, but there was nothing he could do for her. He had no idea where she was, and searching for her in the madhouse that the mall had become in a matter of seconds would be useless. He would look for her later if he got a chance.

If he wasn't dead.

He wasn't going to just stand around and let the sons of bitches kill him. He raised the Shield, flicking off the safety with his thumb as he did so. Somebody was shooting about thirty yards away, fire licking from the muzzle of his weapon as he sprayed bullets into the screaming crowd.

Tobey caught only glimpses of the madman through gaps in the terrified throng of people, but he might have been able to draw a bead on the shooter anyway if he hadn't hesitated when he realized the guy was wearing a security guard's uniform. That confused Tobey for a second, so he kept his finger out of the trigger guard.

The next moment, somebody tackled him from behind.

This couldn't be happening, Calvin thought as the violence and pandemonium spread around him.

Not after he had promised his mother that this job was going to be safe.

But all hell was definitely breaking loose in the American Way Mall.

He had just emerged from the sporting goods store, so far unsuccessful in his effort to locate Dave Dixon, when he heard the shots. That was bad enough, but then everybody started yelling and pushing and running, so it was impossible to tell what was going on.

Calvin looked back toward the center of the

mall. He spotted somebody in a guard's uniform standing near the entrance to one of the service corridors. Calvin's first thought was to start toward the guy and link up with him so they could work together to put a stop to the trouble.

That was when he noticed the funny-looking gun in the other guard's hands. That didn't look right at all.

But for all Calvin knew, some of the guards were armed with automatic weapons. This man could need his help.

Before anything else could happen, a huge explosion rocked the mall. Smoke roiled out from the center of the building. Calvin couldn't see much, but he knew a blast that big must have killed a lot of people. The thought made him sick to his stomach.

He forced that reaction to the back of his mind and started again toward where he had noticed the other guard. He couldn't see the man anymore but knew he was probably still over there. In this mob, nobody could go very far in a hurry.

Calvin had taken one step in that direction when he saw a big man in a denim jacket pull out a smaller pistol and raise it, using a two-handed grip that made him look like he knew what he was doing.

To Calvin's horror, he realized the man was trying to aim at the other security guard.

Calvin didn't stop to think. If he had, he might

have considered the fact that the guy was considerably taller and heavier than he was.

However, during football practice Calvin had tackled guys who were bigger than he was. He hadn't always brought them down, but sometimes he had. Anyway, this gun-wielding man was facing away from him, so Calvin could take him by surprise.

Calvin lowered his head, darted through an opening in the panicked crowd, built up some steam, and rammed his shoulder into the guy's back.

The impact knocked the man forward, off his feet. He went down hard with Calvin on top of him. Calvin had hoped the tackle would jolt the gun out of the man's hand, but the guy hung on to it.

Scrambling for an advantage, Calvin tried to slide an arm around the man's neck so he could get a chokehold on him. Before he could manage to do that, the man's right elbow came shooting back and slammed into his jaw. The blow made Calvin roll to the side.

That hurt worse than any hit he had ever taken in practice or a game, but he tried to shake it off. He pawed at the man's muscular arm, which felt as big around as the trunk of a small tree.

The man rolled toward Calvin, clamped his free hand around the smaller man's neck, and pinned him to the floor.

"Stop that!" he snapped. "What the hell are you doing, kid?"

Calvin couldn't answer. He was having enough trouble just breathing with that big hand squeezing his neck.

The man seemed to understand that. He went on, "If you think I'm one of the bastards doing this, you're wrong. I think the mall's under attack by terrorists. Do I look like a terrorist to you?"

Actually, he didn't. He had a pleasantly homely face, ears that stuck out a little, and close-cropped dark hair. He looked about as American as anybody could be.

Of course, Americans could still be terrorists, Calvin supposed, but something about this man told him that wasn't the case.

When the guy eased up on his grip, Calvin said, "I . . . I'm sorry. You've got a gun . . . I thought—"

"That's okay." The man rose to his feet in a single smooth surge of muscles. He reached down, and when Calvin automatically grasped his hand, he pulled him upright with little or no effort. "Understandable mistake."

"You . . . you were aiming at another guard."

Both of them were shouting to be heard over the bedlam going on around them, but the big man exuded a sort of calm that made Calvin relax a little, too. He said, "I don't think he's a real

164

guard. He's got some kind of machine pistol and is shooting people."

"My God!"

"Yeah." The man looked back and forth. "Sounds like multiple shooters. We need to get somewhere there'll be some cover." He gave Calvin a push back toward the sporting goods store. "Get in there and try to get everybody calmed down. Tell them to find cover and stay low. Anybody who knows how to use a gun better arm themselves, too, including you. Plenty of weapons and ammo in there." He paused. "I'm Tobey Lanning, by the way."

"Calvin Marshall." Calvin started to turn toward the sporting goods store. Tobey had the sort of presence that made people tend to do what he told them, and it wasn't just his size, either.

But Calvin paused and asked, "What are you going to do?"

"See if I can find out what's going on here," Tobey said grimly.

Chapter 20

Aaron didn't know what was going on, but when the madness started, his first thought was for his sister Jennie.

He was turning to look toward the kiosk where

her friend worked, but before he could locate her, some sort of explosion rocked the mall. Then some big guy grabbed another man, shoved him into Aaron's face, and yelled at them to get in the store. He seemed to be used to giving orders, so Aaron figured he was a cop.

Aaron got all tangled up with the skinny nerd who stumbled into him. For several long, maddening seconds, they both struggled to stay on their feet as each tried to disengage from the other. Aaron finally shoved the guy away and caught his balance.

The air was full of smoke from the blast. The mall's ventilation system was still working, circulating smoke that stung the eyes and nose. People ran everywhere, and Aaron couldn't take a step without somebody bumping into him.

He was about to start trying to fight his way toward the place he had last seen his sister when the skinny guy clutched at his arm and babbled, "We've got to hide, we've got to hide! They're killing everybody!"

Frustrated and angry—and scared, really scared, no point in denying it—Aaron pushed the guy away and said, "Leave me alone, dude!"

"They're shooting!" the guy wailed.

Something about the man was vaguely familiar, but Aaron couldn't place him and didn't care.

"Hide if you want," he snapped. "I gotta find Jennie!"

Then the mob surged against Aaron and pushed him in the opposite direction from the way he wanted to go. The skinny guy grabbed his arm and dragged him toward the sporting goods store. It was like trying to fight an ocean of panic. The wave pushed him into the store.

Feet tangled with his and he started to fall. He reached out for whatever he could grab, suddenly afraid that if he fell, these crazy people would trample him to death. That was a very real danger in situations like this. Aaron had been at rock concerts where people had almost been killed that way.

The thing he grabbed to hold himself up as he half-fell was the arm of a wheelchair. As Aaron braced himself, he was shocked to find himself looking into the buzzard-like face of the old man who had nearly shot him the day before.

Pete wanted to yell at the crazy priest to stop, but he couldn't find the breath. Maddened shoppers banged into them as Father Steve pushed the wheelchair toward the sporting goods store. Pete was afraid the chair was going to turn over, and if it did he would spill out of it and be dead meat. The mob would stomp the life out of him.

Father Steve somehow kept the wheelchair upright and moving, though. It was like riding the bumper cars at an old-fashioned state fair midway.

Pete didn't know what was going on, but obviously it was bad. He hadn't heard shooting like that since the Battle of the Bulge, and when the explosion went off, it was like an artillery shell landing nearby. For a second Pete felt like he was back in France or Germany, fighting the Nazis.

Then he snapped back to the present. It sounded like there was a war going on, all right, but it wasn't *his* war. That one had been over for more than seventy years.

Father Steve pushed the wheelchair into the sporting goods store. The craziness still swirled around them, but Father Steve stopped behind a display of camping equipment just inside the entrance.

That stuff won't stop a bullet, Pete thought. He didn't know if the priest would be able to hear him over all the yelling and shooting, but he opened his mouth to say, "You need to . . . find some better—"

Before he could finish the warning, somebody bumped into the chair and grabbed its arm to steady himself. The guy almost fell into Pete's lap. Pete looked at him.

The punk!

With all the hell breaking loose in the mall, Pete had almost forgotten about spotting the kid who'd busted down his door a day earlier. Pete's outrage boiled up until he couldn't contain it.

The world might be going mad around them, but fate had provided him with an opportunity to see that this punk got what was coming to him.

He clawed at the pocket on the side of the wheelchair and dragged out the Browning Hi-Power. As he brought it up, he gasped, "Don't . . . move! Father . . . This guy . . . is a thief!"

The punk's eyes bulged out at the sight of the 9mm. He reacted with the speed of youth, reaching down and clamping his hand around the BHP's barrel. That kept the slide from working. Pete tried to pull the trigger anyway, but the punk easily wrenched the gun out of his hand.

"Are you crazy, old man?" the punk yelled. "Try to shoot me again, will you?"

"Stop it!" Father Steve shouted. "I don't know what's going on here, but just stop it, both of you! The mall is under attack!"

The punk straightened and took a step back, still holding the Browning. He said to the priest, "Are you with this crazy old coot?"

"Yes, but there's no need to—"

"Push him back farther into the store," the punk went on. "Somebody's shootin' out there. You need to get him out of the line of fire."

Pete said, "He's . . . a thief!" but Father Steve ignored him.

Instead the priest asked the punk, "What about you?"

The kid turned the gun around so he was

holding the grip. He said, "I gotta find my sister," and turned toward the store's entrance.

"Hey!" Pete yelped. "He's stealin' . . . my gun!"

The protest was too late. Father Steve was already turning the wheelchair away from the entrance and pushing it toward the rear of the store.

Jennie's brother Aaron had been right. Holly Stevens looked embarrassed when she caught sight of Jennie coming toward her. But then Holly laughed and shook her head.

"I was hoping nobody who knew me would see me in this outfit," she said as Jennie came up to her. "I should have known better."

"Surely I'm not the first one from our school to come by."

"Well, no," Holly admitted. "I've seen quite a few people I know, but well . . . you know how it is. Just because I know who they are doesn't mean they know who I am."

"Yeah, tell me about it," Jennie said. She was well aware that to the kids who were even borderline popular in their school, the outsiders and the misfits might as well not even exist. She went on, "You really don't have to worry, though. You look fine."

"In this?" Holly waved her hand to indicate the German milkmaid's costume she wore. "I look like a lunatic!"

"No, you don't. It's sort of . . . cute?"

Holly rolled her eyes so hard they threatened to come out of their sockets. She changed the subject of her appearance by asking, "What are you doing here today?"

"Shopping, of course. Why else would somebody be at the mall on Black Friday?"

"In my case . . . trying to earn money." Holly paused. "You know, I'll bet they could use a couple more girls part-time through Christmas, if you want me to put in a word for you."

That actually wasn't a bad idea. If Jennie was going to make it to college next year, she would need quite a bit more money than her scholarships would provide, unless she was lucky and happened to get a full ride from one of the schools she'd applied to. She didn't expect that to happen, though. Her grades were very good, but not at the absolute top. And her extracurriculars . . .

Well, it was hard to come up with impressive extracurriculars when your father was a drunk, your brother was an ex-con, and your family was struggling just to barely get by.

Jennie wasn't going to say that to anybody, though, even her best friend, so she just nodded and told Holly, "Yeah, that'd be gre—"

The sudden, unexpected sound of gunshots interrupted her, followed instantly by screaming and yelling.

Holly let out a startled cry and looked around, wide-eyed with fear. So did Jennie. She searched for Aaron in the crowd, which began to swell back and forth in panic. Sure, he was a petty criminal and stayed high way too much of the time, but he was her big brother. Instinctively, she looked to him for protection.

She didn't see him, though, and then Holly grabbed her hand and jerked her away from the kiosk.

"Let's get out of here!" she said. "We'll be safer outside!"

Jennie didn't know about that. In school, they'd had it drilled into their heads that if there was ever a shooting, it was best to lock the door and stay right where they were.

That idea had never fully made sense to Jennie. It seemed logical to her that if somebody was shooting *inside* the school, it would be safer *outside*.

Maybe the same thing was true of a mall.

And there was a *lot* of shooting going on. She could hear the swift reports hammering above the tumult of the panicked crowd. She really wanted to know where Aaron was, but as Holly tugged at her, Jennie gave up and let her friend pull her away from the kiosk.

Just then, something blew up. Both girls stumbled and went to their knees. The jeans Jennie wore protected her, but Holly's legs were bare under the milkmaid's skirt and she cried out in pain as the floor scraped her knees.

Jennie helped her up. There was an exit not far from there, and they joined the shoppers headed in that direction.

Before they could get there, a couple of men moved to block the doors. Both of them held guns of some sort. The weapons looked odd to Jennie, but dangerous at the same time.

One of the men yelled, "Stay back! Stay back!" while the other ordered, "Everyone down on the floor!"

The second man punctuated his order with a burst of gunfire over the heads of the crazed shoppers. Most of them stopped in their tracks, but a few continued charging toward the doors.

The two gunmen opened fire for real. No more warning shots.

Jennie was horrified as she saw men and women jerked to a sudden stop by the impact of the bullets pounding into them. Skin burst and crimson sprays of blood flew around them. It was like something from a movie, just special effects, Jennie thought, but at the same time, she knew it was real. Hideously real.

The people who'd been shot began to crumple. The men kept firing, and slugs zipped past the first targets to smash into the people who had been behind them. More screams added to the chaos. Even as the gunmen continued firing, they shouted, "Get down! Get down!"

Jennie practically tackled Holly and dragged her off her feet. Both girls sprawled on the floor. Staying on their feet was asking to be killed.

She kept an arm around Holly as they huddled there with terrified people pressed against them all around. Her heart slugged so hard in her chest that it felt like it was going to burst right through her ribs and out of her body.

She expected the killers to start moving through the crowd and shooting them one by one. That was what mass murderers did, wasn't it? Like everybody else, she had read about those bloody incidents and seen the news reports on TV.

This didn't seem to be the usual spree killing, though. Shots were coming from all over the mall, on both levels. That bomb had gone off. This was something different. This was . . . an attack.

A terrorist attack.

Jennie knew she was right as soon as that phrase went through her head. She had gotten a good enough look at the gunmen wielding the automatic weapons before she and Holly dived for the floor to know that they were both men in their twenties, with dark skin, dark hair, and beard stubble. Young men from the Middle East.

They stopped shooting. One of them dropped the empty magazine from his weapon and

174

replaced it with a full one, then the second man did likewise. Jennie recognized what they were doing from action movies she'd seen.

"Stay down!" one of them called to the shoppers who had stretched out on the floor. "Stay down and no one else will be hurt!"

Jennie looked at the bloody shapes sprawled on the floor closer to the doors, the figures that had been chopped up so much by bullets that they barely looked human anymore, and she knew the men were lying.

The killing wasn't over.

It had barely gotten started.

Jennie wept silently for herself and her brother and hoped that Aaron was all right and then wished that he was here to hold her hand, the same way he had when they were little and she was scared.

But he wasn't, so she clung to her friend instead and waited to see what was going to happen and how long they were going to live.

Chapter 21

All the department stores that anchored the mall had wide entrances into the mall itself, plus at least two entrances/exits that opened onto the parking lot.

When the shooting started, Jamie heard gunfire

from enough different directions at once, including the store's second floor, that she knew instantly this was a coordinated attack. She'd heard enough talk about Taliban ambushes to recognize what was going on. Those were insurgents doing the firing.

No. They were insurgents in their own country.

Here in America they were terrorists, plain and simple.

She dropped the pair of driving gloves she'd been considering buying for Tom and turned swiftly toward the nearest doors that opened onto the parking lot. She didn't want to be trapped in there. The terrorists would have posted guards at the exits to keep everybody inside, but Jamie thought if there was only one man she might be able to get past him.

If she could put him down, then maybe some of the other shoppers and mall employees could escape, too.

Everybody in the place was panicked in one way or another. Some people ran around aimlessly, shouting questions. Others huddled behind store displays as if that would save them. Some just stood and stared, apparently frozen by fear.

Jamie moved through them like a shark through a school of smaller fish, cutting a path toward the doors. She wished she was armed. She'd always carried a sidearm when she was flying, but since coming home she'd gotten out of the habit.

Those guys doing the shooting had guns, she thought. Maybe she could take one away from them. That would help even the odds.

As she neared the exit she heard a man shouting for everyone to get down on the floor. More shots blasted. People screamed. Jamie saw several of the terrified shoppers dropping to the floor. More and more followed their example.

Jamie knelt behind a rack of dresses. She couldn't stay at her full height without being noticed. Moving at an awkward gait between a crouch and a crawl, she began to work her way toward the yelling gunmen.

She hadn't gone very far when a loud blast shook the floor under her. She stopped where she was and wondered for a frightening few seconds if the entire mall was going to collapse, or if more explosions were imminent.

After a moment, though, as the echoes died away, it appeared that there weren't going to be any more blasts, at least for now. The stench of smoke drifted through the store, along with another smell that Jamie, unfortunately, recognized.

The smell of burned human flesh.

She swallowed the impulse to gag at the grisly odor and forced herself to start moving again.

She reached a glass-topped and -fronted jewelry counter laid out in the shape of a square with an opening at one corner so a clerk could get inside it to work. A dozen people were lying on the floor nearby. Jamie gestured to get their attention, then pointed to the opening in the counter and motioned for them to crawl into the square. The wood and plastic and glass display case wouldn't offer much protection from high-powered bullets, but it was better than nothing.

Several people started moving in that direction, including a middle-aged woman and a teenage girl who looked enough like her that Jamie knew they were mother and daughter. The sight made her think of her own daughters, and her breath caught in her throat at the idea she might never see them again. She knew Tom would do a good job of raising the kids if anything happened to her, but she should have made sure that they all knew she loved them.

If she got the chance to tell them again . . .

Jamie pushed that thought out of her head. Her best chance of ever seeing her family again lay in concentrating on the situation in which she found herself now.

Not everyone tried to crawl into the scant cover of the jewelry counter. Some of the shoppers continued hugging the floor. Jamie couldn't do anything about that. She eased on past, staying low.

The shooting had stopped now, at least in this part of the store. Jamie could hear gunfire in the distance. Men were still shouting orders to stay down, though. They had their cowed victims on the floor and wanted to keep them there.

Jamie risked a glance around a rack of men's coats and saw that there were two gunmen standing near the exit doors. Both appeared to be Middle Eastern, looking a lot like members of the Taliban she had seen in Afghanistan.

That came as no surprise. The Taliban, al-Qaeda, ISIS, the names might change, but in the end they were all the same.

Barbarians. Killers that had no place in a civilized world.

Too bad there were two of them. One would have been easier to deal with. Jamie knew she would just have to do the best she could, though.

A sudden throb of pain from her leg reminded her that she was no longer whole. She asked herself what she was thinking about doing. She couldn't attack two ruthless terrorists armed with automatic weapons. Those guns would chop her to pieces as soon as she made a move toward the men.

Then a possible answer to her dilemma presented itself as one of the men strode forward, stalking past the bloody corpses of the luckless shoppers who had been killed in the first moments of the attack.

"Everyone stay on the floor," this man said as the other one swung his weapon back and forth, covering the crowd near the doors. "If you stay down and do as you are told, you will not be hurt."

Jamie didn't believe that. She knew all too well the bloodlust that men such as these directed at people they considered godless infidels. To them, nonbelievers were less than human, and slaughtering them was the same as stepping on bugs . . . or possibly even better, since spilling the blood of infidels would buy them rewards in their deranged version of paradise.

She had seen the behavior with her own eyes, again and again, but she still couldn't wrap her mind around the concept of having such sick brains. You couldn't negotiate with Islamic terrorists, you couldn't reason with them . . .

All you could do was wipe them off the face of the earth.

Jamie edged to her left, keeping one of the clothes racks between her and the first man as he approached. She had gotten a better look at their weapons by now and knew the killers carried Steyr TMPs, German-made machine pistols. The long magazines extending below the grips probably held thirty rounds, fully loaded. The men had fired quite a bit already, though, and Jamie didn't know how recently they had switched magazines.

The terrorist was only about fifteen feet from her now, stepping carefully among the huddled, trembling shoppers. Jamie couldn't see him, but she could track his movements easily enough by the sounds he made.

The two killers were outnumbered, maybe as much as fifty to one. Why didn't the people rise up against them and overwhelm them by sheer force of numbers?

Jamie knew the answer to that. These were civilians, and they were scared, and you couldn't fault them for that. When they woke up this morning, they had thought they were just going to the mall. They'd had no idea they were going into battle, despite all the jokes people made about how crowded the stores were on this day after Thanksgiving.

Nobody expects the Spanish Inquisition, Jamie thought wryly.

For all Jamie knew, she was the only veteran here, the only one who'd seen combat. So it was up to her to do something, and the time was almost here. The guy was right on the other side of the clothes rack that concealed her . . .

She surged upright and shoved the rack into him as hard as she could.

The move seemed to take the terrorist completely by surprise. He staggered under the impact and tried to bring up the machine pistol he held, but his arms tangled in the clothes on the rack. Behind him, people on the floor screamed and yelled and tried to get out of the way as Jamie kept pushing the man back.

Over by the doors, the second terrorist shouted angrily in a foreign language but held his fire, probably because he didn't want to take a chance on hitting his friend.

That restraint wouldn't last long, though, Jamie knew. Their so-called holy cause took precedence over everything, including friendship.

Anyway, the other guy probably figured this one would be happy to die for Allah.

Not all the people on the floor could scramble out of the way in time. The terrorist finally tripped over some of them and went down. As he did, Jamie vaulted over the clothes rack and landed on top of him. She drove the heel of her right hand up under his chin with all the strength she could muster, which slammed the back of his head on the floor and stunned him.

As she lunged toward the machine pistol now gripped loosely in his hand, the other man opened fire. Bullets ripped through the air above her head. In his killing frenzy, the terrorist was letting the Steyr ride up.

Jamie yanked the weapon loose from the senseless man underneath her and raised it. She didn't know how many bullets were left in the magazine, but at full auto, it wouldn't take long to burn through them. She pressed the trigger and fired a short burst.

The terrorist probably didn't expect a woman to fight back like that. He was just standing there out in the open, not trying to take any evasive action. He looked shocked when the three rounds slammed into his chest and knocked him back a step. His eyes opened impossibly wide as blood began to well from the wounds.

The Steyr slipped from his fingers and thudded to the floor. A second later, the dying terrorist followed the machine pistol as his knees folded up.

The man Jamie had knocked down chose that moment to regain his senses, roar something incoherent but obviously furious, and buck madly beneath her. He swung his left arm and crashed it into the side of her head, knocking her off of him.

She lost her hold on the machine pistol at the same time. It slid across the floor in the open space where everybody had tried to get out of the way of the fight.

The man rolled after Jamie, punching at her. His fists smacked into her body. She tried to fend him off, but he was caught up in the twisted emotions that fueled him and was fighting like a berserker. A wild, looping punch crashed into her jaw, jerked her head to the side, and threatened to knock her out.

Jamie struggled to hang on to consciousness. That was all she could do. She couldn't muster up enough strength to keep fighting. She struck out feebly as both of his hands closed around her neck. He dug a knee into her belly and leaned into her with his stranglehold.

He was going to crush her larynx, cut off her air, and suffocate her. She would die in a matter of minutes, she knew.

And there didn't seem to be anything she could do about it except stare up helplessly into his cruel, hate-distorted face. He hated her because she was an American, a woman, and an unbeliever. Any one of those things was enough to enrage him. Taken all together . . .

He was going to enjoy killing her. She could read that unholy glee in his eyes.

That was the last emotion he ever felt, because the next instant his head seemed to explode as bullets slammed into it from behind. A gruesome rain of blood, gray matter, and bone fragments pelted Jamie in the face. It sickened her, but the need for air was much more overpowering than her revulsion. She grabbed his hands, ripped them away from her throat, and hauled him to the side. He toppled off of her.

She rolled away from the corpse and lay there for a moment gasping for breath. A trembling hand pawed gore away from her mouth, nose, and eyes. She pushed herself up on her other elbow and looked around to see who had saved her.

A few yards away, the teenage girl Jamie had noticed earlier, the one in the University of Illinois sweatshirt who'd been with a woman who was obviously her mom, was on her knees with the Steyr TMP cradled in both hands. Her eyes were wide with awe.

"Son of a *bitch!*" she exclaimed. "This thing can really shoot!"

Jamie sat up, still a little breathless, and said, "Give it to me."

Jamie reached over, tore the gun out of the girl's hands, and then twisted back toward the dead terrorist. She started slapping the man's pockets, searching for extra magazines.

The two terrorists charged with blocking this exit were dead, Jamie thought, but that didn't mean the battle was over.

Chapter 22

The attackers had done the smart thing by making everybody get down on the floor. That way anybody who was upright and moving around could be considered an enemy and a safe target.

For that reason, Tobey dropped to the floor as well, but he didn't remain still. Most of the shoppers were petrified by fear, but Tobey was able to crawl slowly and carefully among them, using their bodies to shield his own movements.

Several people noticed the Smith & Wesson 9mm in his hand, and as their eyes widened, he worried that they would call out to the terrorists and reveal that there was a man with a gun among them. They might try to curry favor among their captors in hopes of being spared.

In the long run, that wouldn't buy them a thing, Tobey knew. They would still be killed.

They must have realized that, too, because they remained quiet.

He came to a kiosk that rented small, motorized scooters in the shape of zoo animals. Little kids rode them through the mall on normal shopping days, when it wasn't as crowded. The kiosk was closed today, since mall management had anticipated that shoppers would be packed in too tightly for such an amusement. Somebody would get run into and be hurt. The ranks of scooters provided cover for Tobey now, though.

He eased around until he could see the man he had tried to draw a bead on earlier, before that security guard tackled him. The terrorist was pacing back and forth among the terrified shoppers huddling on the floor, ranting about how Allah and his followers were going to destroy the United States and all the godless infidels who lived here. Islam was going to spread across the world and only when it reigned supreme would there be peace.

Tobey could think of another, better way to achieve peace: kill all the lunatics. He was fine with anybody practicing their own religion however they wanted, as long as it didn't involve anybody else being hurt.

But once it crossed that line, it wasn't religion anymore. It was a sickness that had to be eradicated if humanity was going to survive.

He could hear the guy talking, saying, "By now this mall, this symbol of Satan, is under the complete control of the Sword of the Prophet."

Cute. This nutjob even had a name for himself and his buddies.

"The world will soon know that we have struck a blow in the holy name of Islam against the sinful decadence of America. The rest of your evil nation will cower in fear at the realization that your time is done. Today is the beginning of the caliphate, and soon it will spread across the world!"

At this range, Tobey figured he could put a couple of rounds through the madman's head without much trouble. Whether the caliphate ever took over the world or not, *this murderer* would never know it, because he would be dead, as he deserved to be.

But as satisfying as that might be, it would also give away Tobey's position, and he wasn't sure he could afford to do that just yet. He didn't know how many of the terrorists there were or just how bad the situation was. It might be better to wait and get a better idea of what he was dealing with.

Then the guy paused in his ranting and pacing and swung around so Tobey got a good look at his face.

What he saw felt like a punch in his gut.

The guy was young, little more than a kid, and the sight of him knocked Tobey all the way back to Iraq. He was there again on that miserably hot, dusty day when his patrol had been ambushed and he was the only one to make it out alive. He carried souvenirs of it in the form of the scars on his leg and the memories of his dead buddies.

Tobey had heard plenty about survivor's guilt. The army shrinks were big on it. So he knew what it was but had never really suffered from it. He would have if he had abandoned the rest of the patrol and they'd died because of it, sure.

But it had been pure luck or fate or whatever you wanted to call it that he and Sagers had dropped off the truck to take a piss at just the right time to save their lives. After that they had both fought with equal determination to save their lives, and again some power beyond their control had decreed that Tobey lived and Sagers died. Tobey couldn't feel guilty about that.

The memories had stayed with him, though, as vivid as if the ambush and firefight had happened yesterday, and among those recollections was the kid whose life Tobey had spared because he looked young and scared and like he didn't want to be there.

That kid was now strutting around in the American Way Mall, waving a Steyr machine pistol, and evidently masterminding a terrorist attack that had cost the lives of many innocent people already.

Tobey's finger was outside the trigger guard on the Shield. He wanted so badly to slide it in there, aim the gun, and blow out that son of a bitch's lights. *Now* he felt guilt. Now he knew that if he had just killed the kid that day in Iraq, instead of taking pity on him, all those innocent folks who had been gunned down or blown up when the bomb went off would still be alive, going happily about their Black Friday shopping.

All Tobey would have needed to do was pull a trigger . . .

He could pull a trigger now.

But it was the wrong thing to do, a stern voice in the back of his head warned him. Sure, he could kill the little bastard, but it wouldn't bring back any of the people who had died, nor would it prevent any more killing. If Tobey fired a shot, the guy's buddies would swarm him and cut him to pieces with those machine pistols. He would get a few of them, but ultimately he would lose.

As gut wrenching as the idea was, it made more sense to wait. Maybe he could figure out a way to save some of the people who had been taken hostage in the attack on the mall.

Because that's what they were, Tobey realized

—hostages. If all the kid and his terrorist cohorts were interested in was wholesale slaughter, they wouldn't have stopped killing until everybody in the place was dead.

No, there had to be another reason, something else they wanted, even if it was just to draw things out and make the whole country suffer more, knowing that thousands of lives were hanging in the balance.

So he had a little time—how much, he had no idea—and a chance to use it to fight back more effectively. That kid might have a small army with him.

Tobey needed an army, too.

He thought he might know where to find one.

Aaron hadn't gone very far toward the area where he had last seen Jennie when he encountered a group of frightened people being herded out of a gift shop at gunpoint. It made sense that the guys who were behind this attack would have men posted in the stores to take them over as well.

In this case, the terrorist was a short, chunky guy in his thirties who waved a machine pistol around as he shouted orders. Aaron quickly tried to blend in with the people in the group, but the man spotted the Browning in his hand, yelled something that Aaron didn't understand, and jabbed the automatic weapon at him.

Aaron had never fired a gun like this before,

but he knew enough to point and shoot. Video games had taught him that. He hurried too much, yanked the trigger on the first shot, and the bullet went high.

Luckily for him the terrorist's nerves must have been jumping around like crazy, too. The burst of slugs from the machine pistol went wide. Aaron settled his sights on center mass and fired three rounds. He tried to make the trigger pulls as smooth as he could.

The guy dropped his gun and doubled over as the slugs punched into his guts. They went a little low and left, Aaron saw, but they did the job. The terrorist folded up and went down.

"Scatter!" Aaron yelled at the people from the gift shop as he ran past them. "Find some cover!"

He didn't wait to see if they did what he said. He raced on toward the kiosk where Jennie's friend worked.

It was close by, right around a slight bend in the mall. Aaron skidded to a halt as he saw maybe a hundred people stretched out on the floor, being covered by two more guys with guns.

He had fired four rounds. He couldn't remember how many shots the Browning held. He lined the sights on one of the terrorists and fired a single shot. The man twisted as the bullet tore through his right shoulder and spun him halfway around. He dropped his gun, fell to his knees, grabbed the wounded shoulder, and howled in pain.

The other man laced bullets through the air at Aaron.

A desperate dive was all that saved him. The slugs went over him. He landed on his belly, slid up against a fat guy who was so afraid he was crying. Aaron fired over him, which made the guy yell as the sound of the shot pounded against his ears. Couldn't be helped.

Aaron knew he had missed. The guy with the machine pistol ran behind the kiosk. Aaron fired again but hit a cheese ball, splattering it all over the place. The terrorist raised up and sprayed more shots. Flame spewed from the weapon's muzzle. People screamed.

Aaron aimed and fired again.

The man lurched against a display of summer sausages and sent them flying. He flopped loosely onto his face among them. Aaron hoped the limp way he fell meant he was dead.

"Jennie!" he yelled as he stood up. "Jennie!"

"Aaron!"

Her scream came from his left. He wheeled in that direction and saw her scrambling to her feet. She reached out to help the girl who'd been lying beside her. That was probably her friend, he thought. He ran over to them, leaping over people who were still on the floor.

"The doors!" he cried. "Head for the doors! We gotta get outta here!"

That idea spread rapidly among the other

people, now that the two gunmen were down. People jumped up and got in Aaron's way. He shouldered them aside and cursed as he struggled to reach Jennie and her friend. A stampede started toward the exit.

Suddenly, just as Aaron finally made it to Jennie's side and grasped her arm, two more gunmen appeared from outside, charging into the mall with machine pistols blazing. They must have been posted at the doors to watch for trouble outside, Aaron realized, and now they were retreating to cut off this potential escape.

Aaron didn't know how many bullets he had left, but not enough for a shoot-out with those killers. He hauled Jennie around, and since she still had hold of her friend's hand, that girl came along, too. Aaron fought against the crowd, which was now being hosed with lead from the two new shooters, and tried to get to the only place he knew that might offer shelter—that sporting goods store.

There would be ammo there, too, and he really wanted to reload so he could kill as many of the bastards as possible.

Charles Lockhart had never been this frightened in his life. Although he wouldn't have wanted to admit it, he had been scared in his classroom. High school kids had no respect for authority, and some of them were flat-out dangerous. There had been a few confrontations over disruptive behavior when Charles had believed that a student might attack him.

That was nothing, though, compared to all those gunshots and things blowing up and people screaming and dying right in front of him.

He hoped he had found a safe haven here in the sporting goods store, but that probably wouldn't last.

"That damn . . . punk . . . took my gun!" the old man in the wheelchair complained to the priest. "You didn't even . . . try to stop him!"

"I couldn't have stopped him, Mr. McCracken," the priest said. "I didn't have time, anyway."

"Well, find me . . . another one . . . and a box . . . of ammo."

"I don't think I can—"

The old man interrupted the priest's tentativeness. He glared at Charles and said, "You there . . . Slats . . . we need . . . guns and ammo."

Baffled, Charles asked, "Are you talking to me?"

"Don't see . . . anybody else around here . . . skinny enough . . . to be called Slats. We need . . . pistols . . . shotguns . . ."

At that moment, screams erupted elsewhere in the store. Charles's head jerked around toward the source of the disturbance.

His heart leaped into his throat at the sight of two men with guns herding frightened shoppers ahead of them toward the front of the store.

Obviously they intended to force everyone in here out into the mall proper.

Back into that violent madhouse.

Charles didn't think he could stand that.

He looked around for anything he could use as a weapon. The concept of fighting back seemed utterly alien to him, but at the same time, he wasn't going to be herded out there into the mall and slaughtered. That was what this was like. Those horrible men were turning the mall into a slaughterhouse.

He didn't know anything about guns. He wouldn't even be able to load one.

But there was a display of bow-hunting equipment nearby. The crossbows, which he had seen pictures of so he knew what they were, looked too complicated for him to master.

Charles saw a regular, old-fashioned bow sitting there, however, although it appeared to be made of plastic instead of wood. Whatever. It was simple. Put an arrow on the string—"nock," that's what it was called, he remembered from somewhere—just nock an arrow, pull it back, and let fly.

Doing that would probably get him killed, he thought, but he was too scared *not* to fight back. It seemed he had some survival instincts after all.

He grabbed one of the bows, as well as a box of arrows, and ducked behind the display. When he risked a glance around it, he saw that the old man in the wheelchair was watching him, as was the priest. The old man's face, one side of it sagging because of a stroke, was twisted in a grimace, and it took Charles a second to realize the man was grinning at him. The old man raised his right arm slightly and gave him a thumbs-up.

The priest just looked aghast. Charles frowned and made a slashing motion, hoping the priest would understand he was telling him to cut it out. He didn't want the gunmen warned that resistance was developing.

Charles fumbled one of the arrows from the box and managed to fit it onto the bowstring. He had never used a bow and arrow before—his parents hadn't believed in violent toys—but the procedure was simple enough. Charles drew the string back a little, testing its strength. It was hard to pull. He would need to put a lot of effort in it.

He couldn't hope for much accuracy, since he was a complete novice, so he needed to wait until his targets were as close as possible. Would he have time to shoot one of the men, fit another arrow to the bowstring, and fire again before the second man shot him? Not likely, Charles realized, but the slight chance was better than waiting to be killed.

Of course, the most probable outcome of this insanity was that Charles would miss with the first arrow and then both men would shoot him. He knew his life was nearly over and could be numbered in minutes, perhaps only seconds.

But the madness was on him, he supposed, because he found to his utter shock that he wanted to do this. No, he *had* to do this.

He heard one of the men ordering prisoners along, threatening to kill them if they didn't cooperate. The terrorist was only a few feet away now. Charles took a deep breath, pulled the bowstring back more, and suddenly wheeled around the end of the display. He shouted wildly as he put all of his strength into holding the bow as tight as he could with his left hand and pulled back on the arrow with his right.

The string and the arrow slipped from his grasp without him really meaning for it to happen. The shaft flew so fast that Charles's eyes couldn't really follow it.

He saw where it ended up, however.

The point struck the terrorist in the hollow of the throat with such force that it went right on through and emerged bloodily from the back of his neck. He staggered and dropped his gun as both hands went to his transfixed throat. He clutched at the arrow. Blood welled out over his fingers in a crimson flood.

Charles was so shocked by what he'd done— and he knew it was almost entirely pure luck —that he stood there staring for a couple of heartbeats before he remembered the second terrorist.

The curses that the other man screamed jolted Charles back to awareness of his perilous situation. He turned and saw the second terrorist lunging toward him, gun outstretched to end his life. All the noise around Charles receded into an echoing silence as he watched his doom about to overtake him.

Chapter 23

The big guy—Tobey, Calvin recalled—had told him to gather people in the sporting goods store, arm them with the guns and ammunition that were there, and organize a defense.

That was all well and good, in fact it was a great idea, but Tobey had entrusted the task to a kid less than a year out of high school, a rent-a-cop who wasn't carrying a gun himself and didn't exactly command a lot of respect.

Calvin wished he'd been able to find Dave Dixon. He had a feeling the older guard would have known what to do.

But he hadn't found Dixon, still had no idea what had happened to him, and now it was up to him to try to forestall this catastrophe in the making, Calvin thought as he hurried around the store. He wasn't sure what to do first . . .

Any plans he might have started making evaporated abruptly as he found himself face to face with a black-bearded man holding an ugly, boxy pistol with a stubby barrel. The long magazine extending down from the gun's grip told Calvin it had plenty of firepower.

"Go into hall!" the man screamed at him. "Everybody go into hall! Now!"

Eyes bulging in surprise and fear, Calvin backpedaled. He held his hands up in front of him, palms out. The gunman stalked after him and swung the gun from side to side to gather up more of the people who'd either been in the store when the trouble started or retreated there hoping it would be safer.

Clearly, the terrorists had made sure that it wouldn't be safe here or anywhere else in the mall.

Calvin was certain now that the men behind all the bloody chaos *were* Islamic terrorists. He didn't like the idea of racial profiling, but really, what else could you think when there were a bunch of swarthy, bearded guys waving guns around and screaming orders in foreign accents?

Calvin supposed he was lucky this man hadn't shot him on sight, since he was dressed in a guard's uniform. Maybe the terrorist had seen that he wasn't armed, not even with a Taser or a baton.

Partway across the store, another man with a

gun herded shoppers toward the mall proper. Calvin glanced out there, saw people cowering on the floor and knew that they were being threatened, too.

That was what these guys intended for the people in the store. Herd them out like sheep, force them to lie down with the other prisoners, and then wait . . . for what?

Nothing good, Calvin knew. When an attack went on as long as this one already had, it usually turned into a hostage situation. The terrorists hadn't been content just to smuggle bombs into the mall and set them off. That would have been bad enough.

The fact that they were taking prisoners told Calvin they wanted to make some sort of statement by doing so. They knew they would be getting a ton of media attention very shortly.

He and all the other people being rounded up were pawns in a game, Calvin thought. He didn't like being a pawn.

He was still pretty close to one of the men. Close enough to jump him, maybe take the gun away without getting killed? It would be a risk, but if he could do that, maybe he could accomplish the task the big guy out in the mall had given him.

Maybe he could get people to start fighting back.

All he had to do was overcome his fear, move

faster than he had ever moved in his life, and out-fight a crazed, ruthless terrorist like the hero in a movie or a video game. And not get killed in the process.

Calvin was working up the courage to give it a try when across the store, a tall, skinny guy jumped out from behind a display, gave a crazy yell, and shot an arrow through the throat of the other terrorist.

That was such a shocking development, for a second Calvin couldn't believe what he had just seen. Evidently, neither could the other terrorist, because he just stared as his comrade fell to the floor to bleed out.

Then the man yelled furiously and charged the guy with the bow, who still stood there looking as shocked as everybody else at what he'd done.

Something about him was vaguely familiar to Calvin, but he didn't take the time to try to figure out what it was. He just ran after the terrorist and left his feet in a diving tackle as the man raised his gun.

This was his second tackle in a matter of minutes, which was one more than he'd ever managed to make in a game, and it was a good one, too. His arms wrapped around the man's thighs from behind and his shoulder drove against them. The man pitched forward as he pressed the gun's trigger, but instead of shredding flesh, the bullets just shattered floor tile in front of him because everybody had leaped out of his way when he started his murderous charge.

The man didn't drop the gun, but the weapon fell silent. Calvin hoped that meant it was out of bullets. He started punching at the back of the man's head.

The terrorist drove an elbow up into Calvin's guts. Calvin gasped and felt sick. The man bucked out from under him, spilling him off to the side. Calvin rolled away and clutched his belly. His eyes watered from the pain, but his vision was clear enough for him to see the man surge to his feet and grab a big knife from a sheath that must have been hidden under his coat.

He snarled and took a step toward Calvin as he raised the shining blade.

Two shots boomed. The terrorist stopped short and did a little jittering dance. Calvin saw a pair of bloodstains bloom like crimson flowers on the man's shirtfront. The knife slipped from his fingers and dropped point down, piercing the top of his shoe and probably the foot inside it. The guy didn't even seem to feel that, probably because he was practically dead on his feet already from being shot twice in the chest.

Then there was no more practically about it. His eyes rolled up in their sockets and he fell like a puppet with its strings cut.

Calvin, still hurting from that elbow in the

breadbasket, pushed himself up on one hand and looked toward the front of the store.

Tobey Lanning stood there, both arms outstretched as he held the black semi-automatic pistol in a two-handed grip.

It had taken Tobey a little while to work his way back to the sporting goods store, staying low and using all the cover he could find so the terrorists wouldn't be as likely to notice him. Once he was there, though, he had to abandon that discretion because one of the bastards was about to go after the security guard kid with a knife.

He squeezed off two swift rounds and was rewarded by the sight of the bastard dropping the knife and falling in a limp sprawl that signified death.

The body of another terrorist lay a few feet away, an arrow through his throat and a pool of blood slowly spreading around his body.

To Tobey's right stood the tall, skinny guy he had shoved toward the store earlier. The man held a bow in his left hand. "You got . . . the son of a bitch!" the old man in the wheelchair exclaimed. He was there, too, leaning forward avidly. The priest stood behind the chair. He hung on to it tightly as if it were the only thing holding him up. His face was pale and drawn, and he kept swallowing hard.

"Any more of them in here?" Tobey addressed

his brisk question to the skinny guy with the bow.

"I . . . I don't think so," the man replied.

Tobey looked around, saw the security guard getting up. The kid had told him his name, but Tobey didn't remember it. He pointed and said, "Kid, get his gun."

The young guard picked up the Steyr and said, "I think it's empty."

"Check his pockets for more magazines."

The kid looked down at the corpse. Seeing his hesitation, Tobey added, "He's dead, he can't hurt anybody now."

"Yeah," the kid said. He swallowed, and bent to search the dead man's pockets.

Tobey turned back to the skinny guy. "You're good with that bow."

The man shook his head.

"It was luck, pure luck. I never fired an arrow before."

"Well, for your first time, you did good. Can you handle a gun?"

Again a shake of the head as the man said, "I never shot one of them, either."

Tobey pointed and said, "Go up there to the front of the store, then, and stand behind that pillar. Keep an eye out. If you see any of those bastards with the machine pistols heading this way, let out a yell and get back here as fast as you can."

"Should I . . . should I take this with me?"

The guy held up the bow.

Tobey shrugged and said, "Couldn't hurt."

The man grabbed a quiver from the bow-hunting display, spilled some of the arrows out of the box they came in, and crammed them into the quiver. He slung it over his shoulder and started toward the lookout spot Tobey had pointed out to him. His movements were awkward and nervous, but he didn't hesitate to do what Tobey had told him.

The kid came up and showed Tobey the three full thirty-round magazines he held in his left hand. The Steyr was clutched in his right.

"I found these," he said.

Tobey slipped the S&W Shield back into his pocket and took the machine pistol and magazines from the kid. He figured he could put them to better use.

"Round everybody up and get them to the back of the store, behind the gun counter. Anybody who knows how to shoot needs to grab a gun and some ammo for it. What was your name again?"

"Calvin."

Tobey nodded and said, "Get moving, Calvin."

Calvin nodded and started to turn away, then paused and asked, "Are you a cop?"

"No," Tobey said. "I'm just a guy. I used to be a soldier, but I was a grunt, not an officer or anything."

"Maybe so," Calvin said, "but I'm really glad you're in charge here."

Tobey grunted. He hadn't actually given any thought to being in charge. He'd just started giving orders because somebody had to.

He dropped the empty magazine from the Steyr and seated a full one, then turned to the priest and the old man in the wheelchair and told them, "You guys need to get back away from the front of the store, too."

"Yes," the priest said, but as he started to turn the chair the old man told him to wait a minute.

"I can . . . shoot," he said to Tobey. "During the war . . . I was in . . . the First Infantry."

"The Big Red One," Tobey said. He didn't have to ask which war the man was talking about.

"Damn . . . straight."

"Get him a gun," Tobey told the priest. "And you'd better get one for yourself, too."

The priest looked shocked and said, "I can't . . . I'm not . . . I mean, I'm a man of God."

"I believe in him, too, Father, but I'm pretty sure he doesn't want us to just stand around and let ourselves be murdered in the name of religion."

"I don't know . . ."

The old man said, "I'll handle . . . the shootin' . . . for both of us."

Tobey grinned and said, "You were a sergeant, right?"

"Corporal . . . Corporal Pete McCracken."

"All right, Corporal McCracken. I'm counting on you."

"I won't . . . let you down," the old man wheezed.

Tobey didn't doubt him for a second.

Chapter 24

Jamie found a couple of loaded twenty-round magazines in the dead man's pockets. As she yanked them out, the girl who had shot the terrorist crawled over to her and asked, "What kind of gun is that?"

"It's a Steyr machine pistol," Jamie answered. She looked around quickly, checking for any new threats. She figured all the shooting in this area of the store would bring somebody to check on it.

"I'm gonna get the one the other guy had!"

The girl started to stand up. Everybody else was still huddled on the floor or behind the jewelry counter. The girl's mother looked over the counter and called in an urgent half whisper, "Kaitlyn, stay down!"

Jamie caught hold of the waistband of the girl's jeans and kept her from rising.

"Your mom's right," she said. "You don't want to make yourself a target."

"But we killed both those guys," Kaitlyn

protested. "I don't see any more, do you?" She looked back and forth hurriedly, then called to her mother, "Mom, come on! Let's get out of here while we can!"

That idea spread instantly. Several people leaped up and charged toward the doors. Jamie wanted to yell at them to stop, but she knew it wouldn't do any good. They were too panic-stricken to listen to her or anyone else.

The ones in the forefront of the stampede reached the doors and pushed outside. Jamie expected something to happen: an explosion, a burst of gunfire, *something* to spread more death and destruction.

But instead the people just charged out into the sunlight and ran wildly away from the mall.

Jamie's jaw tightened. She had figured more terrorists would be waiting outside to stop any escape, but clearly that wasn't the case. If the people who had just fled had listened to her and been more cautious, they might have been doomed. That knowledge was a bitter pill to swallow, but Jamie knew it was the truth.

Kaitlyn appeared to have forgotten about getting the gun that the other dead terrorist had dropped. Instead she pulled loose from Jamie's grip, turned toward the jewelry counter, and waved a hand as she called, "Mom, come on!"

Her mother stood up and started to hurry out the opening in the counter, and at that moment shots blasted from somewhere else in the store. The pretty, middle-aged woman with brown hair arched her back as bullets tore into her.

Kaitlyn screamed, *"Mommmm!"*

Jamie shouted, "Everybody down!" as she twisted toward the new attack. She spotted a man charging through the store, shooting on the run, and dropped to one knee as she raised the Steyr. She fired a burst and saw the terrorist stumble. He didn't go down, though, and he was able to keep shooting.

Kaitlyn's mother fell forward with her body draped over the jewelry counter's glass top as her arms hung limply in front of it. Kaitlyn was still screaming as she ran toward her. The terrorist swung his weapon in that direction. Bullets struck the counter and sprayed glass everywhere as the slugs tracked toward the girl.

Jamie fired again and saw blood fountain from the terrorist's throat as lead stitched across it. The man's gun fell silent as he crumpled into a bloody heap.

Kaitlyn reached her mother's body and grabbed hold of it, shaking it as she cried, "Mom, wake up! Wake up! We've got to get out of here!"

It was too late for that, Jamie thought grimly as she stood up and moved toward the counter. Kaitlyn could still get out of here alive, though. Jamie took hold of the girl's arm and tried to pull her away.

"Let's go," she said firmly, in the same tone she had always used to issue orders.

Kaitlyn wasn't a soldier, though. She was a grieving girl, and she clung to her mother's body.

"No! She's gotta wake up! She's just got to!"

"Kaitlyn. Kaitlyn!"

She turned a tear-streaked face toward Jamie.

"What's your mother's name?" Jamie asked, her voice a bit gentler now.

"Her . . . her name?"

"That's right."

"It's . . . Vanessa."

"I never knew Vanessa," Jamie said, "but I know good and well she'd want you to get out of here and be safe. I have daughters of my own, and that's what I'd want for them if they were in your place."

"But . . . but she . . ."

"I know," Jamie said. "I'm sorry. But there's going to be more of those bastards coming, and this may be our only chance to get out of here."

She glanced over her shoulder as she spoke. People were still fleeing unmolested out the doors and into the parking lot. So many of them were trying to escape, though, that they were jammed up a little in the openings. Despite that, the store looked like it was almost clear of shoppers and employees.

Kaitlyn drew in a deep, shuddery breath and said, "I'm all right now."

Jamie didn't really believe that—Kaitlyn was far from all right and probably wouldn't be for a long time; none of them who had been trapped in this madhouse would be—but at least maybe she could get out alive. Jamie relaxed her grip on the girl's arm . . .

With no warning, Kaitlyn rammed into her and knocked her back against the counter. Glass crunched under Jamie's shoes. Kaitlyn twisted away and ran.

Toward the mall.

Toward the monsters who shared responsibility for her mother's death.

Jamie bit back a curse and went after her, but running wasn't that easy with her prosthesis. Despite being taller, she wasn't gaining any ground. She didn't know what Kaitlyn was thinking, maybe some crazy notion of getting revenge for her mother's death, but all she was going to succeed in doing was getting herself killed.

Kaitlyn had almost reached the mall proper when a small door, almost unnoticeable behind a rack full of purses, flew open and a figure about the same size as her dashed out. Jamie watched in surprise as another girl, this one with black hair caught back in a ponytail, grabbed Kaitlyn, twisted an arm behind her back, and forced her toward the door.

Both girls disappeared through the opening.

The door started to swing shut behind them, but Jamie reached it in time to catch it, which was good because there was no handle on this side. It could only be opened from the other side. Jamie figured the door had something to do with mall maintenance. With the gun up, she went through and found the two girls in a dimly lit corridor, still struggling.

"Let me *go!*" Kaitlyn cried.

The other girl—who was older, probably in her early twenties—hung on to her and said sharply, "Stop it! Do you want to get killed, you fool?" She had some sort of accent, maybe eastern European.

Jamie caught hold of the push bar on this side of the door and pulled it closed behind them. It was dim and oppressive back here, with cinder-block walls and visible ductwork and bundles of electrical cables on the walls, and the whole thing made her feel a little claustrophobic, something the control cabin of her helicopter had never done.

But at the same time, she felt safer now than she had so far during this ordeal, which had lasted only a few minutes although it seemed much longer.

"Stop it!" she snapped at both girls. "And be quiet. You don't want them to hear us and figure out we're in here."

"The lady is right," the black-haired young

woman said. She wore gray coveralls, some sort of uniform, and Jamie figured she might be a member of the mall's custodial crew. She put both hands on Kaitlyn's shoulders and hissed, "We must be silent!"

Kaitlyn stopped fighting but started to cry. The young woman embraced her, and Jamie stepped forward to put her arms around both of them, still holding the liberated Steyr as she did so.

The shock and anger she had felt started to fade. The wheels of her brain began to revolve quickly. For the moment the three of them were safe . . . but maybe they could be more than that.

Maybe they could be the worst nightmare for some damned Islamic terrorists.

American women, pissed off and ready to kick ass.

The blond woman was tall and lean, with a hardness around her eyes and mouth that told Irina she was a soldier. Irina had seen women like her, Russian women who were in the army and knew they had to be harder and tougher than their male counterparts just to survive. They were frightening.

So, too, was this American woman, although not as much so. When she spoke to the young one, there was compassion in her eyes and voice.

"I know how much you're hurting right now, Kaitlyn—" the blonde began.

"No, you don't," the girl said, her voice shaking with both anger and grief. "You don't know. My mother is *dead*."

"How old are you?"

"What? I'm fourteen, but what—"

"My mother died when I was sixteen," the blonde said. "Cancer."

"That's different. She wasn't *killed*."

"She was all right one week, and then she got sick, and then it was six weeks of pure hell for her before she died. You can't say one is better or worse than another." The older woman's tone softened again. "So I know you're hurting. I know you're hurting bad."

Kaitlyn started to cry again.

Since they were sharing things, Irina said, "Two years ago soldiers came for my mother and took her away. I never saw her again. Whether she is still alive, I don't know." She shrugged. "She had made me promise that I would leave and come to America if I could. I kept that promise."

"Russia?" the blonde asked.

"Chechnya."

"I'm sorry."

"So I know the pain," Irina went on. "And I know men like those out there. They live only to kill those who offend them."

The blonde said, "It sounds like you're well acquainted with them, all right." She put out her hand. "I'm Jamie Vasquez."

"Irina Dubrovna," Irina said as she shook Jamie's hand.

Sniffling, the girl said, "I'm Kaitlyn Hamilton. What are we gonna do? Where *are* we?"

"We are in bowls of the mall," Irina said.

Jamie smiled and told her, "I think you mean the bowels of the mall."

"Yes, bowels, that is right. Sometimes the English words, they are still not there for me in my head."

"I think you speak just fine," Kaitlyn said. "This is, like, where all the air-conditioning and heating and electrical cables are, right?"

Irina pointed along the narrow, dimly lit corridor.

"This comes out in service area. These passages are all over the mall, behind the stores and between some of them."

"So you can get around without being seen," Jamie said.

"This is true. I was in break room when I hear shooting and then a bomb goes off. Many times, I have heard the same sort of things where I am from. So I come here and hide. I hear more shooting and open the door just a crack so I can look out. I saw you going out there where you will be killed, Kaitlyn, so I stopped you."

"You should have let me go," Kaitlyn said dully. "I wanted to kill some of them."

"How?" Jamie asked, her voice blunt and no-nonsense now. There was a time for coddling and this wasn't it. "With your bare hands? You didn't even grab that other Steyr before you tried to charge out there."

"If you'd just let me—"

"That's enough of that," Jamie interrupted. Irina thought she must have children. She sounded like a mother. Or an officer. Or both. "We're here now, and we're safe for the moment. We can't go back out there. More of those terrorists have probably shown up by now to see what happened."

"So what do we do? Just hide in here until they all leave?"

"We can't take a chance on that. They may rig the whole place to blow up." Jamie smiled, but there was no warmth or humor in the expression. "That bunch, they're big on suicide bombings. They don't mind blowing themselves up if they can take enough infidels with them, and I'm betting they have plenty of hostages by now."

"Then we'll have to find some other way out—" Kaitlyn began.

"No," Irina said.

The other two turned to look at her.

"You wanted to fight them," she said to Kaitlyn. "You want to avenge your poor mother."

"Yes." Kaitlyn's resolve stiffened visibly. "Yes, I want to fight them."

Irina turned to Jamie and said, "And so do you. Men like that, they are your natural enemy."

"You're right." Jamie's smile was a little more genuine now as she added, "What did you have in mind?"

Irina waved a hand to indicate their surroundings and said, "I know this mall. I work here for more than a year. Anywhere you want to go, I can get us there."

"Some place with guns?"

"Of course."

"Then that's where I want to go." Jamie lifted the Steyr. "We'll need more firepower than this."

"We're going to fight?" Kaitlyn asked with eagerness in her voice again.

"We're going to do more than that," Jamie said. "We're going to win."

Chapter 25

The entrance to the sporting goods store was about thirty feet wide, with a pillar on each side separating the opening from the big glass windows that took up the rest of the store frontage. Tobey had put the skinny guy with the bow and arrow behind the pillar to the left. The fellow was thin enough that the pillar actually did a pretty good job of concealing him.

"Any movement toward us out there?" Tobey asked quietly as he came up behind the guy.

The man jumped, but thankfully he didn't let

out a startled squawk that might attract attention. He caught his breath and said, "No. They're not far off, though. I can hear them talking, and every so often there's a shot."

The area directly in front of the sporting goods store was clear. The prisoners had been herded away from it. More than likely, the terrorists were bunching them up into bigger groups so it would take fewer men to guard them.

The same thing would have happened to the people inside the store if Tobey and Calvin and the man with the bow and arrow hadn't intervened.

"What's your name?" Tobey asked.

"Charles Lockhart," the man answered without looking around. He was nervous and didn't take his eyes off the main part of the mall, as much of it as he could see from here, anyway.

"You've done really good so far, Charles," Tobey told him.

"I haven't really done anything except try not to defecate in my pants."

"That guy with an arrow through his throat would argue with you."

Lockhart shuddered.

"I didn't know that was going to happen. I mean, I was trying to shoot him with the arrow, of course, but I never dreamed that . . . that . . ."

"It's okay," Tobey said. "Our side needed some good luck. We sure haven't had much so far."

"More of those men will be coming to see why the ones who were here never showed up with their prisoners."

"That's right," Tobey said with a nod. "And we need to be ready for them."

"But how can we possibly fight them? They have guns and bombs and—"

Tobey heard the hysteria creeping into Lockhart's voice and stopped him by saying, "We have guns." He waved a hand toward the back of the store. "There are enough guns in here to arm everyone, and there's plenty of ammunition, too." He added under his breath, "Thank God for the Second Amendment."

"But the bombs—"

"If we kill enough of them, they won't be able to set off any more bombs," Tobey interrupted him again.

"It only takes one man to set off a bomb!"

"So we kill all of them," Tobey said.

Lockhart stared at him for a couple of heart-beats, then said in a hushed voice, "My God, you mean that, don't you?"

"Those guys out there in the mall, forget about where they're from or what their motivation is. *They want to kill you.* They want to kill all of us. They've said that over and over, and it's damn well time we started believing them. So the question is pretty simple: Do we let them kill us . . . or do we fight?"

Lockhart's back stiffened a little as he said, "We fight."

"Good man. We need to close and lock the gates that separate this store from the rest of the mall."

"Gates . . . ?"

"Yeah, they pull down from the ceiling." Tobey tipped his head upward, then down. "Then they lock into the floor."

"I . . . I never noticed such things."

"No reason you would. Keep your eyes open. I'll find somebody who works here who knows what to do and can help us."

Tobey turned away from the opening. He was glad to see that the front part of the store was empty of people except for him and Charles Lockhart. A buzz of nervous conversation came from the back where everybody was bunched up around the gun counters. Tobey hoped Calvin was handing out weapons back there. He started in that direction.

He hadn't gone very far when Lockhart yelped, "Somebody's coming!" A second later he added in amazement, "It's a train!"

Aaron held on tightly to Jennie's hand as he led her and Holly away from the chaos. The sporting goods store where he had taken the Browning away from the old man wasn't far away. That was where Aaron wanted to go. It would be safer there than anywhere else in the mall, his instincts told him.

Sporadic bursts of gunfire were still coming from other places in here. People shouted and screamed. A terrible stink—a mixture of smoke and something else, something Aaron didn't want to think about—hung in the air.

Aaron wasn't sure if he believed in hell, but if such a place really existed, he wouldn't be a bit surprised if it looked a lot like the American Way Mall on this Friday in November.

They came to the miniature train that normally traveled up and down the mall, six cars just big enough for a few kids to ride in, pulled by an undersized "locomotive" that was actually battery powered. It sat empty, surrounded by a short wooden fence with a couple of gates in it.

From the looks of things, the train hadn't been operating today, probably because the people who ran the mall figured it would be too crowded. They wouldn't want anything getting in the way of the hordes of shoppers and distracting them from spending money.

But they had gotten a distraction, all right—a bloody one.

As Aaron, Jennie, and Holly were passing the train, two men carrying guns came out of a store on the far side of the mall behind them and spotted them. Aaron heard the shouts of discovery, then told the girls, "Get down!" as the terrorists opened fire.

All three of them ducked behind the train cars. Bullets spanged off the metal frameworks and chewed splinters from the wooden seats and sides. The mock locomotive looked fairly substantial, so Aaron motioned for Jennie and Holly to crawl up behind it.

He straightened up long enough to snap a shot at the men and saw to his dismay that they were splitting up to circle the train from both sides. Aaron swung the Browning toward the man heading to his left, the front of the train, and fired again.

Blood flew as the 9mm round tore through the terrorist's torso, entering under his left arm as he ran. He spun off his feet, went down, and stayed down.

But that left the other man, and he was still shooting.

Even worse, the slide on the Browning had locked back after that last shot, meaning it was empty.

"Get in the first car!" Aaron yelled at his sister and her friend. "Get down in the floor!"

From that angle, there would be five cars between the girls and the terrorist coming up behind them. That might be enough to protect them.

But they couldn't stay here, Aaron knew,

because the shooting would draw more of the bastards, just like rotten meat draws flies, and with the BHP empty, he couldn't fight back.

As bullets whined through the air, he threw himself into the locomotive's seat and hunkered down to make himself as small a target as possible. He looked at the controls and the switches and frowned in frustration. He could hotwire a car, no problem, but he couldn't figure out how to drive a damn toy train!

Then he spotted a switch below a gauge that was marked BATTERY and threw it. He felt as much as heard the hum of the electric motor. There was only one pedal on the floor, so his foot stabbed at it and shoved it all the way down.

The train rolled forward, knocking aside the wooden gate in the short railing that surrounded it.

"Aaron, he's coming!" Jennie wailed.

A frantic glance over his shoulder told Aaron the killer was almost on them, in fact. He had stopped shooting, though. Maybe the magazine in his gun had run dry.

Or maybe he had something else in mind. The vicious grin on his face said that he did. He had the gun in his left hand. He reached behind his back with his right, under the short jacket he wore, and came out with a knife.

Sucker was going to slaughter these infidels up close and personal, he had to be thinking.

As Aaron steered around bodies and debris littering the floor of the mall, he slammed his left hand against the train's control panel and exclaimed in sheer frustration, "Come on!" The thing just wasn't building up any speed.

He and the girls could get out and run faster than the train was going, Aaron thought. But if they did that, and the guy chasing them had any bullets left, he would just shoot them.

"Jennie! Get up here!"

She lifted her head and stared at him in confusion. He yelled her name again, and she started clambering over the front of the open car.

He twisted in the seat, reached back, and grabbed her hand to help her. As she climbed into the locomotive's "cab," he told her, "Get your foot on the pedal and push it down as hard as you can!"

The train lurched and slowed as his foot came off the pedal, but then an instant later Jennie rammed her foot down on it and the train moved forward again. Aaron twisted around to face the back and jumped into the first car, where Holly was still huddled on the floorboard.

The terrorist had reached the sixth and final car. He leaped, grabbed it, and hauled himself on board.

The guy had shoved his gun back in his waistband. Maybe he really was out of bullets. He still had that knife, though, and he brandished it as he climbed from the last car to the next one.

Aaron went to meet him. He wasn't going to let the son of a bitch get any closer to the girls.

They came together at the third car back. The terrorist, tall and skinny with a shock of black hair, swung the knife at Aaron's face. Aaron might not have been able to avoid it, but at that moment Jennie jerked the wheel and sent the locomotive angling to the side. That threw the guy off balance just enough for Aaron to duck under the blade. He hammered a punch to the man's midsection and then jerked back to avoid a second strike.

A guy had come after him with a shank once, while he was in prison, so he had a little experience fighting unarmed against a man with a knife. He jerked his hoodie off and wrapped it around his left forearm. It wouldn't stop the blade, but it might slow it down.

The man lunged at Aaron. The knife darted back and forth like the tongue of a snake. Aaron leaned to one side, then the other, and most of the jabs missed. The ones that didn't, he turned aside with his forearm. As expected, he felt the blade bite into his flesh, but it didn't go deep.

Jennie weaved the train again, and this time the terrorist almost toppled out. He had to grab the side of the car with his free hand to keep from falling, and as he did, the hand holding the knife stuck far out to the right as he tried to balance himself.

That left him wide open for a second, and Aaron seized the opportunity. He sprang forward and shot three punches to the man's face, a right, a left, and another right. The blows rocked the guy's head back. Aaron bent, grabbed the man around the knees, and heaved upward as hard as he could.

The terrorist went over backward, headfirst into the gap between the third car and the fourth.

It wasn't like falling under a real train, of course. But the cars were pretty heavy and as the man tangled up among their wheels and was dragged along, he bellowed in pain. Aaron hoped some of his bones were broken.

"Hey, kid! Kid!"

The shout made Aaron's head jerk around. They had actually made it most of the way to the sporting goods store. Aaron spotted the big guy he had seen earlier, waving them on.

Now was the time to abandon the train and run. Aaron jumped out and yelled, "Jennie! Holly! Let's go!"

The train shuddered to a halt as the girls leaped from it and joined him. As they approached the entrance to the sporting goods store, Aaron glanced back and saw that the terrorist had managed to crawl free of the train. He stood up just as a shot boomed somewhere close by. A black hole appeared in the center of his fore-head, and the back of his skull exploded out-ward as the 9mm round emerged.

The big guy had fired that shot with a small black semi-automatic. He also had one of the terrorists' machine pistols stuck behind his belt.

As Aaron, Jennie, and Holly ran into the store, staggering and breathless now, the big guy shouted orders, telling somebody, "Let's get this gate down and locked *now!*"

That sounded like a good idea to Aaron.

Tobey had seen some pretty bizarre things in his life, but the sight of a miniature train barreling along through a mall littered with corpses, with streamers of smoke from a deadly explosion still hanging in the air, while a life-and-death struggle took place on one of the brightly painted cars, had to be one of the strangest.

At least it had ended all right, for the moment. He had stuck the Steyr behind his belt and yanked out the Smith & Wesson Shield, figuring the semi-automatic would be better if he had to make a fancy shot to save the kid who had been wearing the hoodie. The kid had done all right for himself, though, and by the time the terrorist got loose from the train, Tobey didn't know if there was any fight left in him or not.

A slug through the brain settled that question quickly and efficiently, though.

Now one of the store employees held down the switch that lowered the barred gate across the entrance, and as soon as it was down Tobey and another employee started dogging the toggles that locked it in place.

Charles Lockhart let out another strident warning.

"There are more of them!"

Tobey looked up from what he was doing, saw half a dozen of the terrorists running toward the store, and yanked the machine pistol from his belt. He stuck the muzzle through one of the openings in the bars and sent a stream of bullets heading toward the guys at full-auto speed.

They scattered and returned the fire. He didn't think he had hit any of them, but he couldn't be sure.

Bullets struck the glass walls on either side of the entrance and spiderwebbed it, but the glass didn't shatter. Tobey glanced over at one of the store employees and asked, "Bulletproof glass?"

"That's right," the man said. "All the glass walls in the mall are like that. The company that built it is very security-conscious." He paused. "They were trying to make it hard for thieves, though, not crazy terrorists."

Tobey knew what the man meant. The glass might stand up to the gunfire for now, but eventually it would weaken and collapse. That probably wouldn't take long, either.

If the terrorists wanted to speed things up even more, they could just lob a bomb down here.

Bullets sparked and ricocheted off the thick metal grating that now closed off the front of the store. Tobey jerked a thumb toward the back and told the men who had come to help him to withdraw. They had done all they could for the moment.

Behind a stacked-high display of ice chests, the kid had unwrapped the bloody hoodie from his left arm and was looking at the slashes on it. Both girls with him were fussing over the injuries, which didn't look too bad to Tobey.

"Is that a Browning Hi-Power?" Tobey asked him, nodding to the gun stuck in the kid's waistband.

"Yeah."

"Plenty of 9mm ammo back there." Tobey pointed with a thumb toward the back of the store. "You'd better reload and stock up."

"Is there a, uh, an old man in a wheelchair back there?"

"Yeah," Tobey said, a little surprised by the question.

"Well, I'm gonna stay as far away from him as I can. Crazy old coot's got a grudge against me."

Tobey could believe that. Pete McCracken had struck him as an irascible sort, but also a good man to have on your side.

"We've got to forget about grudges," he said. "Nobody in here is as much of an enemy as those guys out there."

"This is where we're gonna make our stand, eh?" the kid asked as he looked around the store.

"Some are."

"Only some?"

"The rest of us are going to take the fight to those sons of bitches," Tobey said.

Chapter 26

The first call that came in to 911 was a Shots Fired report, but less than a minute later the lines really lit up with civilians calling to say that something had just blown up inside the American Way Mall.

Within seconds, those reports were echoed by a radio call from the police car that had been cruising the mall parking lots to deter auto burglaries. The officers in that car had heard the explosion and saw smoke rising from the mall. They requested backup and were going to respond to the situation and try to find out what had happened.

The officers who were supposed to be *inside* the mall hadn't reported anything. Their silence was one of the most ominous signs of all.

Moments later, however, there were frantic, terrified calls from people actually inside the mall, reporting that men with automatic weapons were killing everybody in sight, and the chief of police was notified immediately that the thing people had dreaded for years had come to pass.

Terrorism had come to the heartland.

The chief of police said a fervent prayer under his breath and then reached for the phone to call Homeland Security, the FBI, and everybody else he could think of who might be able to help with this catastrophe.

Adele Connelly was tired, which was nothing unusual these days, but she missed her husband and found that not having him with her made her feel even worse.

She had thought that Jake would be back before now. He was probably having a hard time finding the curtains she wanted, or else the mall was just so crowded that it was taking him longer than she had expected.

The poor dear. Adele couldn't help but smile when she thought about her gruff ex-cop trying to deal with those throngs of bargain-hunters.

She had been watching an old situation comedy on one of the cable channels running an all-day marathon of the program. Adele enjoyed it— watching shows like that took her back to the early days of her marriage to Jake—but she had grown bored with it and pushed the button on the remote to turn off the TV.

Just before the image blacked out, she caught a glimpse of what looked like some sort of special report, but she didn't turn the TV back on to see what it was about.

Given her circumstances, there wasn't much that could happen in the news to affect her. Anyway, she thought she might nap a little. She leaned her head back against the chair's comfortable cushion and closed her eyes.

Business had been nice and steady all morning, but it would have been a stretch to say that it was brisk, Mitch Hamilton thought as he looked around the hardware store.

There were twenty or thirty customers in the place, maybe more, but the store was big enough that that many people didn't fill it up, by any means. He had two cash registers open, and the girls working them weren't having any trouble keeping up with the flow of customers. The line at each register was never longer than two of three people.

Yeah, if this was what Black Friday was like, Mitch thought, maybe it really *was* time to just pack it in. He'd hang on until after Christmas and then have a big going-out-of-business sale.

Of course, with three kids to put through college, he couldn't afford to actually retire, no matter how appealing the idea might be. He had a standing offer from the manager of one of the big box stores to go to work there. The manager was a guy who'd worked at Hamilton's Hardware for a couple of years while he was in high school. A good guy, really, but the idea of working for somebody who used to work for him kind of rubbed Mitch the wrong way, plus the wages and benefits weren't that good.

But they were better than nothing. Better than losing money keeping his own store afloat.

Sometimes you had to just bite the bullet and move on.

One of the customers came up to him and said excitedly, "Hey, Mitch."

That was one of the nice things about having a small business like this. You actually knew some of the people who shopped there. Mitch said, "Yeah, hey, Phil, happy holidays."

"You heard the news?" the man asked.

"What news?" Mitch grinned and spread his hands to take in their surroundings. "That we're having some great sales here at Hamilton's Hardware?"

"No. There was an explosion out at the mall, and a bunch of shooting, too. From what I heard, sounds like the shit's really hit the fan."

Mitch's eyes widened. He felt like he'd been punched in the gut. Vanessa and Kaitlyn had been going to the mall this morning. They had promised to come by the store when they finished shopping. So far he hadn't seen any sign of them, though.

Suddenly, Mitch felt cold and sick. He turned and dashed toward his office and the TV in there, dreading what he was going to see and hear when he turned it on.

Eddie Marshall had taken the day off. The garage was closed until Monday. But that didn't mean he wasn't going to do any mechanic work until then. The oil in his wife's car hadn't been changed recently.

Wasn't that always the way? The doctor neglected his own health, and the accountant's books were in a mess.

So around the middle of the morning, after sleeping later than usual, then getting up and having a leisurely breakfast, Eddie went out to the garage, ran the floor jack under Christina's car, and lifted it so he could slide under on a creeper and get to work.

He had the oil pan draining when the door into the garage flew open and Christina rushed out.

"Eddie!" she cried.

He knew something was badly wrong. He wasn't sure he had ever heard his wife sound that frightened. He shoved himself out from under the car, looked up at her, and asked, "What is it?"

"Something's wrong at the mall," she said as she stared down at him with a horrified expression on her face. "Something blew up, and now they're shooting people out there!"

All of a sudden, Eddie couldn't seem to get his breath, but he had enough air left to say, "Calvin."

Then a crushing pain slammed into his chest, almost as if the jack had given out and the car had fallen on him.

Walt Graham had his shoes off, his feet up, and a cup of coffee in his hand as he sat back to watch a college football game on TV, one of several that would be on today. As the first one up, it had an early kickoff time.

He didn't want to be disturbed, but he couldn't turn off his cell phone. It wasn't allowed. Theoretically, he was on call twenty-four hours a day, seven days a week, 365 days a year.

He didn't even get the 366th day off, every four years.

So when the cell phone buzzed as it lay on the table next to his big comfortable chair, Graham wasn't surprised. He didn't sigh, didn't moan, didn't curse his bad luck.

Chances were, somebody somewhere was having lots worse luck, he knew, or else he wouldn't be getting a call.

He reached for the phone.

"Graham."

"Sorry to bother you, Walt."

Graham recognized the voice of the Special Agent in Charge of the FBI office in Kansas City, where he was posted currently. He said, "That's all right, Gerald. You need me?"

"I need you to get on a plane to Springfield, Illinois. I'll have one waiting for you."

"Springfield?" Graham frowned. "I haven't seen anything on TV—"

"We're trying to keep a lid on it nationally, but if that lasts for another ten minutes I'll be surprised. There's trouble at the American Way Mall in Springfield."

Graham sat up, placed the coffee cup on the table where the phone had been lying, and asked, "An attack?"

"Shots fired and an explosion of some sort. Men with automatic weapons. In one of the biggest malls in the country, on the most crowded shopping day of the year." The voice on the other end paused. "You can see why I called you."

This time, Graham couldn't help but sigh. His reputation followed him wherever he went, even though he tried to keep a low profile these days. That business in Texas a few years earlier, and his involvement in it, had angered a lot of people higher up the ladder than him, not only in the Bureau but in other parts of the government as well. He'd heard rumors that he had been cussed roundly in the Oval Office itself.

Of course, the person who had occupied the office then was gone, and there had been several presidents since, although none of them had been any improvement as far as Graham was concerned.

"That Black Friday business down there didn't win me any friends," Graham told his boss. "The administration would have just as soon tried to cover it all up. In some circles I've been trying to live down that day ever since."

"You helped save the lives of a lot of people, Walt. There are plenty of us who haven't forgotten that. And hell, you've got experience at something like this. That has to count for something."

"That counts," Graham admitted grimly. He stood up. "I'll be on that plane."

"I knew you would be."

"Does Washington know about this yet?"

"They're just about to," Graham's boss said, and now his voice was equally grim.

Chapter 27

It hadn't taken long for Habib to realize that he should have recruited more men. The mall had too many entrances, too many ways for the hated infidels to escape.

His men had shot up the room next to the

security office where all the closed circuit camera feeds were located, and that had proven to be an unwise move as well since the cameras would have come in handy for keeping track of what was going on. It was difficult to rein in the men's enthusiasm, though, when they had guns in their hands and jihad in their hearts.

All of them carried burner phones they used to communicate with him, and by the time a half-hour had passed since the initial attack, Habib knew that some of the Americans had gotten past his men in three different places. They could only estimate the number who had escaped at around a few hundred.

But considering that close to a thousand of the infidels were dead already, that meant he still had hundreds of living hostages. That was plenty to keep the American authorities from storming the place.

He stood where he could look out one of the glass-doored entrances, staying well back because he was sure the police probably had snipers out there already with their rifles trained on all the doors, each hoping to catch a glimpse of a terrorist so he could take a shot that might make him a hero, at least to the perverted Western media.

Flashing red and blue lights filled Habib's angle of vision from here. Emergency vehicles ringed the outer edge of the parking lot all the way around the mall. Habib's men had reported that to him. They were surrounded.

Which, of course, was exactly what he had expected. In truth, what he had hoped for.

Some of the members of the Sword of the Prophet had fooled themselves into believing that they would get away after striking this blow for Allah, but Habib had always known there was no hope of that. Anyway, wasn't it better to become a martyr in a holy cause than to live?

The mall was quiet now. No shooting, and only an occasional whimper from the groups of hostages crowded into blind corners and small shops, approximately a hundred in each group so that two men with automatic weapons could control them.

In the near silence, when Habib listened closely, he would hear the *whup-whup-whup* of helicopter blades as aircraft circled over the mall. He had expected that, too. Those helicopters belonged to the news media and were sending out pictures of the mall to the rest of the world.

At this point, the Americans didn't know the details of what had happened inside the mall, but they knew it was bad, very bad. Soon, the helicopters would have to leave when Homeland Security or the FBI declared the area around the mall to be a no-fly zone. Speculation would grow. Nerves would stretch tighter.

Let them, Habib thought with a smile. Let the

Americans suffer as they wondered how many of their loved ones had died already, and how many would die before this bloody day was over.

Habib would end that speculation soon, but not yet. Not yet.

Mujidan Bashir hurried up to him. With the glorious death of Mahmoud Assouri, Bashir had become Habib's second-in-command. He'd been resentful because he had wanted the job of blowing up the escalators and all the Americans on them, but Habib knew he was a good, dependable man anyway.

"Our losses stand at eight men killed and five more wounded," Bashir reported. Habib had sent him to find out how many casualties they'd had so far. Bashir went on worriedly, "We don't have enough men left. We should have brought more."

Habib had been thinking the exact same thing a few moments earlier, but he wasn't going to admit that to Bashir.

"We're fine," he snapped. "Have all the pockets of resistance been wiped out?"

When Habib's men had opened fire, among their first targets had been the police officers stationed inside the mall, along with all the hired security guards who were armed, even if they carried only stun guns or batons. Those Americans had been wiped out quickly and efficiently.

Some of the civilians had been armed, though,

and foolishly had fought back. Small caliber revolvers and semi-automatic pistols had been no match for Steyrs, however, and the would-be defenders had been killed or wounded and disarmed in short order.

"Except for the sports store," Bashir replied sullenly to Habib's question.

"Sporting goods," Habib corrected him. He prided himself on his English being perfect. It had helped him blend in until the time came to strike in the name of Allah.

"Whatever," Bashir muttered, sounding like an American himself. "We have shot out all the glass at the front of the store, but every time we try to approach, gunfire from inside drives us back."

That cursed place! All the time Habib had spent considering every angle of the attack, and he had failed to take into proper account that there would be an abundance of weapons in that store.

He had known they sold guns there, of course, but he had counted on the men he placed there being able to keep the Americans from getting their hands on the weapons. Everyone should have been herded out into the mall proper before any sort of resistance could be mounted.

But obviously, something had gone wrong. He should have placed more men, or better men, or both inside the store. They should have been more ruthless.

Honestly, Habib hadn't believed that the Americans would be brave enough, or quick-witted enough, to turn those surroundings to their advantage.

"How many of the infidels can possibly be in there?" he asked Bashir now. "A dozen? Two dozen?"

"If there are two dozen, we now outnumber them less than four to one," Bashir replied grimly.

Habib waved away that concern and said, "But we have hundreds of hostages. If need be, we will kill a few of them and force the holdouts to surrender. In the meantime, we keep them bottled up there. If we cannot get in, neither can they get out."

Bashir nodded.

"I will pass along your commands, Habib," he said. "And it matters not, I suppose, whether one group of infidels dies now or dies later. In the end, they will all die."

"Yes," Habib said, nodding solemnly. "In the end, they will all die."

Tobey hadn't planned on being in charge of anything, but since everybody in the store seemed to be looking to him to make the decisions, he figured he'd better determine exactly what the situation was, and what resources, human and otherwise, he had to work with.

They were in good shape on guns and ammo.

They had enough to deal with a siege lasting for days, maybe even longer.

Food was a different story. According to the store manager, who Tobey quickly located, there was an employee break room with a small refrigerator in it, but it didn't contain much to eat.

Plenty of water was available, at least for now, from the faucets in the store's restrooms.

Tobey ran through all that information quickly in his mind, then realized that other than the guns and ammunition, the rest of it was completely irrelevant. There wasn't going to be a siege lasting for days. Those madmen weren't the type for long, drawn-out confrontations. The lust for infidel blood was too strong in them to allow that.

Nor would the authorities wait that long. They would assault the mall with SWAT teams or Special Forces units or some other sort of tactical squad before this mess was allowed to stretch out for days.

Tobey figured, realistically speaking, they were looking at a matter of hours—no more than twenty-four—before all hell broke loose. |Nobody was going to die of thirst or starvation in that time.

Yeah, that was the least of their worries.

Next on the agenda was a head-count of the defenders. There were 127 people in the store, Tobey found, but 35 of them were kids below the age of fifteen. That left 92 adults and older teen-agers, 60 female and 32 male.

That wasn't an issue as far as Tobey was concerned. He expected the women to fight alongside the men if necessary, some of them, anyway. And not all the men were exactly warriors.

As he looked around, though, he thought he ought to be able to muster around seventy-five people who were willing and at least some-what able to put up a fight. All of the store's employees claimed some degree of proficiency with fire-arms, and at least half of the customers had had varying levels of experience handling guns, including a couple of dozen veterans like Pete McCracken.

The hoodie kid, whose name was Aaron Ellis, had already traded shots with some of the terrorists while rescuing his sister Jennie and her friend Holly. Calvin Marshall, the young security guard, had fired a gun only a few times in his life, but he struck Tobey as the sort who'd be a quick study, and Calvin was willing to do whatever was necessary, too. The way he'd tackled one of the terrorists proved that. Pete, the old-timer, was probably too feeble to do much, but Tobey gave him a .22 pistol anyway, figuring he might be able to handle the lighter weight.

Pete had glared at the gun, saying, "A .22? If

I . . . shoot anybody with that . . . it'll just make 'em mad. I could . . . do more damage . . . throwin' the damn pistol . . . at 'em."

"Put enough .22 rounds in somebody, it'll slow 'em down," Tobey had assured the old man. "Hit them in the right place and it'll knock them out of the fight for good."

"I . . . suppose so. Still rather have . . . a 9mm . . . or a .45."

Then there were the ones like Father Steve, who absolutely refused to take one of the guns.

"My conscience just won't allow me to kill another human being," he told Tobey.

"Not even to save your life or someone else's life?" Tobey had a hard time wrapping his head around how anybody could be *that* much of a pacifist. If somebody's brain functioned well enough to let them walk and talk, how could they not comprehend that sometimes violence, even fatal violence, was justified?

"No, I'm afraid I'd die before I could do such a thing," the priest insisted. "To take a life is to interfere with God's plan."

"So you're saying it's God's plan for you to stand by and do nothing while those terrorists slaughter even more people?"

Father Steve glared at him and said, "You don't understand."

"No, Father, I sure as hell don't," Tobey said as he turned away. He didn't bother trying to keep the disgust he felt out of his voice as he spoke.

All this happened quickly, during the first half-hour of the standoff. The terrorists continued sniping at the store, sending bullets through the grating on the pull-down gate and shooting the windows until the damage was more than the spiderwebbed glass could stand and they collapsed under their own weight.

By the time that happened, Tobey had twenty men and five women positioned behind the counter at the back of the store. Displays of merchandise had been shoved aside by men who had risked being hit by ricochets from the terrorist potshots in order to create firing lanes between the counter and the entrance. The defenders were armed mostly with rifles and shotguns, with fully loaded handguns in easy reach in case there was any close quarters fighting to be done.

Tobey expected the terrorists to charge the store as soon as the big windows went down, and that's what they did. Men appeared, spraying lead in front of them from the machine pistols, but the defenders didn't panic. Tobey had told them that the most important thing they could do was to remain cool and steady. They returned the fire, not rushing but keeping up a firm resistance, and within moments the terrorists withdrew.

"Did you . . . get any of 'em?" Pete asked. He hadn't taken part in the shooting.

"They didn't leave any bodies behind," Tobey told the old-timer. "We must've winged a few of them, though."

"Get 'em . . . next time. There'll be . . . a next time . . . you know. The Krauts kept comin' at us . . . at Bastogne."

"Yeah, I know," Tobey said. "I've read about that battle, and seen the movies about it, too."

"What are you . . . gonna tell the bastards . . . if they ask you . . . to surrender?"

Tobey grinned and said, "Nuts."

Pete gave him a thumbs-up with his good hand.

Tobey moved over to where Calvin knelt behind the counter, holding an AR-15.

"You did good," Tobey said. "You handled that gun like a pro."

"Yeah, I doubt that," Calvin said with a rueful smile. "I couldn't seem to get the bullets to go where I wanted them to go. At least I kept it pointed in the right direction, though."

"Sometimes that's all there is to it."

Aaron was all the way down at the other end of the counter, as far away from Pete McCracken as he could get. Tobey hadn't taken the time to find out the story behind the hostility between Aaron and the old man, and under the circumstances he wasn't sure it mattered.

Normally, he wouldn't have liked the looks of Aaron. The kid was a punk, as Pete called him. He reminded Tobey of some of the guys he had gone to school with, the ones who spent most of the time high and were involved in all sorts of shady things. Aaron just reeked of "petty criminal."

On the other hand, he had risked his life to help his sister and her friend, and he had killed a couple of the terrorists. That excused some of his personal failings as far as Tobey was concerned.

"You're pretty good with that Browning," Tobey told him now.

"Yeah, I never used one until today. Nice gun." Aaron hefted the Hi-Power, now fully reloaded, and looked toward the other end of the counter. "I guess I'll have to give it back to the old geezer once this is all over."

"Well, it *is* his gun."

"We'll worry about it then, right?" Aaron said. Tobey heard the bleak tone in his voice and couldn't argue with it.

Right now it didn't make sense to worry about anything except sheer survival.

More shots blasted just then as the terrorists tried for a second time to get into the store. Tobey knelt beside Aaron and used the Steyr he had taken off one of the dead men. Gunfire roared all along the counter as the defenders fought back.

For a long moment, the air was filled with flying lead going in both directions. Stray bullets hit a stack of ice chests and blew them apart in an explosion of brightly colored plastic. A display of mugs emblazoned with hunting logos met the same fate. One of the defenders behind the counter fell backward, blood welling from a shoulder wound. The racket inside the store was deafening.

Then it ended abruptly as the terrorists pulled back again, unable to stand up to the firestorm any longer.

Tobey moved quickly along the counter. The one wounded man was the only casualty, and another man replaced him on the line of defenders.

With his confidence growing that the people in the store could hold off the terrorists, at least for a while, Tobey's thoughts moved on to the other part of his plan, the one he had mentioned earlier to Calvin.

He didn't know how many terrorists there were—dozens, he guessed—but there had to be hundreds of hostages, even with all the killing the bastards had done. They would have their hands full controlling that many prisoners.

Of course, faced with the threat of automatic weapons, most of the hostages would be terrified and willing, if not eager, to cooperate.

But give them a chance to revolt against their brutal captors, and some of them would seize it and go on the attack.

Tobey intended to give them that chance.

He just needed to pick the right people for the job.

Chapter 28

The agent who met Walt Graham at the airport in Springfield was a gorgeous young woman who appeared to be of Indian descent, despite having the very nonethnic name Helen Shaw. Graham wanted to ask her about her ancestry and also felt like saying, *Are you sure you're an FBI agent, or do you just play one on TV?*

The first question would have been very culturally insensitive, and the other, since it was an indirect reference to her appearance, could be construed as sexual harassment. Graham had endured many agency-mandated seminars on how to avoid giving offense to anybody, ever, and although he had spent most of the time in those seminars trying not to doze off, a few things had stuck in his brain, he supposed.

"I'm glad to meet you, Agent Shaw," he said as he shook hands with her. His big black hand completely enveloped her slim brown one, but her grip had plenty of strength in it. "Wish it was under better circumstances."

"Yes, sir," she said, her tone brisk and cool. "I have a car waiting to take you to the mall."

Graham didn't have anything but a small carry-on bag, so they didn't have to wait for his luggage. As they walked out of the terminal to the dark government-issued sedan, he asked, "Down here from the Chicago office?"

"That's right."

"Brendan Zimmer's still the SAC there, correct?"

"Yes, sir." Shaw waited a beat before asking, "Do the two of you know each other?"

"We were at Quantico together," Graham said. "Seems like a hundred years ago."

"You're not that old," she said with a slight frown.

Now *that* could be taken as a comment on his appearance, he thought, but he didn't point that out to her. Instead he just said, "Older than I look."

Once they were in the car with Shaw behind the wheel, headed away from the airport, Graham said, "Fill me in on what we're dealing with."

"An unknown number of suspects appear to have opened fire and set off an explosion inside the American Way Mall," Shaw said. "Their identities and motives are also unknown."

Sure they are, Graham thought, but he just nodded and said, "Go on."

"They've inflicted an unknown number of casualties, but according to phone calls and text messages and social media posts from people inside the mall right after the incident started, a relatively large number of people have been killed. Also according to that intelligence, the suspects appear to be exclusively males in their twenties and thirties of Middle Eastern descent."

"So we kind of *do* know who they are," Graham said, "even though we don't know much of anything else."

"We can make an educated guess, sir. At this point, however, it would be unconfirmed speculation."

Graham wanted to ask her how long it had been since she'd graduated from Quantico. Not long, he was willing to guess. But there was really no point in it, so he didn't.

"This intelligence from inside the mall, is it ongoing?"

"No, sir. The messages had all stopped within half an hour of the time the incident began."

"That's pretty ominous," Graham said.

"Not necessarily. The suspects would have been likely to collect all phones and other devices from the hostages."

"So we're officially calling it a hostage situation?"

Shaw grimaced just slightly, but the reaction was enough for Graham's keen eyes to detect. She had said something that wasn't strictly by-the-book, and that bothered her.

"There's been no communication with the suspects, so it can't be considered an official hostage situation. The local police have tried to make contact with someone inside the mall, but as far as I'm aware, they haven't had any success so far."

"I assume they tried to get into the mall?"

"Yes, sir," Shaw said. "Tactical units attempted to gain access to the premises at two separate entrance points, at opposite ends of the mall, at the same time. But both units encountered heavy fire and were forced to withdraw."

"Casualties?"

"Some wounded, no fatalities, at least not that I heard of."

"So the local cops are pretty steamed by now, I expect," Graham said, nodding slowly. "But SAC Zimmer has taken charge, I suppose, and is keeping a tight rein on them."

"Yes, sir."

"Is Homeland Security on the scene?"

"They arrived ten minutes after we did."

Shaw was probably happy that the FBI had beaten DHS to the mall, given the interagency rivalries that permeated the federal government, but if so, she didn't show any actual signs of it, Graham noted.

"Who's running the show for them?"

"A woman named Yolanda Crimmens."

Graham nodded and said, "Know of her. Don't recall ever meeting her."

"She's rather . . . severe." Again, as soon as Shaw spoke, she looked like she regretted saying something she shouldn't have.

"A dragon lady, that's the reputation I've heard," Graham said.

"Sir?"

He waved a hand for her to ignore the comment and said, "Before your time, Agent Shaw."

"Yes, sir." Shaw handled the car with smooth precision. She had carried on the conversation without ever taking her eyes off the road or missing an opportunity to make good time. She changed lanes, went through a yellow light, and continued, "The FAA has established a no-fly zone for three miles around the mall. All roads are shut down a mile from the mall. Nothing is going in or out."

"If those fellows are who they appear to be, they don't *want* out," Graham said. "They never intended on getting out. At least, their leaders don't. Who knows what bill of goods they've sold to the foot soldiers?"

"Do you think they intend to blow up the mall?"

"That depends on what their capabilities are. If they have enough explosives to do something like that, then yeah, that's what I'd expect. If they don't, they probably intend to kill the hostages once they get good and ready, then lure us in and blow themselves up with suicide vests once we get close enough they can take some of us with them. It doesn't take near as much C4 for that as it would to take down the mall."

Her tightly controlled façade showed the smallest of cracks as she asked, "Those men down in Texas . . . they had a nuclear device, didn't they?"

"A briefcase nuke, yes."

"I remember when it happened, all the news reports afterward claimed that when the terrorists said they had a nuclear bomb, it was just a bluff."

"It was no bluff," Graham said, his voice flat and hard now. "The White House made sure the media toed the line on the story they put out. The president didn't want the country panicking over the thought that terrorists were able to smuggle a nuclear device into the country and almost get away with detonating it."

"Do you think there's any chance the suspects in this case might have a nuke?" Shaw asked, clearly worried about the possibility, as she should have been.

"There's no reason to believe they do, as far as I'm aware. My boss didn't say anything about it when he called me."

"Then with all due respect, why did the director want you involved with this, sir?"

Graham gave her an honest answer.

"I don't know, unless it's because I have experience with crazies taking over a place like this. But you know, in the end it wasn't anything we on the outside did that saved the day down in Texas."

"Sir?"

"It was the people in the inside," Graham said.

"The hostages. A bunch of brave men and women who did what had to be done . . . and the one man who got them to do it."

"I wonder if there's anybody like that in the American Way Mall."

"We'd damned well better hope there is," Graham said.

Empty brass clattered on the floor behind the counter as Tobey moved along it to the spot where Calvin was positioned. The young security guard was reloading his rifle.

"You all right?" Tobey asked.

"Yeah. A little rattled." Calvin nodded toward a couple of bullet holes in the wall behind him. "Some of those shots didn't miss by much."

"An inch is as good as a mile, they used to say."

"Well, they were wrong," Calvin said. "I swear, I *felt* some of those bullets go past me."

"I wouldn't be a bit surprised. But you didn't panic, did you?"

"Well, no. Couldn't afford to."

"That's why I'm putting you in charge."

Calvin's eyes widened as he said, "Wait . . . what? You're putting *me* in charge? Why? If it's because I'm one of the guards, that doesn't mean anything. This is my first day on the job!"

And with luck, maybe not his last, Tobey thought, but there was no reason to say that to the young man.

Instead he said, "Everybody kind of just decided to put me in command, and now I'm returning the favor with you. You're steady, and people will listen to you."

"I don't think so. I'm just a kid."

"Then grow up in a hurry, because I'm not going to be here to keep everybody fighting."

Calvin seemed utterly confused. He asked, "Where are you going?"

"I've been thinking about it. There are bound to be ways to get around behind all these businesses. Workers have to be able to get to all the electrical wiring and the heating and air-conditioning units. If some of us can use them to get around without the terrorists being able to see us . . ."

"It'll be like secret passages!" Calvin exclaimed, finishing Tobey's thought.

"Exactly."

"You might be able to escape."

"That's not likely," Tobey said, shaking his head. "I'm not sure any of those corridors would lead outside. Probably not. But we could come out in different places, where those murdering sons of bitches aren't expecting us, take them by surprise, kill some of them, free some of the hostages, and then duck back out of sight."

"Like a guerrilla war. We read about that in history class."

"Yep. It's the way the Iraqis fought us. But *we're* the insurgents now."

"And you want me to take over here and keep the terrorists from capturing the store."

It wasn't really a question, but Tobey nodded anyway.

"That's right. I'll only take about half a dozen men with me. You'll still have plenty of fighters to defend the place. You've seen how they've been attacking us. I don't expect them to change their tactics. With the logistics of the situation the way they are, there's not much else they can do."

"What if they try to throw a bomb in here?"

"I think if they were going to do that, they would have already done it. But if you see anything like that about to happen, you'll just have to shoot the guy before he can lob it in."

Calvin drew in a deep breath and blew it out. He said, "That's not exactly a pep talk."

"I'm not a cheerleader," Tobey said. "But I'll spread the word before I go. I'll let everybody know that you're in charge and that they should do what you say."

"Thanks." Calvin paused. "Who are you taking with you?"

"That's what I've got to figure out," Tobey said.

Most of the people who weren't handling the fighting had withdrawn into the large storeroom in the back. They were safe there, as long as the terrorists didn't get into the store. Charles

Lockhart was among them, as well as Pete McCracken and the priest called Father Steve.

Pete had been complaining because he wasn't on the front lines with the others. The way he waved around the .22 pistol Tobey had given him made Lockhart nervous.

"Perhaps Mr. Lanning wanted you in here to help protect these people in case the terrorists get past our first line of defense," Lockhart told the old man.

"If those bastards . . . make it this far . . . we're all done for anyway," Pete said. "Pardon my language . . . Father."

Father Steve sighed and said, "At this point, I think it hardly matters, Mr. McCracken."

"Yeah, we're all . . . screwed anyway."

Tobey came into the storeroom with three men, one of whom Lockhart recognized as the store manager, Herb Dupont.

"I need three more men to come with me," Tobey announced. He nodded to Lockhart. "I'd like for you to be one of them, Charles."

"Me?" Lockhart said, trying to keep the tendency to yelp out of his voice. "I don't know what you have in mind, Mr. Lanning, but I promise, I wouldn't be of any use to you."

"I don't know about that. You handled that bow pretty good earlier."

"I told you, that was pure luck." Lockhart felt panic rising inside him. He still had the bow in his left hand and the quiver full of arrows slung over his right shoulder. He wished he had left them in the front of the store. Then maybe Tobey wouldn't have gotten this crazy idea. "If you're going to launch some sort of attack on those terrorists, I . . . I'm not the man you're looking for."

"What I had in mind is more of a commando operation."

Lockhart waved a hand to indicate his tall, skinny, awkward body and asked, "Do I *look* like a commando to you?"

"They come in all shapes and sizes," Tobey said with a grin. "Stealth is probably going to be very important on this mission. Can you be sneaky, Charles?"

"Well, I . . . I don't know. I suppose . . ."

Tobey looked around and said, "I'm not going to order anybody to come with me. This is strictly a volunteer effort. But if we're successful, we might be able to whittle down the number of those terrorists until they won't be able to control the prisoners anymore. If everybody rises up against them, they won't stand a chance."

One of the men asked, "What if they're all wearing bombs? What you're talking about, mister, is a suicide mission."

"There's only so many of us they can kill," Tobey said, his face and voice grim. "We're talking about saving the lives of hundreds of hostages."

"I'll go," another man said. He was older, probably in his sixties, and on the small side, but there was a look of rawhide toughness about him. "I was an MP, a long time ago. I know about dealing with troublemakers."

Tobey nodded and said, "All right. Sounds good to me."

"Count me in," a second man said. "I'm a high school football coach."

Tobey nodded, then looked at Lockhart.

"How about it, Charles?" he asked. "Are you the third man?"

"You haven't explained exactly what we're going to do," Lockhart said.

Herb Dupont, the store manager, pointed to a small door in the wall across from the entrance to the employee break room and restroom. The door didn't have a knob on it, just a place for a key.

"That leads into the maintenance access corridors," he said. "They connect up and form a network that runs all the way around the mall."

Tobey said, "We're going to use those corridors to get to where the terrorists don't expect us to be. We're going to kill as many of them as we can, duck back out of sight, and then go somewhere else and do it again, as many times as we can."

"And you honestly think this is something I'd be good at?" Lockhart asked.

"Heroes are made, not born," Tobey said with a

smile. "And you might have a better shooting eye with that bow than you think you do. We're liable to need to kill quietly, without drawing a lot of attention. An arrow can do that."

"You don't think we could take some of them prisoner and negotiate with them?"

Tobey shook his head and said, "Fanatics like these don't negotiate, Charles. They may pretend to, when it suits their aims, but really, all they want to do is kill us. All of us."

Lockhart thought about the way the terrorists had blown up the escalators in the center of the mall, killing hundreds of people already, and how they had mowed down more innocent shoppers with those machine pistols. Tobey was right, he realized. It was kill or be killed.

"I still think you're making a mistake," he said, "but I'll come with you."

Tobey nodded and said, "Good. We'll be leaving in a few minutes."

While Tobey was talking to some of the other men, one of the members of the "commando squad" he had brought with him from the front of the store came over and said, "You're Mr. Lockhart, aren't you?"

This was the young man he'd seen earlier who looked vaguely familiar, Lockhart realized. He said, "That's right. Do we know each other?"

"I was in your English class a few years ago," the young man said. "Aaron Ellis."

"Mr. Ellis," Lockhart said as the memory came back. He frowned. "As I recall, you weren't much of a student. No offense."

"None taken. You're right. Hard to make much sense of all that symbolism and grammar crap when you're high."

"I always suspected as much."

"But I'm clean. Right now, anyway," Aaron went on. "It looks like we're both gonna be in class again."

Lockhart frowned and shook his head, saying, "I don't understand."

"Asshole Killing One-O-One." Aaron pointed at Tobey. "And there's the teacher."

Chapter 29

When Tobey had come to him and asked him to be part of what might turn out to be a harebrained scheme, Aaron's first impulse had been to say no. Not just no, but hell no. He wasn't going to abandon his sister. He planned to stay right there and keep fighting to protect her.

But the longer the standoff continued, the more danger Jennie was in, Aaron realized. Those Muslim crazies might get tired of fighting and just blow the place up. That was the kind of thing they did.

If there was even a chance that Tobey's idea

could bring this mess to an end without everybody in the mall dying, maybe they ought to give it a try, Aaron decided.

He had given his answer to Tobey, then added, "But whoever takes my place here better be willin' to give it everything he's got to protect those folks back there. He'd better be ready to fight to the death."

"I think we all are," Tobey had said. "We don't have any choice."

Tobey had called some guys up front to replace the men he was taking with him, then they had gone into the back room to recruit the others. While Tobey was talking to the tall, skinny guy with the bow and arrows, Aaron had finally remembered where he'd seen him before. He might have recalled who Mr. Lockhart was before now if he'd paid more attention during his various short stints in school.

Now, after talking to the teacher—who seemed like a really odd choice to take along on a dangerous mission like this, Aaron thought, but hey, he wasn't in charge—he went over to Jennie and Holly.

Jennie threw her arms around his neck, hugged him hard, and asked, "Are you all right? You weren't hurt in all that shooting?"

"I'm fine except where that son of a bitch cut me earlier," Aaron assured her. His left arm had makeshift bandages tied tightly around the slashes. "And he got what was comin' to him, didn't he?"

Holly said, "That big guy can really shoot." Her voice held a note of hero worship and maybe something else.

"Yeah, he's good at it," Aaron said, suppressing the urge to point out that *he* had shot some of the terrorists, too. He told himself it didn't matter what some little high school girl thought of him.

"What are you going to do now?" Jennie asked. "Something's up, isn't it?"

"Yeah. Me and Tobey and some of the other guys are gonna see if we can sneak around and kill us some terrorists."

Jennie's eyes widened with surprise and worry. She said, "That sounds dangerous."

"Yeah, it will be, I guess."

Holly asked, "How are you going to sneak around?"

Tobey had already explained all that to the group, but Aaron went over it again with his sister and her friend. Holly was kind of cute, though, he had to admit, if only to himself.

"We'll probably be safer than you guys here, when it comes right down to it," he concluded. "We'll be out of sight most of the time."

Jennie squeezed his arm and said, "Be careful."

"As much as I can," he promised. He was glad she hadn't tried to talk him out of it. It wouldn't have taken much to sway his resolve.

Tobey came over, nodded to Aaron, and said, "Let's go."

"Yeah, just gimme a second." He hugged Jennie again and then went to hug Holly, but she was gazing at Tobey with a dumb expression on her face. The big guy was ignoring her, of course. He had more important things on his mind right now.

"Hey," Aaron said to Holly. "I'm goin' off to fight here."

"Oh, yeah, sure." She put her arms around him, and her hug had some enthusiasm to it that made him feel kind of good, the way her trim little body was pressed against his, whether she meant anything by it or not. "Take care of yourself."

"I will," Aaron said. "And I'll be back for you girls."

"We'll be here," Jennie said, smiling. Aaron could tell she was trying to sound brave. She succeeded . . . sort of.

Then Dupont, the guy who ran the sporting goods store, opened the narrow door in the wall with a key he took from his pocket and led the six-man group into a cinder-block corridor barely wide enough for one man at a time to get past the bundles of wiring.

The tunnel-like passage was lit by an occasional small, bare bulb, and when the door was closed behind them, it was gloomy enough in here that

266

Aaron felt a little claustrophobic, like the walls were trying to close in on him.

Tobey was second in line behind Dupont, then Mr. Lockhart, then Aaron and the other two guys. It didn't add up to much of an army, Aaron thought.

But if anybody was going to save the day, looked like it would have to be them.

"Just how much time have you spent back here, Herb?" Tobey asked Dupont as they moved along the corridor.

"Not that much," the manager of the sporting goods store replied. "I've had to check that breaker box we just passed a time or two, and last summer one of the air-conditioning guys called me back here and tried to explain to me why the AC wasn't working that day, but that's it."

"So you don't really know where all the corridors lead or how they link up."

Dupont shook his head and said, "No, I'm afraid not. You really need one of the mall maintenance guys, but there weren't any of them in the store when the trouble started."

"Well, you were able to show us how to get back here," Tobey said. "I guess we'll just have to figure out the rest of it for ourselves."

Dupont carried two Glock 9mm semi-automatic pistols. Tobey had his Shield tucked in his jacket pocket as a backup gun, but his primary weapon at the moment was the Steyr machine pistol. Two of the Colt 1911s he had been looking at earlier—that seemed like hours ago, if not days—were fully loaded and stuck in the waistband of his jeans.

Charles Lockhart had refused a gun, insisting that he would probably pose more of a danger to his allies than their enemies if he was armed with one.

Aaron Ellis still carried the Browning Hi-Power that belonged to Pete McCracken, and he also had a Taurus Judge, generally regarded as an inferior weapon, but Tobey thought its ability to fire shotgun rounds might come in handy. Each of the other men carried a pair of semi-automatic pistols of various makes and calibers, and all the members of the team had their pockets stuffed full of extra ammunition.

They couldn't match the firepower of the terrorists, but they could put up a damned good fight, Tobey thought. And if things worked out as he hoped, they might be able to get their hands on more of the Steyrs.

To do that, they'd probably have to pry the machine pistols from the cold, dead fingers of the terrorists, a prospect that didn't bother Tobey one little bit.

They passed another of the narrow doors. Tobey figured it opened into the business next to the sporting goods store. There was no point in going out there; they needed to get farther away. Somewhere close to one of the entrances, so that when they popped out and wasted any terrorists who were nearby, the hostages in that part of the mall could flee safely. The more of them who were able to get out, the better.

After passing two more doors, the group approached a bend in the cramped passage. It made a ninety-degree turn to the left, and there was no way of seeing what was around that corner until they got to it.

Tobey tapped Dupont on the shoulder, then signaled for everyone to stop. He listened intently but didn't hear any movement on the other side of the turn. Motioning the store manager closer, he asked in a whisper, "What's around this corner in the mall?"

"I . . . I don't know. It's hard to visualize this stuff in my head. I'm kind of turned around."

"Stop for a second and think about it," Tobey told him. "You've probably walked around the mall a lot."

"Yeah, sure . . . We're close to the center, you know, where the big bank of escalators are."

"Where they were," Tobey said. "Those bastards blew them up."

"Yeah. I know." Dupont swallowed hard and looked a little sick. "All those people . . ."

"Don't let yourself think about it," Tobey said. "Just concentrate on the job at hand."

"Yeah. All right. When we make this turn, we'll be behind a candle store, then there's a place that does jewelry repair, then a toy store that's next to one of the department store anchors."

Tobey nodded. The mention of jewelry made him think of the ring in his pocket, and that made him think about Ashley, and the fear for her that lurked inside him tried to well up. He pushed it down stubbornly and followed his own advice to Dupont, focusing his attention on the task ahead of them.

"The department store has exits to the parking lot, right?"

"Two of them."

"If there are any hostages still in there, they'll be able to get out if we kill their guards. That's where we'll start." Tobey motioned for Dupont to crowd against the wall. "Scoot over and let me past. I'll take the lead now."

"Sure."

It was an uncomfortably tight fit, but Tobey managed to wedge himself past Dupont. He put his back to the wall and eased along it toward the corner, listening intently again. He paused as he heard something he thought might be breathing.

The sound didn't come again as Tobey waited for several long moments. He held the Steyr in his left hand and drew the Shield. He didn't want to fire a burst from the machine pistol, because the terrorists might hear that and realize someone was back here in this labyrinth behind the stores. Firing the Shield would be bad enough, but there was at least a chance that a shot or two from it would go unnoticed.

He drew a deep breath, held the Shield in front of him, and wheeled sharply around the corner.

A huge shape loomed up in the shadows, moving toward him, and his finger tightened on the pistol's trigger.

"Don't shoot!" a man's voice pleaded. "For God's sake, please don't kill me!"

Tobey released the pressure on the Shield's trigger at the last possible instant and took an involuntary step back. His eyes widened in surprise as he said, "Santa?"

Even in the gloom of the passage, the fat man's suit was bright red. The white, fake fur trim stood out in sharp contrast to the rest of the outfit, as did the gold buttons on the coat and the black belt and boots. The beard that hung down over his chest was just as snowy as the trim on the coat.

"Holy crap!" Santa blurted out. "You nearly gave me a heart attack."

From behind Tobey, Herb Dupont asked, "Is that you, George?"

"Herb? Herb Dupont? Oh, hell, I'm so glad to see you, man!"

Tobey looked over his shoulder at Dupont,

quirked an eyebrow, and said, "I take it you two know each other?"

"That's George Hendricks, one of the mall Santas," Dupont said. "He's been working here for, what, three or four years now?"

"Four," Santa—or George Hendricks—said.

"What in the world are you doing back here?"

Hendricks took off the red cap and ran his fingers through the thatch of white hair on his head. He said, "I was taking a break . . . you know, tending to the reindeer . . . when all hell broke loose. Stuff was blowing up and people were shooting . . . I didn't want to go back out into that, so I stayed in the men's room where I was. But then I started worrying that whoever was causing all the trouble might come looking for other people . . . you know, to make sure they hadn't overlooked anybody . . . so I found one of those access doors in the bathroom, got it open, and came back here to hide."

"You have to have a special key to open one of those doors from the outside," Dupont said with a frown.

"Hey, Santa can fit down a chimney, right . . ." Hendricks spread his hands. "What can I say, I picked the lock. I haven't always played Santa, you know. Sometimes I didn't exactly *leave* presents . . ."

Tobey said, "Never mind. You're back here, and you're safe for right now."

"Yeah. Whew. When you came around that corner and I saw that gun, I thought I was a goner for sure. What the hell are you guys doin', anyway? What's going on here?"

"Terrorists have taken over the mall."

"No kidding? Damn! When you say terrorists, you mean . . . ?"

"The Islamic kind," Tobey said.

Hendricks winced and said, "The kind who kill everybody and blow themselves up, right?"

"We're not going to let it come to that. We're going to see if we can't whittle them down to size and help the hostages to escape."

"Like in a movie!"

Dupont said, "You should come with us, George."

Hendricks put his red cap back on, frowned in apparent thought, and then said, "Santa's coming to town to deliver presents and kick ass . . . and he's all out of presents."

Tobey gritted his teeth for a second to hold back an angry response, then said, "Come with us or not. One of our guys can let you have a gun. But one way or another we've got to get moving again."

"Much as I might like to, son, I'm not really the terrorist-fighting type. I think I'll just scuttle along . . ."

Dupont said, "The fourth door on your left as you go along this corridor opens into the sporting

273

goods store, George. Some people are forted up there. You can go help them, if you want. You ought to be about as safe there as anywhere."

"I don't know, I kind of like it back here, just me and the rats."

"There are rats back here?" Aaron asked, sounding nervous.

"Yeah, but they won't bother you. They're probably more scared of you than you are of them."

"I wouldn't count on that," Aaron said.

Tobey said, "Everybody scoot over and let Santa by." There was a sentence he wouldn't have thought he would ever say.

With some grunting and wheezing and puffing, Hendricks got past the other men. He looked back at them and said, "Good luck to you boys. I admire your bravery."

Tobey just grunted and started moving along the corridor again. Dupont called back, "Good luck to you, too, George."

"Never thought we'd run into Santa back here," Aaron said when they were all around the bend in the corridor. "I guess that song's right about him seein' you when you're sleepin' and seein' you when you're awake. *And* when you're sneaking around to kill terrorists. Does that count as naughty or nice?"

"Shut up," Tobey said.

Chapter 30

Emergency vehicles, all of them with their lights flashing, completely surrounded the American Way Mall at the outer edge of the parking lots. The lots were full of cars, pickups, vans, and SUVs that belonged to the shoppers who'd been trapped inside the mall. It would have been nice if those vehicles could be cleared out some way, but it would have taken all day, if not longer, for tow trucks to haul them off.

All the cars and trucks would provide extra cover if the terrorists decided to open fire from the mall entrances, Walt Graham thought as he and Agent Helen Shaw walked along the perimeter toward the command post that had been set up inside a square of heavily armored tactical squad vans.

Graham recognized his old academy-mate Brendan Zimmer, who was talking to someone on a cell phone. Zimmer was impeccably dressed, as always, today in a dark gray suit. The suit, as well as the dark glasses Zimmer wore, made his pale skin and hair seem even more washed out than usual. His hair had been a light blond when Graham knew him at Quantico. Now it was pure white.

Zimmer must have spotted them coming because

he broke the connection with whoever he was talking to, lowered the phone, and stepped forward to extend his hand to Graham.

"Walt," he said. "Long time no see."

"Yes, but is that a good thing or a bad thing?" Graham asked as he gripped Zimmer's hand.

The Special Agent in Charge from the FBI's Chicago field office grunted and said, "Still as blunt as ever, aren't you, Walt?"

"Not blunt. Efficient."

And not a brown-nosing politician like some agents, Graham thought.

That probably wasn't fair—from everything he'd heard, Zimmer was a good agent—but even back at Quantico, the man had always had an angle, some way to push himself ahead of others who were doing work that was just as good.

"It wasn't my idea for the director to call you in on this, but I'm glad you're here."

"Have we established communication yet with the terrorists?" Graham asked.

"We're not calling them terrorists," Zimmer said. "There's no official confirmation of who they are or what they want." He gave a little shake of his head. "So far, they're not talking."

"Well, it's only been, what, a couple of hours?"

"Not even that. An hour and thirty-eight minutes since the first reports of shots fired."

Graham looked around at the giant circle of

flashing lights and said, "You've been busy since then."

"Everybody has." Zimmer jerked his head in an indication for Graham to follow him. "There's somebody over here I'd like for you to meet."

Zimmer hadn't given any orders to Agent Shaw, but Graham looked at her and inclined his head in a similar, though not as curt, gesture, letting her know that he wanted her to come along, too. He felt an instinctive liking for the young female agent, and it didn't have anything to do with the fact that she was so attractive, he told himself. Well, that didn't have *much* to do with it, he amended.

The three of them walked over to a middle-aged woman in a tan suit. Her brown, curly hair was cut so that it hung almost to her shoulders. She didn't look happy as she said to whoever was on the other end of the phone connection, "Yes, sir. I'll inform you right away if there are any develop-ments. Of course, sir."

The call ended, and as the woman lowered the phone, Zimmer asked her, "The president?"

"Yes, and the president is not happy."

"Neither are the director and the attorney general. I've been on the phone with both of them in the past few minutes. They want this resolved."

"That's not actually up to us, is it?" The woman looked at Graham, her dark eyes curious and hostile at the same time. "Who's this?"

"One of our agents, Walt Graham." Zimmer nodded toward the woman and went on, "Agent Graham, this is Yolanda Crimmens, assistant director of the Department of Homeland Security."

Graham would have put out his hand, but instinct told him she would ignore it. Her eyes narrowed as she said, "Graham . . . You were part of that debacle down in Texas a few years ago."

"A nuke going off in the middle of the country would have been more than a debacle," Graham said.

"Officially, there was no nuclear device involved in that incident."

Graham shrugged. There was no point in arguing with anybody who spent most of their time in Washington, D.C. Might as well just ask them what color the sky was in their world, because they sure didn't understand—or care about, for the most part—the rest of the country, except for Wall Street and Hollywood.

"What are you doing here, Agent Graham?" Crimmens asked.

"I don't really know. I was just told to come. I'll help any way I can."

"Just stay out of the way unless we need you," Crimmens said.

Graham was tempted to point out that he didn't actually work for her, but he didn't see what good it would do so he didn't say anything. Crimmens turned to Zimmer and went on, "We still don't have any word as to the identities of the suspects?"

"That's right," the SAC said.

"We need to identify them as soon as possible. The press corps is hounding the White House for a statement. The president would like to reassure the American people that this is just another case of workplace violence, you know, some disgruntled employees perhaps stressed out by the pressure of Black Friday—"

Graham couldn't stop the scoffing sound that came from his throat.

Crimmens fixed him with a baleful stare and said, "You disagree with that assessment, Agent Graham?"

"There have been phone calls and texts from people trapped inside the mall saying that the shooters are young, Middle Eastern males. I suppose the mall might employ a few workers who fit that description, but not enough for them to be able to take over the whole place. These suspects don't work here, and we all know it." Zimmer had called him blunt, and Graham supposed he might as well be. "They're terrorists. Whether they're al-Qaeda or ISIS or Hizb ut-Tahrir or some other splinter group that's sprung up recently, it doesn't matter. They want to kill us."

Crimmens' chin lifted angrily as she said, "Where are you normally posted, Agent Graham?"

"The Kansas City office, ma'am."

"Then I suggest you go back there—now. I don't want you on this scene."

Zimmer said, "All due respect, but Agent Graham works for me, not you, Assistant Director Crimmens, and *my* boss wants him here."

Graham appreciated Zimmer standing up for him like that. It was out of character for the guy, who was very much from the "go along to get along" school.

Before the argument could continue, a man in the uniform of the Springfield Police Department came up to the little group and said, "Excuse me, Agent Zimmer?"

"What is it, Chief?"

The officer, who was evidently the chief of police, held out a phone and said, "This call was forwarded to me by the local nine-one-one dispatcher."

"Who is it?" Zimmer asked with a frown.

"Guy who says he's the leader of the Sword of the Prophet. The group that's taken over the mall."

As much as Habib enjoyed the thought of the Americans suffering from the uncertainty of what was going to happen next, he knew the time had come to put an end to that. He walked through the food court toward the glass doors, although he stayed close to the wall and didn't move up far enough toward the entrance that he could be spotted easily.

He kept an eye on the burner phone's display. All the metal in a building like the mall sometimes interfered with wireless service, and the phone was a cheap one. The signal looked good where he stopped, though, so he thumbed in 911.

He figured the dispatchers might be overloaded with calls so he was prepared to wait for a while. However, the call went right through, and a brisk female voice said, "Nine-one-one. What's your emergency?"

"The emergency is that the United States and the rest of the decadent West has defied the will of the glorious and divine Allah," Habib said. "They have spread their sin and evil across the world until the planet is drowning in a cesspool of immorality. Islam is the only thing that can save it. The world must be washed clean in the blood of the unbelievers."

"Sir?" The woman sounded utterly baffled. The fact that a female would be in such a position of power was yet another slap in the face to Habib and his holy cause.

Deliberately, he said, "My name is unimportant. I am a servant of Allah. My brothers and I call ourselves the Sword of the Prophet. We have taken control of the American Way Mall as a demonstration of Allah's mighty power."

"Could you, ah, stay on the line, sir?"

"There is no need to trace this call. I have told you where I am, and as a devout follower of

Islam I am always truthful, even with unbelievers. Please allow me to speak with whoever is in charge of the authorities surrounding the mall."

"Yes, just . . . just hold on, okay?"

"Okay," Habib said with exaggerated politeness.

He turned to look back along the food court while he waited. Tables and chairs had been shoved aside to create a large open area in which hostages were packed in like sardines as they sat on the floor. Habib thought there were under a thousand infidels in this group. Ten guards stood along the walls, five on each side of the food court, and five more were near the wrecked escalators, cutting the prisoners off from the rest of the mall.

The Americans had been split up into five such groups spread out through the mall so that Habib's men could control them with the menace of the machine pistols. Taken by surprise, shocked and stunned into submission, disarmed and in mortal fear for their lives, the prisoners were like sheep being driven to the slaughter, cooperating freely in their own doom. They could have risen up against their captors, but they were too craven to do so. Many more would die if they did, and none of them wanted to be in that number.

They still clung to the hope that some of them would survive.

Most of the Americans looked terrified. Many

of them were crying as they held tightly to each other, trying to draw strength from loved ones or, in some cases, strangers caught in the same trap.

A few wore angry, defiant expressions. As Habib held the phone to his left ear with that hand, he strolled toward one of the prisoners glowering at him, a stocky man with iron-gray hair. A blond woman sat on the floor next to him, holding tightly to his arm.

"You don't like me, do you?" Habib said to the man.

"Ken, no—" the woman began.

Her husband—Habib assumed they were married—cut her off by saying, "No, I damn sure don't."

"I don't want to harm you."

The woman plucked at the man's sleeve, but he ignored her as he said to Habib, "You've got a mighty funny way of showin' it."

"You don't have to die today," Habib said. "Just renounce your sinful beliefs and embrace Islam. Accept Allah as the one true god."

"Go to hell, you damn—"

Habib fired a three-round burst from the Steyr into the man's face, blowing his head apart and spraying blood, bone chips, and brain matter onto the woman, who screamed hysterically. Habib put three rounds into her chest, knocking her back-ward and silencing her shrieks. The prisoners crowded in around the two people Habib had just executed cried out and cringed, trying to get out of the line of fire if he continued shooting.

But at that moment, a man's voice said, "Who is this?" in Habib's ear. He swung away from the prisoners, the couple he had killed already forgotten.

"I am the leader of the Sword of the Prophet," he said. "We strike in the name of Allah to cut away the disease that infects your country."

"Listen, mister—"

"No, you listen," Habib interrupted him. "We have nearly a thousand hostages. We can kill a hundred of them every hour for the next ten hours. Is that what you want?"

"What do *you* want?" the man asked.

"Who am I speaking to?"

"I'm Richard Dodson, the chief of police for Springfield—"

"Chief Dodson, I'm sure you're not the highest ranking person out there. By now the FBI is bound to be on the scene, along with perhaps other representatives from the federal government. I want you to find the person who's in charge and let me talk to them."

"I can handle any negotiations—"

"Chief," Habib said, "I'm going to kill five hostages right now if you don't—"

"Wait, wait!" Dodson cried. "Just hold on. I'll

find who you're looking for. It'll just take a minute. Don't hurt anybody."

"Go on, then. You've got a minute."

Habib hummed to himself as he waited. He didn't bother counting off the seconds or anything like that. When he felt like enough time had passed, he would shoot more of the infidels.

"Hello? This is Special Agent in Charge Brendan Zimmer."

"Really?" Habib said. "In charge of what?"

"The Chicago field office of the Federal Bureau of—"

Before Zimmer could finish, Habib heard a woman's voice saying, "Give me that."

Zimmer said, "You can't just—"

Habib heard some faint sounds and realized the two people were struggling over the phone. He laughed at the ludicrousness of the Americans.

Then the woman's voice spoke again, louder this time, which meant she had won the battle.

"Listen to me," she said. "This is Yolanda Crimmens. I'm the assistant director of the Department of Homeland Security, and I'm willing to listen to your demands."

"I don't deal with women," Habib said coldly. "Give the phone back to the FBI man."

"Now, listen—"

Habib lifted the Steyr, and the Americans started screaming again. That was enough. He didn't even have to press the trigger.

"Wait, wait!" the woman cried. "Don't—"

A man's voice abruptly replaced hers, but it didn't belong to the FBI man. It was deep and resonant and sounded like a black, Habib realized.

"Take it easy," the man said. "My name's Walt Graham. I'm with the FBI. Let's see if we can figure out a way to end this without any more bloodshed."

There wasn't a way to end it without bloodshed. There never had been. Blood and death were vital components in what was happening here today.

But the Americans didn't have to know that yet. Let them hope, so they would suffer all the more when that hope was dashed.

In the meantime, Habib could accomplish some good for the holy cause of jihad. He said, "Listen carefully, American. These are our demands . . ."

Chapter 31

Herb Dupont led Tobey and the other men behind several more businesses, then the service corridor made another ninety-degree turn. When they came to the next door, Dupont stopped and said quietly, "This should open into the department store on this side of the mall. I can't be sure, though. I've never been back here in this part. I'm just going by what I can figure out from where we should be."

"I understand," Tobey said. "You've done great getting us this far. I guess I need to just have a look."

He motioned for the other men to remain silent, then held the Steyr in his right hand while he carefully used his left to depress the latching bar on the door. When he felt the latch disengage, he pushed gently. So far, nothing had made enough noise to draw any attention—he hoped.

The door swung outward. Evidently its hinges were well oiled, because they didn't make any sound, either. Tobey was thankful for that. He eased the door open a couple of inches and peered through the narrow gap.

The first thing he saw made him stiffen with shock and anger. A woman and two children under the age of ten lay on the floor not far away, their bodies covered with drying bloodstains where bullets had ripped through them, killing them. That wanton slaughter made fury well up inside Tobey. He controlled it and shifted slightly so he could look elsewhere.

He saw other bodies, but no one who was alive. He didn't hear anyone moving around or talking, either. The grim hush of death hung over the store.

He turned his head and said over his shoulder

to Dupont, "I'm going out to have a look around."

"Be careful." The man swallowed. "Not to be a pessimist, but . . . what do we do if you don't come back?"

"That's up to you," Tobey said. "You can carry on with what we planned, or you can go back to the store and defend it with the others."

"And hope that we'll be rescued before those bastards kill everybody?"

Tobey shrugged.

"Life's a crapshoot, Herb," he said. "It always has been, and it always will be."

"Yeah, I guess. Just take care of yourself, that way I don't have to make the decision."

Tobey gave the man a curt nod, then opened the door wider and stepped out into the department store with the machine pistol gripped in both hands now.

Everywhere he looked, corpses littered the floor. Men, women, and children, gunned down indiscriminately, their bodies twisted in grotesque attitudes of death. Tobey felt both anger and sickness and couldn't tell which one was stronger. Both fueled his determination to find some way to end this before any more innocent people died.

In all likelihood, that wasn't going to be possible. More killing lay ahead. More blood would be spilled. But Tobey would do everything in his power to see to it that it was the terrorists who bled and died.

He stayed low, moving in a crouch through the aisles of merchandise so he wouldn't be spotted as easily if any of the terrorists walked past in the mall and looked in through the store's broad entrance. The leaders of this atrocity probably had patrols out, sweeping through the mall on the lookout for anyone who was hiding.

He didn't hear any shots at the moment, which was good. That meant they weren't attacking the sporting goods store right now.

Or else they had already overwhelmed the defenders and captured the place, but Tobey didn't want to think about that.

He didn't look too closely at the bodies when he stepped over them, or else rage would have blinded him and obscured his other senses. He needed to be as alert as possible right now. He worked his way toward the entrance into the mall, and after a few minutes, he was close enough to see that two armed men stood just outside the store, evidently on guard.

Tobey didn't spot anyone else alive, although scores of murdered shoppers were sprawled on the floor of the mall itself. Clearly, the terrorists had just gone through the place on a killing spree, mowing down anyone who had the bad luck to be in front of their guns.

The death toll, Tobey thought, might stand at upward of a thousand already. That was almost inconceivable. He had a hard time wrapping his mind around such evil.

The two terrorists didn't seem to be paying much attention. The killing was over for the moment, so they were bored, Tobey supposed.

Close by, a rack of blouses had been over-turned. From the looks of things, the dead woman who lay next to it must have grabbed the rack as she was falling after being shot. Tobey bent, reached down, and picked up a plastic hanger that had slipped out of one of the blouses.

He straightened partially and whipped out his arm, flinging the hanger across the store. It spun through the air for a long way, propelled by the powerful throw, and finally came down with a clatter.

The two guards responded instantly, stiffening to attention and swinging their machine pistols in the direction of the sound.

They couldn't see anything, of course, since nothing was moving in that part of the store. Tobey stood stock-still, peering through a gap between garment racks at the terrorists as they talked urgently and quietly to each other. Tobey didn't have to be able to hear them to know that they were trying to figure out what they should do.

Finally, one of them stepped into the store and started reluctantly toward the area where the hanger had landed. Tobey could tell he was nervous by the way he hunched forward a little and thrust the Steyr out in front of him. He swung the gun from side to side as his head swiveled back and forth.

That terrorist didn't know it, but he was in no danger at the moment . . . because Tobey had started creeping up on the other one. The second man was focused on watching his comrade search for the source of the racket, and he never even glanced in Tobey's direction.

Tobey stopped just inside the store entrance. The second terrorist was about fifteen feet away from him, just outside the opening between store and mall. Tobey could have killed him easily with a burst from the machine pistol, but he didn't want the attention that was bound to attract. Instead he waited, gambling that his quarry's nerves would get to him.

Sure enough, after a few more moments, the man stepped into the store, still with his back to Tobey, and called out to his companion in a foreign language. Tobey understood just enough of it to know he was asking his friend if he saw anything over there on the other side of the store.

The first man turned, glared, and made a sharp gesture for the second one to be quiet. Then he went back to his search.

Tobey was like a ghost as he came up behind the second man. The Steyr was tucked behind his belt now, so he could strike with both hands.

His left arm went around the man's neck and jerked back, snapping shut like an iron bar across his neck to choke off any outcry.

At the same time, his right hand reached around and across and caught hold of the man's jaw on the left side. Tobey's fingers hooked under the jawbone and he pulled as hard as he could.

He heard the sharp crack as the terrorist's neck broke.

The man went limp and dropped the Steyr he held. Tobey lunged and caught it with one hand before it hit the floor and made a racket. With his other hand, he lowered the dead man to the floor.

When the first man looked around, he would see that his friend was gone, but he wouldn't have any idea what had happened. Tobey could wait for him to come back and investigate.

He didn't have to wait for very long, either. A minute later, a low-voiced call floated across the store. When there was no response, the first man repeated it, more urgently this time. Still no answer, and Tobey eased away from the body of the man he had killed as he heard footsteps approaching. They grew more rapid as they came closer.

Then the first terrorist spotted the body and rushed past the place where Tobey was hidden behind a rack of coats. Tobey uncoiled from his crouch and smashed his Steyr against the back of the man's head.

The terrorist went down hard, too stunned to allow his muscles to work properly. He tried to roll over but succeeded only in flopping clumsily. Tobey kicked him in the head, and the man became still.

Tobey used his foot to push the Steyr away from the man's hand, then searched him. He found a couple of fully loaded magazines and put them in his pocket. Then Tobey slid a knife with a curved blade from a sheath inside the man's waistband and used it to cut his throat.

He stood with one foot on either side of the terrorist's torso, grabbed his hair, and yanked his head back to draw his throat taut, then slashed the keen blade across in a deep cut. Blood shot out away from Tobey, pumping hard for a few seconds before the flow began to ebb.

Tobey let go. The dead man's face thudded against the tile floor.

Two of the bastards dead. It was a start. Not necessarily a *good* start . . . but Tobey was far from finished.

Bleak lines were etched in Walt Graham's face as he handed the phone back to Springfield's chief of police.

"Bastard hung up on me," Graham said. "But not before telling me what they want."

"Never mind that. Just tell us what the guy said," Zimmer asked.

"They want all Muslim prisoners released."

"The ones we used to have at Guantanamo, you mean?"

A couple of years earlier, there had been an abortive effort to move all terror suspects from Guantanamo to a federal prison in Texas. When that had turned into a bloody mess, the prisoners had been dispersed to a number of different black sites, according to the scuttlebutt Graham had heard. The real truth of the matter was probably well above his pay grade.

"No, I'm not talking about just the guys we had at Gitmo," he said in answer to Zimmer's question. "They want *every* Muslim prisoner released, no matter what the charge, from the CIA's black sites down to the county jails and small-town lockups."

Zimmer, Crimmens, and Shaw all stared at Graham for several seconds before Crimmens said, "But that's insane! We don't even know who's locked up in all the jails in the country, let alone which of them are Muslims."

"What about the NSA?" Shaw asked. "That sounds like something they might keep track of."

"They keep track of everything else," Zimmer muttered. He shook his head. "But it doesn't matter. Coordinating such a thing would be impossible, even if you could get everyone involved to agree to it, which you couldn't in a million years. Anyway, most of the Muslims who are locked up aren't political prisoners, by any stretch of the imagination. They're just criminals, pure and simple."

"I'm just telling you what the man said they wanted," Graham said. "I think it's impossible, too."

"What else?" Crimmens asked. "That couldn't have been all of it."

"They want twenty million dollars put in an off-shore account. The guy said he would give me the number once we'd agreed to the terms."

"It's a stall of some sort," Zimmer said. "We know good and well that at least three-fourths of the Islamic terror groups are bankrolled by Saudi oil money. Some of those families are worth billions. Twenty million would be small change to them."

Graham nodded and said, "I agree."

"I suppose they want safe passage to the airport, too, and a jet waiting there to take them to, where, Mecca?"

"That's right."

Zimmer shook his head.

"They're full of hot air, and they're bound to know that. They're just stringing us along. What is it they *really* want?"

Graham rubbed his chin, frowned in thought, and said, "Maybe just to string us along."

"Keep us waiting," Shaw said. "Keep us

hoping. Keep us *scared*. They know the whole country's watching by now, sitting around their televisions and computers, praying that the hostages make it out alive."

"I think you're right, Agent Shaw," Graham said. "There's another angle to consider, too, and I'm not sure those guys in there have even thought of it. This is going to make a huge dent in Black Friday shopping. In fact, the hangover from it is liable to damage the numbers for the entire holiday season. That'll hurt the economy. It's not going to collapse or anything like that because of it, but it's still not good."

Crimmens folded her arms across her chest and asked, "Then what do we do? If we can't give them what they ask for—and I agree that we can't—what happens next?"

"They're threatening to kill hostages, of course."

The chief of police spoke up, saying, "When I talked to the leader of the suspects, he told me they could kill a hundred hostages an hour for the next ten hours."

"No way they're that patient," Graham said. His voice was firm with conviction as he went on, "This whole thing is a sham. Like Agent Shaw said, they're going to torture the whole country for a while, and then they'll jerk the rug out from under all of us by killing the hostages."

"You're talking about a bloodbath unlike

anything this country has seen in the past fifteen years," Crimmens said.

"Yes, ma'am. I certainly am. That's what they want. A sea of infidel blood."

Zimmer said, "We have to get in there. There'll be heavy casualties among the hostages and among the personnel who carry out the assault, but if we wait, everybody's going to die."

A uniformed officer hurried up and broke into the tense silence that followed Zimmer's declaration. He said, "Chief, we've got another call from inside the mall."

"That terrorist bastard again—"

"No, sir. This guy says he's a cop, he's armed, and he's on the loose in there."

Chapter 32

As a cop in Chicago, Jake Connelly had attended anti-terrorism seminars and other training sessions along those lines, but he'd never been assigned to any of the units that dealt with such matters. Everyday street crime had been his focus. He had paid attention during the seminars, but he'd never expected to have to use any of it.

That was before that punk kid had gunned down Ray Napoli and tried to kill him, too.

The explosion a moment later, followed by waves of shooting and screaming, pretty well confirmed all Jake's suspicions. The two guys he'd been watching were up to something, all right . . . something as bad as it could be.

After the kid took off, as Jake stood up in the corridor, his hands and clothes sticky with Napoli's blood, he felt an unusual sensation: indecision. He didn't know what to do. When he was on the street, he'd never been bothered with that. His instincts had always told him the proper course of action.

Sometimes he had ignored those instincts out of sheer stubbornness, and mostly that hadn't worked out too well. So he'd learned to trust his gut.

Today his gut couldn't make up its mind whether he should charge out there into the mall with his gun blazing, or retreat deeper into the warren of service corridors.

If he chose to fight, he'd be one guy against who knew how many terrorists. He would almost certainly be killed, probably within minutes, but he could take some of the bastards with him and that might save some lives.

But if he played it safe—and God, how he hated the idea!—he could survive longer and maybe do more good in the long run.

What made up his mind in the end, though, was actually simple.

Adele.

He couldn't throw his life away while she still

needed him. He might not survive today either way—hell, he knew he probably wouldn't—but he had to do whatever gave him the best chance of living. If he made it out of here, he could return home and spend with Adele whatever time she had left.

He knew that if she were here, she would tell him not to worry about her, just to go ahead and do his duty however he saw fit. He knew that. She would say that he needed to help as many of those other people as he could. That was her way, to think about everybody else before herself.

Jake couldn't help it. He was going to be selfish for a change. He wanted to see her again, to hold her and stroke her hair and kiss her forehead and tell her how much he loved her. Sure, she knew that, but he wanted to say it again.

Clutching the .357, he faded back away from the opening into the mall, away from Napoli's body, until he reached the open door of the storage room where the kid in the security guard's uniform had come out.

Curious what the guy had been doing there, and figuring that he wouldn't be coming back any time soon with all that chaos going on out in the mall, Jake ducked into the room.

The light was still on, revealing stacks of crates and boxes, buckets and mops, big push brooms, and a floor-buffing machine. This room was used by the mall's custodial crew, Jake realized.

Some open, empty crates were scattered around. On a hunch, Jake reached into one, picked up a handful of packing material, and sniffed it.

Gun oil. Somebody had hidden the automatic weapons the terrorists were using in here. That told Jake this attack had been planned for a while, and that the bastards had an inside man.

That could be sorted out later, if anybody survived. Right now Jake was more interested in firepower. Maybe one or two of the machine pistols had been left unused. He started opening the other crates.

While he was doing that, he spotted a man's shoe sticking out from behind one of the stacks. With a bad feeling in his gut, he pushed that stack aside and saw the body of a security guard lying there. This guy was the real thing, Jake thought. The front of his uniform shirt had a small bloodstain on it, probably from a stab wound to the heart. Jake had seen corpses like that before.

The guard had found out what was going on, and the terrorists had killed him. Quite possibly, he had been the first one to die in the mall today.

Unfortunately, not the last, by far.

"Sorry, buddy," Jake muttered. "I'll see what I can do about getting even with the sons of bitches."

A moment later, he found two of the machine pistols like the one the kid had used to kill Napoli. Jake recognized them as Steyrs. He had never fired one before, but operating them wouldn't be difficult for him. He found a number of loaded magazines as well and stuffed as many of them into his pockets as he could.

Then, feeling a little better because he knew he could put up a hell of a fight, anyway, he ventured out again.

Around a corner, he found a door with no knob, just a place for a key. Acting on a hunch again, he returned quickly to the room where he had come across the dead guard and searched the man's pockets. He found a ring of keys, took them with him, and tried them until he came to one that opened the lock. Holding tight to the key, he pulled the door open and blocked it with his foot while he removed the key.

The door opened into a narrow corridor with cinder-block walls. Jake nodded. That was what he'd been hoping to find.

He stepped into the dimly lit passage and pulled the door closed behind him.

Jake spent the next hour wandering the network of tunnel-like corridors without encountering anyone. The American Way Mall was so big it would take all day to explore these shadowy, twisting passages.

No more explosions rocked the mall, but from time to time Jake heard shooting. The gunfire sounded distant, but he knew that was because the thick walls muffled it.

The shots meant more people were dying out there, and although the knowledge gnawed at Jake's guts, he resisted the temptation to go out and die in a blaze of glory. Throwing his life away wouldn't be glorious, he told himself. In fact, it would be damned stupid.

Finally, tucked away in a little alcove, he found what he'd been looking for: a ladder of sorts, iron rungs set into the wall that led up a shaft to the mall's upper level. When he tilted his head back to look up, he saw light at the top of the shaft. There was some sort of ventilation opening up there.

He didn't know if he could use that opening to get out of the mall, but he didn't really want to get out. He had been checking his phone every so often, but he couldn't get a signal in here. There was too much concrete and steel all around him. Up there, though, it might be a different story.

He tucked the machine pistols behind his belt and started to climb.

He hadn't gone very far before he realized that he was too old and fat for this crap. The workmen who clambered around in here were all younger and slimmer than he was. He stopped and hung on the ladder while he puffed and caught his breath.

Then he climbed again, past the landing on the mall's upper level and higher still until he reached a square opening on the side of the shaft covered with a heavy iron grate.

Jake got a good grip on the ladder with his left

hand and used his right to take his phone out of his shirt pocket. When he held it up this time, a good strong five bars appeared on the display.

He used his thumb to press 911.

"You take it, Walt," Zimmer said as the cop held out the phone. "You've got more experience at this sort of thing than any of us do."

Graham took the phone and said, "This is Walt Graham. I'm an agent with the FBI."

"Jake Connelly, Agent Graham. Formerly of the Chicago PD."

"Jake," Graham said. "I hear that you're inside the mall. Are you injured?"

"No, I've got a bunch of dried blood on me, but it's not mine."

"It belonged to one of those terrorists, I hope."

"I wish it did. I was with a guy named Ray Napoli, the head of security for the mall, when he was shot and killed by one of the bastards. That's what started the ball rolling in here."

"I see. What's your location now?"

"I'm in a combination ventilation and service shaft near the top of the mall. Getting up here higher seemed the best way to get a phone signal."

"What can you tell us about what's going on in there?"

"Not much, I'm afraid. I heard an explosion and a lot of shooting. There are bound to be quite a few casualties by now."

"Yes, too many. You don't know where all the terrorists are located?"

"No, but I think I may have gotten a look at the guy who's in charge." Quickly, Jake Connelly explained to Graham about the two men he had seen exchanging a signal just before the killing started. "The kid I saw came out of the storage room where they had their weapons hidden," he went on. "He must have been passing them out to the others so they could scatter around the mall and wait for his go."

"You didn't happen to get his name, did you?" Graham asked.

"No, all I can give you is a description. He's young, early twenties, dark hair, brown skin, Middle Eastern in appearance. He doesn't really *look* like a killer. He looks more like a college kid."

"They don't all look like movie terrorists," Graham said. "What else can you tell us, Mr. Connelly?"

"Not much. But I was thinking . . . They've got the entrances to the mall covered, don't they?"

"We're not getting in without a firefight," Graham replied, his voice grim. "We've determined that already."

"Maybe you need to come in from a different direction. I haven't found it yet, but there has to be some sort of access from the mall to the roof, otherwise they couldn't get to the heating and air-conditioning equipment up there to work on it. If you could land guys on top and have them work their way down, you might take those terrorist sons of bitches by surprise."

Graham frowned. He was proud enough to think that they didn't need some retired cop coming up with their tactics, but on the other hand, he wasn't too proud to let that keep him from putting people's lives first.

Anyway, he was certain that he and Zimmer and Crimmens would have come up with the same idea. They just hadn't had time to get around to it yet, that was all.

"We'll discuss it out here, Mr. Connelly, but you may be onto something. In the meantime, can you get out and make it to safety?"

"Maybe, but I'm not going to. I'm staying here so I can lend a hand when it all hits the fan."

"I could order you to escape if possible, you know."

"And I could ignore that order, Agent Graham. What're you gonna do, arrest me?"

Graham had to chuckle at that. He said, "All right, Jake. I think under the circumstances we can call each other by our first names. I'm Walt."

"Sounds good, Walt. I may not be able to stay in touch, but tell your guys that when they come busting in, they should keep their eyes open for a fat, gray-haired guy who looks like a flatfoot. That'll be me, so don't shoot."

"I'll pass the word along," Graham promised.

"It's going to take a while to discuss all this, settle on a course of action, and then implement it."

"Just don't take too long," Jake Connelly said. "I don't know how much time the folks in here have left."

Chapter 33

The other men in Tobey's squad—he couldn't help but think of them that way—were waiting with anxious expressions on their faces when he got back to them.

"I killed a couple of guards out there," he reported. "Managed to do it without raising a ruckus, though, so the rest of them probably won't know anything about it for a while."

"What did you do with the bodies?" Herb Dupont asked.

"Dragged them into the ladies' room." Tobey grinned. "I figured their buddies wouldn't think to look for them in there and wouldn't want to, even if it did occur to them."

"Good one," Aaron said.

"Is the way out clear?" Dupont asked.

"Now, that I couldn't tell you," Tobey replied. "I couldn't see the door to the parking lot from where I was. I wouldn't be surprised if the guy in charge of this bunch has men posted at all the entrances and exits to keep the authorities from getting in without a fight. But if you want to go and see for yourself, I won't stop you."

Dupont shook his head and said, "No, I'd rather stay here and fight. Those bastards shot up my store. Somebody's got to pay for that."

"And all the people they killed," Lockhart added.

"That'll be up to somebody besides us," Tobey said. "Let's just say I figure they'll wake up surprised, disappointed, and pretty hot under the collar when they realize they're not in their sick version of paradise after all."

"Because the devil will be waiting for them," Lockhart said. Tobey just nodded.

"What do we do now?" one of the other men asked.

"We see if we can find some more of them to kill without them catching on to what we're doing," Tobey said.

Habib wasn't happy. He had men roaming through the mall to root out any of the Americans who were trying to hide, as well as to check in with the men guarding the hostages and make sure everything was all right. One of those patrols had returned with the news that two men were missing.

"Missing, you said?" Habib repeated. "Not dead?"

"No, Habib. They are gone from their post, and we could not find them."

"Did you see any of the infidels in the area?"

The man who was making the report grinned,

his lips drawing back from his teeth in a savage expression. He said, "Only dead ones, praise Allah."

Habib nodded slowly. This was troubling news, but not completely unexpected. While he hoped that all of his men were as devoted to the cause of jihad as he was, it was possible that some of them were not as courageous. Perhaps the two who were missing had gone off to hide somewhere in hopes of living through this.

That would never happen. Everyone in the American Way Mall was going to die today. It was ordained in heaven.

"Pass the word to the guards that some of them are to reinforce the men at the entrances," Habib decided. "The Americans have heard our demands. They will refuse to honor them, of course, although they may lie and say that they will. All the while, however, they will be plotting to attack us. Everyone stay in contact. When the attack comes, we will rush to meet it with all the strength of the Prophet in our arms."

"Taking guards away from the hostages, I don't know—" the man began.

Habib didn't let him continue. He snapped, "The infidels are beaten down and too afraid to oppose us. They cower on the floor like animals and pray we will not kill them." Habib shrugged. "They're wrong, but for now their false hope is useful to us. It keeps them cowed."

The man nodded and hurried off to relay the order. Habib felt the skin on the back of his neck crawl. He had hoped to prolong the Americans' ordeal until the holy hour of sunset, but that might not be possible. Despite his confidence, those two missing men worried him.

Were they just the start of trouble he hadn't expected?

Perhaps he might need to move up his plan and start the killing early.

All the Americans had been herded down the staircases at each end of the mall so the upper level was now empty except for a few guards roaming along the walkway overlooking the vast central area on the ground floor.

The children's play area was not far from the center of the mall, and it was now packed with hostages sitting shoulder to shoulder. A few of the prisoners talked in low voices, some whimpered in fear, but most sat in stunned silence, unable to believe that their day of festive shopping had turned out this way.

The bodies lying everywhere just made things worse. Loved ones of the dead sobbed uncontrollably.

Guards strutted around, machine pistols in their hands, sneers on their faces.

This scene was repeated in the food court, in the entrance areas at the north and south ends of the mall, and in one of the department stores that anchored the complex. The prisoners were spread out that way to keep them from acting in concert. Together, they would have had overwhelming numbers on their side. Separated, terrified, they still outnumbered their captors by seven or eight to one, but the automatic weapons, along with the fear they generated, evened the odds.

Jake Connelly figured that out from the half-hour of reconnaissance he did, slipping out of the service corridors at different locations on the upper level and discovering that it was mostly deserted. He kept an eye out for the roving guards and steered clear of them, and so far nobody had spotted him.

He was about as far from a ninja as anybody could get, though, and he knew it. He wasn't going to push his luck too much.

He hoped that FBI guy had taken him seriously about sending men in from above. That was the best chance they had of turning the tables on the terrorists and getting some of the hostages out of here alive.

Whoever had put this attack together wasn't a pro, Jake mused as he crouched behind the counter in a vitamin and health food store. The leader of the terrorists hadn't taken everything into account. If it was that kid he had seen earlier, then Jake wasn't surprised. The guy was too young to be anything but an amateur.

Problem was, even an amateur terrorist was way too deadly.

He heard footsteps outside and knew the patrol was approaching. Jake drifted into the store's back room, where he had left the door to the service corridor propped open. He went into it and eased the door closed behind him.

He wasn't doing any good here on the upper level, he told himself. When the authorities struck back, as they were bound to do, the action would be down there on the ground floor. That was where he needed to be, he decided. That way when things started to pop, he could get out there and give the good guys a hand.

He headed for the ladder and ventilation shaft he had found earlier.

It took him a while to find it, since he had gotten a little turned around in this rat's nest. But when he came across it, he tucked his guns away again, took hold of the iron rungs, and started down.

His feet had just touched the concrete floor on the ground level when he heard a faint noise behind him. He started to turn as he reached for the guns at his waist, but then he froze as he felt a hard ring of metal jab against the back of his neck.

That was the muzzle of a gun, he knew, and he realized he was only a few ounces of pressure on a trigger away from dying.

Irina appeared to know every inch of these service corridors, Jamie thought, and that was good. You always needed a trustworthy guide when you were operating behind enemy lines.

Today, this entire mall had become enemy territory.

They needed guns, too, and in talking it over with Irina, Jamie's hunch had been confirmed. There was a large sporting goods store attached to the mall as one of the anchor businesses, and it carried a supply of guns and ammunition.

"Do they have any guns like that?" Kaitlyn had asked as they were talking about it. She gestured toward the machine pistol in Jamie's hands. The girl was more composed now, although her eyes were still red from crying and from time to time she wiped the back of her hand across her nose.

"I doubt it," Jamie said. "You can't just go into a store and buy a fully automatic weapon like this. There are rules against that."

"Those terrorist guys have them," Kaitlyn protested.

"Terrorists tend not to follow rules, except for the ones that tell them to kill anybody who doesn't believe exactly the same way they do."

"*You've* got one of those guns."

"I don't follow the rules all the time, either," Jamie said. "Anyway, I didn't buy this Steyr. I took it off one of the bad guys, remember?"

"And I used it to save your life. Remember that? I'd sure like to get my hands on one again."

"We'll see," Jamie said, although she hoped they wouldn't run into any more of the terrorists until after they reached the sporting goods store and armed themselves better. After that, if they had a chance to grab a couple of the machine pistols for Kaitlyn and Irina, it wouldn't be a bad idea.

Irina knew how to lead them to their destination, but to get there they would have to cross a couple of the hallways that were open to the mall.

"There could be guards," the young woman from Chechnya warned. "And even if there are not, all it takes is one terrorist walking by to look down the hall and spot us."

"We'll have to take that chance," Jamie said. "We can't fight them with just one gun." She paused. "Unless, of course, you and Kaitlyn would rather find a place to hunker down and wait, instead of engaging them again. That would be the smartest thing to do."

And she wouldn't hold it against them if they decided to do that. Neither of those young women was in the business of waging war the way she was.

Or at least, the way she had been. Technically, she was a civilian now, just like they were.

"No, we fight," Irina said.

"Hell, yeah," Kaitlyn added. "For the sake of

my mom and everybody else those bastards have killed."

Jamie said, "Your mother wouldn't want you talking like that."

"How do you know? You never even met her."

"I just know, all right?"

"So it's all right to want to kill those men, but not to curse?"

"Don't ask for logic at a time like this," Jamie said. "Come on. Let's go."

She cracked open the narrow door that Irina pointed out and peered up the hallway toward the mall. It appeared to be empty. The mall was to the left, some restrooms back to the right, according to Irina. Jamie couldn't see those doors from where she was, so she had to risk opening the door even farther. She peered around it.

The restroom doors were closed. No one was in sight.

She turned her head, nodded to the other two, then stepped out, holding the Steyr level with both hands. Irina and Kaitlyn hurried out behind her and darted across the hall to another of the narrow service doors. Irina thrust her key into the lock and twisted it. She pulled the door open and ducked inside. Kaitlyn was right behind her.

Jamie was about to enter, as well, when she caught a flicker of movement from the corner of her right eye, toward the restrooms. When she turned her head, she saw one of the terrorists stepping out of the men's room as he zipped up his fly. His machine pistol was tucked under his right arm.

He saw her at the same instant. His eyes opened wider in surprise. He moved his arm and let the machine pistol drop into his grip.

Jamie had no choice. She pressed her Steyr's trigger and fought the gun's tendency to rise as she laced a string of slugs into the man's chest.

The bullets drove him back against the restroom door, which swung open under the impact. He dropped the machine pistol just outside the door as he fell into the restroom.

Jamie glanced toward the mall. No one was there yet, but somebody was bound to have heard the shots and would come to check them out. But she might have a few seconds . . .

Irina was peering anxiously out the service door, holding it ready to close. Jamie said, "Be right back," and raced along the hallway to the man she had just killed. She scooped up the Steyr he had dropped, used her foot to shove his legs inside the restroom, and pulled the door closed. Anybody who came looking for him would have to go down the hallway and open the door to find him.

She ran back to the service door and ducked through it. Irina closed it behind her. Jamie handed the Steyr to the young woman.

"Hey, no fair!" Kaitlyn said.

"You get the next one," Jamie promised, although a part of her hoped it wouldn't come to that. She had a feeling that Vanessa Hamilton wouldn't want her daughter turning into a killer, no matter what the circumstances.

Sometimes circumstances forced people to do things they never would have done otherwise, though.

They continued making their way toward the sporting goods store, according to Irina. They weren't far from it when Jamie heard something up ahead and motioned for the others to stop. She cocked her head a little to the side, tightened her grip on the Steyr, and listened intently.

It was an odd, regularly spaced sound, sort of like footsteps but not exactly. Jamie heard what sounded like a grunt of effort. It came from around a corner in the shadowy corridor. At least it was only one man, she decided, although she still couldn't figure out what he was doing.

Then it came to her. He was climbing up or down a ladder. Since the sounds weren't fading, she decided he was climbing down.

Toward them.

Had to be one of the terrorists, she thought. They had finally realized this network of passages was back here behind the scenes in the mall, and he was exploring it, looking for people who had hidden themselves away from the massacre.

Like her and Irina and Kaitlyn, she thought.

But the bastard wouldn't find them defenseless.

She motioned to her companions for them to stay where they were, then leveled the machine pistol and stepped around the corner in time to see a stocky, gray-haired man in slacks and a lightweight jacket reaching the bottom of a ladder formed by iron rungs cemented into the wall.

Jamie frowned. From this angle, he didn't *look* like the other terrorists she had seen. For one thing, he was a lot older. But maybe he was the mastermind of the whole attack. Until she knew for sure, she couldn't afford to take a chance.

As quiet as a cat, she stepped up behind him and pressed the Steyr's muzzle to the back of his neck. At this range, if she pulled the trigger the stream of bullets would saw his head right off his shoulders.

"Don't move," she said.

The man obeyed the order, she had to give him credit for that. He stood absolutely motionless with his hands still on one of the ladder rungs.

Then he said, "Lady, you don't sound like a terrorist, gun or no gun."

Jamie's breath hissed between her teeth in surprise as she heard the American tones in the man's voice. She said, "You're—"

"Hoping that we're on the same side," the man broke in. "My name's Jake Connelly. I used to be a cop, and right now I'm trying to find a good place to fight back against the men who have taken over this mall."

For a second, relief flooded through Jamie. The emotion was so strong she wanted to lower the gun and cry. That would have been too stereo-typically feminine a thing to do, though, so she kept the Steyr level as she moved back a step and said, "Turn around, Mr. Connelly. Carefully. And keep your hands where I can see them."

"Like I told you, ma'am, I used to be a cop. I know the drill."

He turned, and again Jamie fought the urge to break down as her tension eased even more at the sight of his broad, friendly, bulldog-like face.

He was observant, too, because he said, "Ex-military?"

"Captain. Air Force. Three tours in Afghanistan."

Jake's face creased in a grin as he said, "Then I was right. We're on the same side." He glanced past her and added, "Who's this?"

Jamie looked over her shoulder and saw that Irina and Kaitlyn had come around the corner, unable to resist the temptation to find out what was going on. Irina held the Steyr Jamie had given her a short time earlier.

"Friends of mine," Jamie said. "I'm Jamie Vasquez. This is Irina Dubrovna and Kaitlyn Hamilton."

"Ladies," Jake said as he nodded to them. "All of you look like you have a fight in mind."

"That's right. We're on our way to the sporting goods store, since that's where we'll find the most guns and ammo."

"Sounds like a good idea to me." Jake sketched a salute. "I'm at your command, Captain Vasquez. We'd better get moving, though. I don't know how much time we have left."

"How much time before what?"

Jake pointed up with a thumb and said, "Before a bunch of Special Forces guys drop down on the roof and all hell breaks loose in here."

Chapter 34

There was too much to keep up with, Habib thought. Too many things to remember. He summoned Mujidan Bashir and told his second-in-command to check on the situation at the sporting goods store.

"I don't have to go check," Bashir said. "I just talked to one of the men down there. The Americans who took refuge there are still trapped inside."

"We haven't gotten them out yet?" Habib didn't try to keep the irritation out of his voice as he asked the question.

"No, but you said we should just keep them penned up and deal with them later."

"I know what I said," Habib snapped. "But such

defiance of Allah's will cannot go unpunished."

Bashir shrugged and said, "It won't. There can't be more than a few dozen of them in there. Once we're finished with the others, we can all attack the store and finish them off."

What Bashir said made sense, but Habib wasn't going to tell him that. Instead he said, "I'll think about it. But I don't like the idea of them sitting in there thinking that they can get away with what they're doing."

"No one gets away," Bashir said. "Destiny catches up with everyone."

Habib couldn't argue with that, either.

Calvin used the back of his hand to wipe sweat off his forehead. A few feet away, Pete McCracken said, "Hot in here . . . ain't it . . . kid?"

"The AC must've gotten knocked out in that explosion," Calvin said.

"The AC . . . wasn't on. It's . . . late November."

"Yeah, but the weather's been warm."

"Not . . . that warm . . . You're sweatin' . . . because of all the people . . . crammed in here. And because . . . you're scared."

Calvin turned his head to frown at the old man in the wheelchair.

"You're not even supposed to be up here in this part of the store. Where's Father Steve?"

"Probably back there . . . prayin'. I can . . . get around without him . . . you know."

Pete moved the knob on the wheelchair's arm with his clawlike left hand, making the chair swing back and forth slightly as its motor hummed.

"Well, you need to go back where you'll be safe if those terrorists attack again."

"Is anybody . . . in here . . . really safe?"

Calvin couldn't answer that question, or rather, he didn't *want* to answer it, he thought. That would have meant admitting that they were just holding off the inevitable. Sooner or later the terrorists would storm the store, he thought, and he knew how that pitched battle would end.

Already, the defenders had fought off half a dozen attacks. Three men had been killed so far. Their bodies had been carried into the back room, and others had replaced them. Those deaths had caused spirits to run low. People were beginning to sense that the end was looming.

The gunfire, the deaths, the sheer desperation had all combined to make Calvin feel numb. He could still force his brain to think, but everything else inside him had gone dead. Things weren't supposed to be this way, but they were and there was nothing he could do about it except to keep fighting.

He wondered how Tobey, Mr. Lockhart, and the others were doing. Calvin wished he had gone with them, rather than having Tobey pick him to be in charge of the store's defense. He would have rather been on the move, even if it was more dangerous.

He heard a quick patter of footsteps behind him as he knelt at the counter. Turning his head, he saw a girl about his age with brown hair approaching. She was standing up too straight, so Calvin motioned for her to get down. With a nervous look, she dropped to hands and knees and crawled toward him.

"You're the guy who's in charge up here, right?" she asked.

"Yeah, I guess." Calvin thought her name was Jennie, but he wasn't sure about that.

"The priest sent me to get you. He says somebody's trying to get in at the back of the store, through that door where my brother and those other men left."

Calvin's heart thumped hard in his chest. The door into the service corridors opened into the store if you had a key for it, but anybody could open it from the other side. The doors were designed that way, he supposed, so that mall maintenance workers couldn't get trapped in there.

At Tobey's suggestion before he departed on his commando mission, the store's defenders had barricaded that door with a couple of file cabinets. When Tobey and the others returned, they were supposed to knock on the door in a prearranged signal so they could be let back in.

"It must be Tobey and your brother and the others," Calvin told the girl.

She shook her head and said, "They didn't give any signal. They just tried to push the door open."

Calvin closed his eyes for a second as despair went through him. His emotions weren't as numb as he had believed them to be. The terrorists must have found those narrow passages and were trying to launch a sneak attack.

He motioned one of the other defenders over and told the man, "Keep an eye out front. I've got to go in the back."

"Trouble?" the man asked.

"I don't know yet," Calvin said, but in truth, he did. There was nothing but trouble in the American Way Mall today.

Staying low, he and Jennie made it to the back room. The people who were hiding here had withdrawn to the other side of the room and were staring fearfully at the blockaded door. Most of them were armed, but the people who were more experienced with guns were all up front.

Still, how experienced did you have to be to point a weapon at a doorway and pull the trigger, Calvin asked himself. He pointed to half a dozen of the men and crooked his free hand at them, indicating that they should join him. They came over, albeit a bit reluctantly, and Calvin told them in a whisper, "A couple of you get ready to shove those file cabinets out of the way. The rest of you have your guns ready and start shooting if I give the order."

The possibility that whoever was on the other side of the door was friendly still existed. Calvin wasn't going to take any chances, though. Whoever they were, they'd have to identify themselves in a hurry to keep from getting shot.

The men positioned themselves beside the filing cabinets. Calvin and the others lifted their guns. Calvin nodded, and the men shoved the cabinets aside, causing a scraping sound as they moved on the floor. The door swung open abruptly, and the first thing Calvin saw was the barrel of a machine pistol.

His nerves snapped, and he yelled, "Fire!"

Jake caught just a glimpse of the men standing on the other side of the door pointing guns in the direction of him and the three women. Irina had been confident that the back room of the sporting goods store was on the other side of that door, but when they had tried to open it, they had encountered resistance, as if something was blocking it.

None of them had wanted to call out, for fear that the terrorists were lurking right on the other side. Then they'd heard whatever was blocking the door being moved, and Jamie had snapped, "Get behind me," as she stepped forward with the Steyr in both hands and used her foot to push open the door.

That was when Jake spotted the armed men, and he reacted instinctively, grabbing Jamie's collar and pulling her back and to the side while he lunged forward.

Somebody yelled, "Fire!" and guns roared, deafening in the close confines.

What felt like a giant fist smacked into Jake's upper left arm, spun him halfway around, and caused him to lose his balance as his legs tangled with Jamie's. They both fell, but that was good because they toppled out of the doorway and therefore out of the line of fire. As Jake landed, he saw Irina and Kaitlyn flinching away from the lead storm.

Jake's arm hurt like blazes where he'd been hit, but he didn't think the wound was serious. At least he hoped not. The barrage of bullets stopped abruptly. He thought it did, anyway. His ears were ringing so bad it was hard to tell for sure.

"Hold your fire," a young voice ordered, sounding like it came from far, far away. "You terrorists, come out with your hands up!"

"Terrorists!" Kaitlyn repeated angrily. "*You're* the terrorists!"

"Wait, wait." That was the young man again. "You're Americans?"

Jamie pushed herself up on an elbow and

325

barked in her command voice, "Everybody stand down! That's an order!" She looked over at Jake. "How badly are you hit, Mr. Connelly?"

"Just grazed, I think," he said. "Still hurts like the devil, though."

Jamie stood up, and as the right leg of her jeans hiked slightly, Jake saw the steel shaft of a prosthesis going down into the foot-shaped block of plastic inside her shoe. He hadn't realized until just now that at least part of her right leg was gone. He had noticed that she had a slight limp but hadn't attributed it to such a severe injury.

She didn't let it slow her down much, that was for sure.

A young black man in a security guard's uniform appeared in the opening, holding a gun. He stared at Jake and the three females and said, "Oh, my God. We almost killed you."

"You came too close for comfort, kid," Jake said. "Somebody give me a hand here."

Within moments, Jake was on his feet again and they were all inside the store's back room. Jake looked around, saw the frightened people gathered there, and realized that others had had the same idea of forting up in here where guns and ammo were available.

Briskly taking charge, Jamie said, "Mr. Connelly, you find a place to sit down. There's bound to be a first aid kit somewhere around here. We need to clean and bandage that wound."

A woman who wore the uniform of the store's sales staff volunteered, "I'll get the kit. I know where it is."

With that in hand, Jamie asked, "Who's in charge here?"

"I guess I am," the young security guard said. "My name's Calvin Marshall."

"I'm Captain Vasquez." She nodded toward Jake. "This is Detective Connelly."

Calvin swallowed and said, "Yes, ma'am. I think that makes *you* in charge now. Both of you. You sure as heck outrank me."

"Tell me what's been going on here," Jamie said.

Calvin summarized the past couple of hours, a time filled with so much violence and death that his voice sounded haunted by it. Jake noticed that Kaitlyn appeared to sympathize with him. He knew the girl had lost her mother, back in the opening moments of the terrorist attack, and that loss probably hadn't completely sunk in on her yet. Her moral fiber was strong enough, though, that she could feel for Calvin.

While that was going on, the woman who had gone to fetch the first aid kit returned with it in hand. She seemed to have had a little training in that area. Jake took off his jacket, and she cut away his shirt to reveal that the slug had plowed a bloody furrow across the outer part of his upper left arm. It was a painful wound, but it wouldn't incapacitate him.

A young, blond priest stepped forward to help as the woman cleaned the wound on Jake's arm and then wrapped a strip of gauze around it and bound it tightly in place.

"You should be able to use your arm some," she told him, "but it's going to hurt."

"Let it hurt," he said. "Right now that doesn't matter a whole lot, does it? I really appreciate your help." Jake nodded to the priest. "Thanks to you, too, Father."

"I wish I could do more," he said. "I'm Father Steve, by the way."

"Glad to meet you."

"Are you a Catholic?" Father Steve asked. "I mean, with a good Irish name like Connelly . . ."

Jake chuckled and said, "Sorry, Father. Methodist as far back in the family as I can remember."

"Well, that's all right, too."

Jamie and Calvin came over to join them. Jamie said, "Calvin's been telling me that some of the men who made it safely into the store have gone back out through those passages we were using."

"To try to escape?" Jake asked.

"To kill as many of the terrorists as they can," Jamie replied with a shake of her head.

Jake frowned and asked, "How many left here?"

"Seven men," Jamie said.

"Against a hundred heavily armed terrorists?"

"I know it sounds crazy," Calvin said, "but I wouldn't count them out."

Chapter 35

Tobey stepped through one of the narrow doors into a place that sold eyeglasses in an hour. It was empty except for the bodies of two women and a man. Broken glass covered the floor. The terrorists must have shot up every pair of glasses displayed on the walls for customers to pick from. There couldn't have been any point in that other than sheer, wanton destruction.

Which came as no surprise, considering how easily, even gleefully, these bastards killed innocent people.

The broken glass crunched under Tobey's boots as he catfooted toward the store's entrance. He risked the possibility that some of the terrorists might be close enough, outside in the mall, to hear his footsteps, but he wanted to get an idea of what was going on in this section. According to Herb Dupont, they weren't far from the children's play area. It was just around a slight bend in the mall from here.

The idea of cold-blooded killers strutting around with guns in a place where children should be playing and enjoying themselves filled Tobey with a cold anger. Those bastards had an awful lot to answer for, and the score against them just kept mounting all the time.

He froze suddenly near the front of the store as he heard voices. It sounded like two men were talking, and they seemed to be coming closer. Tobey crouched behind a desk that, before today, had been where store employees sat as they fitted new glasses to customers.

Two of the terrorists walked past the store, never even glancing in Tobey's direction. That's how sure they were that they held the upper hand, he thought. They were speaking English with barely any accents. They had probably been in this country for quite a while, enjoying life here, taking advantage of all the benefits the federal government offered so freely.

He edged up to the entrance and risked a look around the corner. The two men patrolling this part of the mall were still walking away, but as Tobey watched, they stopped and turned back in his direction. He pulled back out of sight before they could spot him and looked at the door to the maintenance corridors.

Aaron stood there, watching him anxiously through the small gap.

Tobey motioned to him. Aaron slipped through the door and hurried to join him.

"There are a couple of guys coming in this direction," Tobey whispered. "We're going to jump them."

"The others won't see us?" Aaron asked.

"We're kind of around a little corner from the

main part of the mall. If we can take care of these guys without firing any shots, I don't think we'll alert the rest of them."

Aaron swallowed hard but nodded. Tobey could tell that the kid was scared. Who wouldn't be, under these circumstances? Tobey had talked enough with Aaron, though, to know that he'd done time in prison. If Aaron was tough enough to survive there, he was tough enough to make it through this.

"Just follow my lead," Tobey said.

The terrorists were closer now. Tobey heard one of them say, "—think Habib is getting impatient with the infidels. He won't wait much longer."

"Good," the other man said. "I'm not anxious to die . . . but martyrdom and all its glories await us."

That didn't sound good at all, Tobey thought. This Habib had to be the leader, and if he was getting ready to put his endgame into action, that didn't bode well for any of them. Maybe there wasn't time to whittle down the enemy forces as much as he would have liked, Tobey decided . . .

The two men appeared at the entrance to the eyeglass store, walking steadily toward the center of the mall. Tobey and Aaron had their backs pressed to the wall, and they didn't make their move until the terrorists had gone a couple of steps past them.

Then Tobey lunged, swinging the Steyr in one hand at a terrorist's head while he bent slightly at the waist and launched a side kick at the other man's back.

It was a devastating attack. The machine pistol smashed into the first man's head with enough force to shatter bone. The kick landed in the small of the other man's back at almost the same exact instant and knocked him forward. The impact was such that he couldn't keep his feet. He fell hard, landing facedown with stunning force.

Aaron landed on the man's back a split second later, pinning him down with a knee while striking with the knife he had taken from his pocket and unfolded. The blade went into the terrorist's throat, ripped across it. The man spasmed once as crimson sprayed from the wound, then he went still.

Tobey was pretty sure he had fractured the skull of the first man, but he slit his throat just to make certain.

Then he and Aaron dragged both corpses into the store, out of sight of any casual glance directed toward this part of the mall. The blood splattered on the floor might attract attention, but there was nothing they could do about that.

The whole thing had taken less than thirty seconds and been almost noiseless.

Tobey was searching the bodies for loaded

magazines when he noticed something odd about one of them. He pulled the man's jacket and shirt aside, and Aaron exclaimed, "Shit! Is that what I think it is?"

"Yeah," Tobey said. "It's a bomb. A suicide belt." He pointed. "All you have to do is jerk that wire loose to set it off. Looks like there's enough C-4 to make a pretty good boom."

Aaron rubbed his jaw and shook his head.

"That's crazy, man. Who's nuts enough to blow themselves up like that?"

"Plenty of this bunch. Over in the sandbox, we even saw women and children carrying suicide bombs. Their husbands and parents made them do it. Sickest bunch of bastards there's ever been on the face of the earth."

"Yeah, no argument from me, man. You think they're *all* wearing those things?"

Tobey frowned and said, "The ones I searched earlier weren't. Either only some of them have the bombs . . . or they're being passed out to everybody now."

"If they're all wearin' 'em . . ." Aaron had to swallow again before he could go on. "How much damage would it do if they all went off at the same time?"

"Yeah, I was thinkin' about that, too," Tobey admitted. "We don't know how many of them there are, but based on what we've seen . . . and how many men it would take to guard all the hostages they have . . . I think there's a good chance a blast of that size could bring down the whole mall."

"Ohhhh, man. That's what they're plannin', isn't it? They're gonna blow this whole freakin' place to hell."

"Wouldn't put it past 'em," Tobey said with a grim nod.

"We gotta do something. We gotta get the word out, let the cops or whoever's on the outside know they've got to storm the place and stop those crazy sons o' bitches. Otherwise everybody in here is gonna die, and who knows how many outside."

"I think that's probably exactly what they have in mind," Tobey said.

Ideas stirred in the back of his brain. He reached into the pocket of the dead man's jacket and found a cheap phone. Maybe that was the way the terrorists were communicating, he thought, although reception in here would be wonky. He opened the phone and checked the recently dialed numbers.

There was only one, but it had been called several times.

Tobey was willing to bet it belonged to Habib.

He could maybe do something about that later. Right now he had something else in mind. Carefully, he removed both suicide belts from the dead terrorists.

"We're not takin' those things with us, are we?" Aaron asked.

"They might come in handy," Tobey said.

Aaron looked at him like *he* was crazy, too.

Maybe he was.

Tobey left Aaron and the bombs at the eyeglass store and went scouting toward the center of the mall. He was being more daring now, but his instincts told him the risk was justified because they might be running out of time.

He reached the bend in the mall and carefully looked around it. The children's play area was about fifty yards away. Hostages were packed into it, sitting shoulder to shoulder on the floor. Guards with machine pistols stood around the perimeter of the group. Tobey counted eight men, but there were probably more nearby that he couldn't see.

As he looked around, his gaze fell on some plush, motorized, wheeled toys in the shape of giraffes, kangaroos, lions, and other exotic animals. They stood about four feet tall and three feet long, and they had handlebars with throttle controls on them, as well as built-in seats and places for a kid's feet to go. There were about a dozen of them inside a plastic corral.

Parents could rent those animals for their children to ride while they were shopping. Tobey figured they couldn't go very fast, since the kids controlled the speed by squeezing the handlebars. It was a weird deal, he thought, but maybe he could make use of it.

And someday, when he and Ashley had kids of their own, they could bring them here and they could ride the animals and laugh and it would be a great day.

Yeah, someday. Tobey wasn't going to allow himself to consider any other possibility.

The corral was located right where the mall made its little turn. Tobey knew he would be taking a big chance if he went out there, but he waited until none of the guards were looking in his direction and then moved as fast as he could, sprinting across the open space and then ducking down behind the dozen or so animals.

Nobody shot at him, so after a minute he figured he hadn't been spotted.

The plastic corral wasn't meant to keep anybody out. It was mostly for show. Tobey moved a section aside, being careful not to make any noise. Then he reached in and took hold of the nearest animal, a lion.

It wheeled backward without any trouble. When Tobey had it clear of the corral, he continued backing, keeping the group of animals between him and the play area where the hostages and the terrorists were. He could only hope no other patrols would spot him.

Suddenly he heard footsteps and voices above

him. Some of the terrorists were on the upper level, too. Going flat on the floor, he left the animal where it was and rolled under one of the mall benches set at intervals for weary shoppers. He froze and stayed there until the terrorists above him were gone.

Then he rolled out, got hold of the lion again, and rolled it back another twenty feet or so before the angle was good enough for him to surge to his feet, grab the thing up into his arms, and trot toward the store where Aaron was waiting, his eyes big with confusion.

"What the hell, man?" Aaron asked as Tobey set the lion down.

Tobey didn't explain. He just said, "Go tell Herb you need to find a place that sells sewing materials. I need some sturdy gray thread."

Fishing line might have been even better, but he didn't want to go all the way back to the sporting goods store.

"Thread?" Aaron repeated.

"Yeah. And hurry up. We don't know how much time we have left."

"Okay, dude. Whatever you say."

Aaron disappeared through the narrow door to the maintenance corridors. Tobey went to work. He used his knife to cut a slit in the plush covering over the lion's framework.

Time seemed to pass maddeningly slowly while Aaron was gone, but Tobey stayed busy with his part of the task, and eventually Aaron showed up with several spools of gray thread clutched in his hand.

"Will this work?" he asked. "I didn't know exactly how much you'd need."

"Yeah, I'll tie some of it together to make it longer if I have to." Tobey took one of the spools, unwrapped some of the thread, and pulled back the padding he had cut loose on the lion.

"Oh, hell," Aaron breathed. "You put those bombs in there?"

"Yep." Tobey tied the thread to the wire that would trigger one of the bombs. "I figure if this one goes off, the other one will, too."

"Be careful, man. If this goes wrong, you'll blow us both sky-high."

"It won't go wrong," Tobey said. He started unwinding more of the thread, being careful to keep it from tangling. Then he handed the spool to Aaron. "Here, hold this. Keep playing it out. Just don't pull on it until I give you the signal."

Aaron took the spool of thread, but he looked at it like Tobey had just handed him a live rattlesnake.

Tobey rolled the lion to the bend, then put his leg over it and stood so that his legs blocked the two footrests and kept the animal from moving as he held down the control on the handlebar. The motor made it push against the back of his calves.

He took a length of thread he had snapped off from the spool and used it to tie the control in place, gauging the tension so the lion wouldn't move too fast. He wanted the toy just barely rolling along. When he was satisfied, he stepped back.

Slowly, the lion trundled past the corner and started toward the play area.

Tobey stayed where he was. Somebody had to watch the blasted thing. He couldn't let it get too close to the hostages.

Looked like that wouldn't be a problem. One of the guards spotted the lion almost right away and let out a yell. Tobey heard the swift rataplan of running footsteps, and as he risked a look around the corner, he saw at least half a dozen terrorists swarming around the lion and pointing their machine pistols as they babbled questions at each other. As far as he could tell, none of them noticed the dark gray thread played out along the floor behind the animal.

Idiots, Tobey thought.

He raised a fist where Aaron could see it and made a sharp tugging motion.

Aaron nodded, wrapped the thread around his hand, and pulled hard.

The blast shook the floor under Tobey's feet.

Chapter 36

The explosion made Habib jerk around and stare wide eyed along the mall in the direction of the blast. That had sounded like at least one of the suicide belts had gone off, maybe two.

Bashir ran up to him and asked, "What was that?"

"I don't know," Habib answered honestly. "None of the men were supposed to detonate their devices yet."

Only about a third of the members of the Sword of the Prophet wore the explosive belts under their clothing. Only the most trusted men had gotten them, the men who could be relied on not to hesitate when the moment came to strike the ultimate blow for Allah.

Although these bombs weren't as powerful as the one that Mahmoud Assouri had set off to destroy the central escalators, they packed enough punch to do tremendous damage to the mall and perhaps even cause the building to collapse. Although Habib would have liked to leave only a huge, smoking crater where the American Way Mall had been, he simply didn't have the resources to manage that. He had been able to funnel off only so much money from the network funded by Saudi oil riches.

Now, in the wake of the blast, he heard screams, shouts, and the sudden chatter of automatic weapons. Something had gone wrong, and he had to act before events spiraled out of his control.

"Tell the men to take that sporting goods store," he snapped at Bashir. "No holding back this time. Take it and slaughter every infidel in there like the pigs they are!"

As Bashir ran off to follow those orders, Habib reached for the phone in his pocket. He was going to tell the men standing guard on the hostages to go ahead and open fire on them. The killing season had begun.

Before he could grasp the phone, it began to vibrate. One of the men was calling him, maybe to report on what was happening. Habib grabbed it, thumbed the button to answer, and practically yelled, "What the hell is going on down there?"

"Hey, Habib," an unmistakably American voice said in a mocking tone. "Things not going according to plan anymore?"

Before the smoke from the explosion that had blown apart the six terrorists had cleared, Tobey charged through it with a Steyr in each hand. He saw two Middle Eastern men in their twenties, armed with machine pistols, gaping at him. He skidded to a stop, and as they started to raise the weapons, he fired both guns and put a burst into each man's open mouth.

Their heads blew apart like blood bags as they flew backward.

To his right, a gun hammered a deadly staccato. Tobey whirled in that direction and triggered both Steyrs again. The slugs punched a line of bullet holes up the charging terrorist's torso from groin to breastbone, opening him up in grisly fashion.

Tobey heard another machine pistol to his left and pivoted that way, holding off on the triggers as he saw that Aaron had joined in the fight. The long burst from the kid's Steyr sent two more terrorists spinning off their feet as blood sprayed from their wounds.

The hostages were all gaping at Tobey, but some of them had already leaped to their feet and looked ready to run or fight, whichever they needed to do. Tobey waved an arm toward the opening to a now deserted department store.

"Out that way!" he bellowed. "There won't be more than two or three guys guarding the exit! Run them over!"

He knew that some of the hostages would probably be killed in the escape, but the terrorists couldn't hope to stop a fear-crazed horde of a thousand or more. The prisoners surged toward freedom and safety like a herd of maddened buffalo fleeing from a prairie fire.

Tobey motioned Aaron over to him and told him, "Go get Dupont and Lockhart and the rest! Send one man back to the sporting goods store to tell them to go on the attack! We're gonna fight our way toward them and try to catch the rest of those bastards in a crossfire. We've got to take them down before they start blowing themselves up!"

"What about the rest of the prisoners?" Aaron asked.

"I hope when they hear hell breaking loose again, they'll decide it's time to fight!"

Aaron jerked his head in a nod and turned to race back toward the eyeglass store where the others were waiting. Tobey stepped behind a pillar supporting the upper level of the mall and reached into his pocket for the phone he had taken from the dead terrorist a few minutes earlier. He thumbed the redial button.

When a frantic voice answered and demanded to know what the hell was going on down there, Tobey grinned and said, "Hey, Habib. Things not going according to plan anymore?"

Walt Graham was seething with frustration as Zimmer and Crimmens argued about who was going to carry out the rooftop assault on the mall. Zimmer wanted to use a special FBI strike team that would have to be called in from the East Coast. Crimmens insisted that Homeland Security personnel be used. Graham wanted to ask them if maybe they ought to call in Delta

Force, Seal Team Six, the British SAS, or maybe even the freakin' Boy Scouts. That would accomplish just as much as their blasted wrangling was.

Didn't they realize that time was growing short?

Maybe even shorter than he'd thought, because he heard a dull boom from inside the mall. The others heard it, too, and Agent Shaw even let out a surprised gasp.

"That was another bomb going off," the young woman said.

Graham thought that was pretty obvious but didn't waste time pointing that out. Instead he snapped at Zimmer and Crimmens, "Better make up your mind, or those terrorists are going to make it up for you."

That warning didn't really make sense, he realized as soon as he said it, but the others seemed to catch his drift. Before either Zimmer or Crimmens could say anything, though, Shaw pointed at the mall and exclaimed, "Look!"

Several people had burst out through the doors at one of the entrances. Shots popped inside, but the stampede continued and strengthened. Then the shots stopped abruptly.

"The hostages are breaking out!" Graham said. "If they can get out that way, it means we can get in!"

The chief of police was already barking orders.

"Get those people to safety!" he said into the microphone attached to his collar. "Deploy the SWAT teams! Get in there now, while we have the chance!"

Graham wanted to charge into the mall himself. He could tell from the eager expression on Shaw's face that she did, too. But he caught her eye and shook his head.

"We need to grab some of those hostages as soon as they're clear and question them," he told the young woman. "We have to find out what's going on in there."

"Whatever it is, it's going to keep happening without us," Shaw said with an impatient look on her face.

Graham nodded and said, "Yeah, I know. Once the lid comes off a pressure cooker like that, there's no putting it on again."

Habib started screaming curses in Tobey's ear. Tobey cut him off by saying, "I'm coming for you. Count on it."

"Who are you?" Habib shouted.

"The man who's going to kill you."

It was a brazen attempt to get in the terrorist's head, and judging by the way Habib started yelling almost incoherently again, it worked.

"I'll be here, infidel!" Habib screamed. "I'll bury my hands in your guts and rip out your heart!"

Tobey didn't point out that Habib seemed to be getting his human anatomy mixed up a little. He just broke the connection and shoved the phone back in his pocket.

As he did so, he touched the ring box and thought about Ashley again. He didn't know where in the mall she had been when the attack started, so he couldn't even guess which bunch of hostages she was with. He had tried to spot her in the group that had just fled from the mall, but he hadn't seen her in the hundreds of people. Maybe she had been among them . . . but if she had been, she should have been able to see him and surely she would have tried to catch his attention.

He couldn't think too much about that now. At the moment, it was more important that he had succeeded in angering Habib and making it personal between him and the terrorist leader. Tobey hoped that would make Habib hold off on giving the order to detonate the suicide bombs. He wanted to kill Tobey himself, not blow him up from a distance.

If at all possible, Tobey was going to give him that chance.

"Mr. Lanning! Mr. Lanning!"

That was Charles Lockhart's voice. Tobey swung around to see the teacher, Herb Dupont, and the other men from his group, other than Aaron Ellis. He asked, "Where's Aaron?"

"He went back to the sporting goods store to order that attack you wanted," Lockhart replied. "He said his sister was there and he was going to keep her safe if he could."

Tobey had expected Aaron to use one of the other men as a runner, but he couldn't fault the kid for wanting to protect his sister. If he had known where Ashley was, he would have battled his way to her side by now.

"Fine," he said with a nod. "We're going to fight our way toward the center of the mall and then on to the sporting goods store from there. We're going to drive the terrorists into a crossfire."

"Do we have enough men to do that?" Dupont asked.

"We'll have to fight bigger than our numbers, that's all. There are dead terrorists scattered around. Grab their machine pistols. We need as much firepower as we can get." Tobey turned to Lockhart. "I've got a special job for you, Charles."

Lockhart was clearly terrified, but he nodded anyway and said, "Whatever it is, I'll do my best."

"Get an arrow nocked on that bow. You're our rear guard. If you see any hostiles coming up behind us, you let us know. And if any of the bastards get past us, it'll be your job to put an arrow in them."

"I'll do my best," Lockhart said again.

Tobey nodded to the other men and said, "Let's go."

Calvin was glad Captain Vasquez was there to take charge, but the woman didn't really do anything different than Calvin had been doing during the defense of the sporting goods store. She just put herself and Mr. Connelly and the young foreign woman Calvin had noticed earlier in the day on the frontlines.

The woman's name was Irina, and she seemed to handle a machine pistol with as much confidence as she had the buffer when Calvin had first seen her. She was a little older than him, a couple of years maybe, but from the way she was smiling now, Calvin was sure she recognized him from the food court.

Calvin felt surprisingly pleased by that. With all of their lives in danger, the last thing he should have been worried about was whether some pretty girl smiled at him, but he supposed some human instincts were so strong it was difficult to ignore them forever.

If he was going to die here today, it might make that fate a little easier to take.

Or maybe make it worse, because he couldn't help but think about what he might be missing.

A sudden explosion from somewhere in the mall forced those thoughts out of Calvin's head.

The blast was followed by a babble of nervous speculation from the store's defenders. Calvin didn't know what had happened, but he figured it wasn't anything good.

Less than two minutes later, he knew he'd been right, when the terrorists launched another attack on the store. The shooting from outside picked up, sending volley after volley of lead crashing and ricocheting through the place. The defenders couldn't do anything except keep their heads down and hope none of the flying bullets found them.

Then, in an abrupt lull in the gun-thunder, Captain Vasquez called, "Get ready! Here they come!"

Calvin raised up and saw at least a dozen terrorists charging the store, leaping through the entrance and the blasted-out windows and firing their machine pistols as they rushed the defenders. Calvin thrust out the two semi-automatic pistols he held and started pulling the triggers. He heard slugs whining past his ears, or maybe he just imagined he did, since it would be almost impossible to hear anything in this savage combat.

In the back room, Pete McCracken raged, "I gotta . . . get out there . . . and help!"

Father Steve tightened his grip on the wheel-chair and said, "No, Mr. McCracken. You need to stay back here where you'll be safe."

Pete glared at the priest and said, "You think anybody's . . . safe . . . no matter where . . . they are?"

"I know Sister Angela would never forgive me if I let anything happen to you," Father Steve said.

Then they both heard Captain Vasquez shouting, "Fall back! Fall back!"

The men and women who had been up front, defending the store, began to appear in the doorway, stumbling in their haste. Some were bleeding badly from wounds.

At the same time, that punk kid who had tried to rob Pete appeared in the doorway to the service corridors, bursting in and calling, "Tobey says we got to counterattack now! He and the others are comin' this way! We'll get the bastards in a crossfire!"

Not a bad idea, Pete thought, but not the greatest timing, either, since the store was almost overrun. In fact, one of the terrorists was in the door now, raising his machine pistol to point it at the punk.

Pete lifted the .22 in his good hand and fired through the melee. He'd always had a good shooting eye.

The .22 round entered the terrorist's mouth, which was open because he was yelling some of that *akbar* shit they always yelled, smashed his spine, and dropped him before he could pull the trigger.

Unfortunately, another one was right there to take his place. Connelly, the cop, shot him, but the second terrorist got a burst off and Pete heard Father Steve grunt. He looked back over his shoulder to see the priest swaying as blood welled from a hole in his left shoulder.

Pete had his hand on the wheelchair's control. He shoved it forward, and there was nobody to stop him now since Father Steve had let go of the chair and stumbled back.

The terrorists were still pouring in as Pete rolled toward them. Everybody was shooting and yelling and screaming. The back room had become a madhouse.

Pete remembered what it was like on Omaha Beach. They'd been pinned down by the Germans, and if they had stayed there they would have been chopped to pieces even worse than they already were. So Pete, like the other officers and non-coms, had passed the word—"Move or die!"—and then led by example.

That's what he did now, somehow summoning up the breath to yell, "Follow . . . me!"

And by God, they did. Every open shot he got, he took it. Head shots, because the .22 wouldn't do any good otherwise. One of the terrorists fell, then another. Pete rocked back in the chair as something slammed into his chest, but his left hand, mostly useless but now important again, was locked around the knob and had it pushed forward, so the chair kept moving.

The others swept past him, the punk kid, the black security guard, that skinny blond Air Force woman, the cop, the custodian, even the teenage girl who looked like she ought to be a cheerleader, not a fighter. They kept going, pushing the terrorists out of the doorway and back into the front part of the store.

Pete's chair didn't stop until the wheels hit the front wall, and even then the motor whined and hummed as it kept trying to drive the chair forward. Pete's hand hadn't budged, even though his head had tipped forward and the front of his shirt was soaked with blood.

When they found him there like that later, the side of his face that didn't droop from the stroke wore a big smile.

A smile of triumph.

Habib ran around, not knowing what to do. What was happening? How had things gone so wrong so quickly? He had had everything under control. Allah was on his side. The Americans weren't supposed to be fighting back like this. They were godless infidels, craven cowards, helpless before the irresistible tide of holy jihad.

If he could find the man who had called him on the phone and kill him, the resistance would collapse. That man was the leader, the one driving the other infidels to defy Allah's will. He had to die.

And as soon as he did, Habib would give the order and his men would ascend to heaven on glorious balls of fire, lifted on high to the martyrdom that awaited them.

The explosion from the play area, where a group of the hostages had been held . . . that was what started this catastrophe, Habib thought.

The American he wanted to kill had to be somewhere around there.

Clutching his Steyr, Habib started in that direction as shooting began to erupt all over the mall.

Tobey had no way of knowing it at the moment, but his hope had turned out to be right. Hearing the explosion and the sudden outburst of shooting, the other hostages had assumed that the mall was under attack by the authorities from outside, and they were seizing this chance to rise up against their captors. For more than two hours, fear had kept many of the prisoners paralyzed, but as if they realized this was their last chance, they threw off those shackles and acted to save themselves.

Some died. Many, in fact, were cut down by desperate terrorists wielding machine pistols.

But this time there was no surrender. This time the former hostages just kept coming, over-running those who would have destroyed them and ripping those evil men to pieces. It was the epic struggle between light and dark, civilization and barbarism, that had gone on for centuries, and though barbarism might well be the ultimate fate of mankind, on this day that would not be the case.

On this day, evil would not win.

Jamie, Irina, Jake, Calvin, Aaron, and Kaitlyn were among the first of the store's former defenders to battle their way out and go on the offensive against the terrorists who were starting to realize that things were not going their way after all. The defenders drove the enemy back toward the center of the mall.

An explosion slammed several of the Americans to the floor. Jamie was one of them. As she sat up, shaking her head to try to dispel the ringing in her ears, Aaron knelt beside her and shouted, "Some of them are wearing suicide belts! We'd better not get too close!"

"Damn it!" Jamie said. "Somebody should've told me that before now." She raised her voice to shout orders. It sounded odd to her, as had Aaron's voice, but at least she could understand the words. "Don't crowd them too close! Riflemen! Aim for their midsections! We'll blow them to smithereens with their own bombs!"

More blasts shook the mall as shots aimed with deadly accuracy found the bombs and detonated them. Even the bullets that didn't set off any explosives punched deep into terrorist guts and dropped them.

The counterattack forged on.

"Would you look at that," Walt Graham said in an almost awed voice as he watched thousands of people flood out of the mall. "I'd say our hostage crisis is over."

"Yes, but we need to round up as many of them as we can," Helen Shaw said, "in order to make sure some of the terrorists aren't trying to slip out with them."

Graham looked at her, smiled, nodded, and said, "Agent Shaw, I think you're destined for a long, successful career in the Bureau."

Charles Lockhart heard footsteps pounding up behind him. He spun around and spotted one of the terrorists running toward him. The man appeared to be fleeing from something.

It quickly became apparent what he was afraid of, as several hundred former hostages boiled around a corner after him.

Lockhart lifted the bow and arrow and cried, "Halt!"

The terrorist skidded to a stop and jerked up his machine pistol just as Lockhart loosed the arrow. The point slammed into the man's thigh and buried itself deep in the muscle, but that didn't stop his finger from pulling the trigger and sending a burst of slugs into Lockhart's chest. The bullets' impact drove him back against the wall. He hung there for a moment before he began sliding slowly to the floor.

His vision seemed to be dimming as a hot flood coursed through him, but he could still see well enough to watch as the wounded terrorist tried to limp away from the mob, only to have it catch up to him and rip and trample him into something that didn't even look human anymore.

Charles Lockhart smiled faintly. He didn't want to die, but there didn't seem to be anything he could do about it. At least he had finally done something in his life worth remembering. He would go down in history as one of the heroes of the Battle of the American Way Mall. A minor footnote, perhaps, but still there.

"The green light," he breathed. Gatsby had seen it, and now so did he.

Tobey, Herb Dupont, and the rest of the make-shift squad had cut down several more terrorists before automatic-weapons fire from their right flank ripped through them, knocking several of the Americans off their feet. Tobey twisted toward the new threat, but before he could fire, a bullet struck the Steyr and knocked it out of his hands. Tobey wasn't hit, but the impact numbed both hands to the elbows.

An instant later, a slug clipped his left thigh and knocked that leg out from under him. One of the 1911 .45s fell from his waistband and skidded across the mall floor.

Tobey glanced over, saw that Dupont was dead, the front of his clothes covered in blood from the gaping wound in his throat. Another man was down and appeared to be dead, too, and the others had their hands full exchanging shots with a trio of terrorists that had closed in from the left.

The man on the right, the one who had ambushed them from inside a store they were passing, came toward Tobey with his machine pistol thrust out in front of him, ready to finish Tobey off. Tobey struggled to reach for one of his other guns, but his arm muscles refused to work.

The .45's boom took both of them by surprise, but the terrorist was even more shocked as the high-powered round smashed into his chest and drove him back a couple of steps. His eyes rolled up in their sockets and he fell to his knees, only to pitch forward a second later in a limp sprawl.

Tobey pushed himself up on an elbow and looked around to see who had saved him.

"Ashley!" he cried.

She stood there, tall, straight, and beautiful despite the smudges on her face and the trickle of blood from a scratch on her forehead. She gripped the Colt in both hands. Tobey knew she had picked it up after it slid away from him. Call it a miracle, call it fate, call it whatever suited whatever you believed, but they had found each other again just in time for her to save his life.

She had said that she couldn't pull the trigger like that, but he had known all along that she could if it meant saving innocent lives.

Feeling was starting to flow back into his numbed arms. He was able to push himself to his feet and lift those arms as Ashley lowered the gun and rushed into his embrace. He caught her tightly against him and murmured, "Ash, Ash," as he raised a hand to stroke her blond hair.

Another shot blasted, and Ashley surged against him as the bullet drove into her body. Tobey let out an inarticulate cry of denial. Ashley's head jerked back, her eyes widening in the realization that she'd been shot.

"Tobey . . ." she whispered. "I love . . ."

Her head tipped back even more now, loose now in either unconsciousness or death.

Tobey didn't have time to find out which as more shots roared and a bullet screamed past his ear. He went to the floor, taking Ashley's limp form with him. He lunged behind one of the seats next to the play area and plucked the .45 from her unresisting fingers.

Then he rolled out into the open, winding up on his belly with the Colt grasped in both hands in front of him. He saw the man who had shot

Ashley standing about fifteen yards away, and for a frozen second in time, once again he was back in Iraq, staring into a young face . . .

Only this time that face didn't look innocent and scared. The man's features were twisted with hate, almost unrecognizable.

But Tobey knew him, and some gut instinct made him yell, "Habib!"

The look of shock on the man's face as he jerked back a little told Tobey he was right. Somehow, the kid whose life he had spared all those months ago had made it to the United States. Not in search of a new and better life, but to carry poisonous hatred inside him, and let that evil loose on thousands of innocent people.

Habib hesitated. Tobey didn't know if the kid remembered him or not, but it didn't matter. His finger didn't tighten on the trigger in time, and Tobey shot.

The bullet ripped through Habib's left shoulder and knocked him back. He stumbled, and then Tobey was on him, batting the gun aside, ramming into him and knocking him down. Tobey landed on top of him and closed both hands around Habib's throat.

Shooting was too good for a snake like this. Tobey was going to choke the life out of him.

Habib writhed feverishly and tore at Tobey's arms and hands, but he couldn't rip them loose. He reached down toward his midsection. Tobey let go of Habib's throat with his left hand and caught hold of his wrist before it could find the wire to jerk loose on the suicide belt he wore.

Tobey's big right hand was still clamped around Habib's throat. He shook his head and said, "You're not going to blow yourself up, you bastard. I'm going to do what I should have done before. I'm going to finish you off myself."

He held Habib's hand away from the bomb and kept choking as the terrorist's struggles grew more and more feeble.

"No virgins where you're going, you son of a bitch. Just the devil, waiting to welcome you home."

Habib spasmed one final time, and then his wide, staring eyes began to turn glassy with death.

Tobey let go of him then and tried to stand up. His wounded leg wouldn't hold his weight. Sprawled on his stomach, he looked toward where Ashley lay.

He started to crawl toward her. Around him, and elsewhere in the mall, the shooting began to fade away. Men shouted. American voices. Cops or soldiers or both, rushing in to mop up the rest of the terrorists. Tobey hoped the killing would soon be over, but he was done, out of this fight.

Instead he whispered, "Ashley," and felt the ring box pressing into his body as he pulled himself closer and closer to her still form.

Chapter 37

Later that day . . .

"Calvin!"

The young security guard was sitting in the back door of an ambulance, a blanket around his shoulders, a foam cup of coffee in his hand, when he heard his mother call his name. There was just enough time to set the coffee aside before she was there, throwing her arms around him and hugging him.

"I'm all right, Mom, I'm all right," he told her as he patted her awkwardly on the back. "Everything's gonna be fine now."

Then he realized she was alone, and a chill went through him. He pulled back a little so he could rest his hands on her shoulders.

"Mom? Where's Dad?"

"He . . . he had a heart attack," she said between gulping, sobbing breaths. "But he's going to be okay. The doctors said so, and he was awake enough for me to tell him that I was coming to get you."

Calvin's heart pounded hard in his chest, even harder than it had during the fighting in the mall. He said, "Are you sure he's going to be all right?"

"I'm sure. He's just going to have to take it easy for a while."

"That's all right," Calvin said. "I'll take care of us. Don't you worry." From the corner of his eye, he saw that another blanket-draped person had come to stand beside them. Calvin said, "Mom, I want you to meet somebody. This is Irina . . ."

Jake had gotten out of there as fast as he could. They hadn't wanted to let him go so soon, but that big FBI guy, Walt Graham, had interceded on his behalf. Jake had promised to talk to the FBI, Homeland Security, and whoever else wanted to talk to him, but later.

After he'd seen Adele and made sure she was all right.

He hoped she hadn't been watching the news all day and worrying about him. The fact that he hadn't returned would be enough to scare her, and if she knew what had been going on at the mall, he was sure she'd be terrified.

Now, as he let himself in, the house was quiet and dark. He stepped inside, spotted the still form in the chair, and all the breath went out of him. He lifted a hand and said, "Adele . . . ," then went toward her, stumbling, falling to his knees in front of the chair, leaning forward and resting his head against her knees, grown thin and bony as the disease stole the life from her.

"Adele," he said again.

Then her hand moved, touched his hair, and she said, "Jake? What are you doing down there? Oh, my, I've been napping for a long time. Jake? Did you get my curtains?"

Aaron, Jennie, and Holly walked across the parking lot toward Aaron's car. Holly said, "Looks like I won't have a job to go back to for a while. They say they're going to have the mall open again before Christmas, but I don't see how. All those explosions . . . there was just too much damage. But they've promised to hire everybody back, not just in the seasonal stores if they're gone, but in the regular stores, too."

"You think they might have a job for me somewhere?" Aaron asked.

Jennie looked at him and said, "You? You're going to work in the mall?"

"Ehhh . . . I'm thinking honest employment might be good for a change."

During the counterattack in the sporting goods store, Aaron had seen how that crazy old man charged the terrorists in his wheelchair like he was Teddy freakin' Roosevelt at San Juan Hill or something. It had been the most . . . what was the word? Valiant? Yeah, it was the most valiant thing he had ever seen. And to think he'd been planning on robbing that old geezer.

Then he wondered how he had come up with

that thought about Teddy Roosevelt. It wasn't like he'd ever paid much attention in history class or anything. Funny the things that stuck in a guy's head.

"I don't think you'll make much money working at the mall," Jennie said.

"Maybe not, but if I'm careful and do a good job, maybe it'll be enough to help you pay for college." Aaron shrugged. "Hey, it's a start, anyway."

Holly put a hand on his shoulder, bumped her hip against his as they walked, and said, "Maybe we can work in the same place."

"I'd like that," Aaron said.

Tobey was sitting in the back door of an ambulance, too, at the edge of the area in the parking lot that had been cleared for triage. His wounds had been cleaned and bandaged, and although none of them seemed serious, he knew the doctors would insist on keeping him overnight in the hospital just to be sure.

He knew that Charles Lockhart and Herb Dupont and Pete McCracken were all dead. He had watched while Kaitlyn Hamilton reunited with her father and brothers and delivered the news among hugs and tears that her mother had been killed. He had witnessed the much happier reunion between Jamie Vasquez and her husband and kids.

All around the mall it continued. The tears of grief and shock, the tears of joy and relief. The miracle of life and the senselessness of death. A vicious wound had been struck today in the soul of America.

But not a fatal one. America would recover . . . this time.

If everyone soon forgot, though . . . if the politicians postured and the pundits pontificated and the apologists deflected the blame onto anyone and anything else instead of directing it at those who had truly caused this tragedy . . . then who could say? More than three thousand innocent Americans had died on September 11, 2001, and it hadn't taken much time at all before things had gone back to normal. About a third that many had been killed today. Tobey gave it a couple of weeks, and then everybody would move on to something else. Christmas was coming, after all.

He sighed and pushed himself to his feet.

One of the paramedics paused in his busy round of activities to say, "We'll be leaving for the hospital soon, sir."

"That's fine," Tobey said. "I'll be in here."

He stepped up into the ambulance and moved over to the gurney fastened into place on one side. Ashley lay there, her face pale, her eyes closed, but when he slipped his left hand into her right one where it lay on the sheet covering her, she opened her eyes and tightened her fingers on his with surprising, reassuring strength.

"Hi," she whispered.

"I've got something for you," Tobey said as he reached into his pocket with his other hand and closed his fingers around the ring box. "I was going to give it to you on Christmas Eve, but I don't think I'll wait."

Somebody outside closed the ambulance doors, and a moment later it pulled away, detaching itself from the sea of flashing lights around the mall. A few tendrils of smoke still rose here and there from the sprawling building, but they were soon lost in the late November sky.

About the Authors

Though known largely for their westerns, *New York Times* bestsellers, WILLIAM W. JOHNSTONE and J. A. JOHNSTONE are the authors of some of the most explosive and timely thrillers of the last decade, including the nationally bestselling *Tyranny*, a ripped-from-the-headlines story of citizens' rights and government wrongs, and *Stand Your Ground*, a chilling depiction of terrorism on American soil.

The Johnstones know that freedom is never free. They fully support our military and regularly donate books to our troops. You can learn more about this as well as upcoming releases and special promotions by visiting williamjohnstone.net, or kensingtonbooks.com.

Center Point Large Print
600 Brooks Road / PO Box 1
Thorndike, ME 04986-0001 USA

(207) 568-3717

US & Canada:
1 800 929-9108
www.centerpointlargeprint.com